UNCORRECTED PROOF - NOT FOR SALE

Title: NEVER MIND THE POLLACKS
Author: NEAL POLLACK
Classification: Fiction
Publication month: October 2003
Price: $23.95/$36.95 (Can.)
Index: No
Illustrations: No
Page count: 272 pages
Trim size: 5 1/2" x 8 1/4"
ISBN: 0-06-052790-0

*Reviewers are reminded that changes may be made in this proof copy before
books are printed. If any material from the book is to be quoted in a review
the quotation should be checked against the final bound book. Dates, prices,
and manufacturing details are subject to change or cancellation without
notice.*

HarperCollins*Publishers*

For Tina:
  Together, we will conquer
  Arkansas.
              Rock on,

              Neal
              Pollack

NEVER MIND THE POLLACKS

ALSO BY NEAL POLLACK

Titles TK

NEVER MIND
THE POLLACKS

A ROCK 'N' ROLL NOVEL

NEAL POLLACK

HarperCollinsPublishers

This book is a work of fiction. References to real people, including the author's friends whose lives have been ruined by major-label record deals, as well as events, establishments, organizations, or locales, are intended only to let you know that corporate rock still sucks. They are all used fictitiously or satirically, but especially the stuff about Kurt Cobain. All other characters and all incidents and dialogue are drawn entirely from the author's fertile imagination and are not to be construed as real, even if they, against your will, stir up unbearable waves of sexual desire.

HarperCollins books may be purchased for educational, business, or sales promotional use. For information, please write: Special Markets Department, HarperCollins Publishers Inc., 10 East 53rd Street, New York, NY 10022.

FIRST EDITION

Designed by Elliott Beard

Printed on acid-free paper

Library of Congress Cataloging-in-Publication Data is available upon request.

ISBN 0-06-052790-0

03 04 05 06 07 ❖/RRD 10 9 8 7 6 5 4 3 2 1

FOR JACK AND MEG

ACKNOWLEDGMENTS

A number of real-life rock critics, both paid hacks and enthusiastic amateurs, endured my annoying, naïve questions over the past two years as this project slowly creaked to life. If the details in this book are correct, they can take credit. If I got stuff wrong, it's not their fault. Here they are, in no particular order: Jim DeRogatis, Henry Owings, Bethany Klein, Dan DeLuca, John Strausbaugh, Kenan Hebert, Andrew Earles, Chuck Klosterman, Monica Kendrick, Elisa Ludwig, Glenn Kenny, and Greg Beets. I'm also tremendously grateful to Jim Roll, who allows my band to exist, and to the other members of The Neal Pollack Invasion, Dakota Smith, John Williams, and Neil Cleary. And many thanks are due Jerod Gunsberg, Joanne Abrams, Jane Lerner, and Shep from The Telegraph Company, my agent, Daniel Greenberg, my editors David Hirshey, John Williams, and Jeff Kellogg, Carrie Kania and Amy Baker from HarperAudio, Carl Lennertz and Jen Hart, Ben Brown and the Book Punk crew, the organizers of Philadelphia's own 215 Festival, my parents, Regina, Elijah, and Hercules, and all the friends I've made along the lonesome road from independent publishing nobody to corporate sellout gutter monkey. People, I have so much love to pass around, but the media wants to destroy the world that we've all built together. If you give an interview without my permission, it's over, do you hear? Over. Sweet Jewish God, I can't take the pressure anymore.

So with that in mind, these acknowledgments really go out to those who have doubted me, mocked me, called me a "one-trick retardo pony," or said I had no business following my dream of becoming the world's leading rock novelist. Well, after ten years of working nearly five hours a day, I'm taking my rightful place at the table of the American literary canon. And where are you now? Nowhere, that's where! This bullet train cannot be stopped, and you don't have a ticket! Not now, not ever. Up yours, wadbutts! You can suck my bug fat best-selling dick!

I want a job

I want a job
I want a real job
I want a job
I want a job that pays.
I want a job
I want a job
I want a real job
One that satisfies
My artistic needs.

—SID AND NANCY, 1986

PROLOGUE
1994

The phone rang in the post-noon dusk, and I answered it, because I'd told them not to call me unless somebody famous died. Sure enough, two days into my vacation, someone had, and I knew him. In the rock world, which I chronicle, our friends and heroes are always dying, and we're always eulogizing. But at deadline time, I've learned, mere grief is never enough.

It was Wenner on the line.

"St. Pierre," he said. "We've lost Pollack. I want you to write a piece about him. A short piece, for the back of the book."

My mouth was full of fish taco.

"How," I said, "did he die?"

The answer wasn't as simple as might be indicated by my brilliantly researched prologue to this book, which you are about to read. As I constructed my story through press accounts, on-site witness interviews, and pure historical conjecture, I realized that Neal Pollack's death, in retrospect, had been inevitable since his birth. What is death, after all, but the absence of life? In Pollack's case, as in so many others, not much.

Pollack mattered to me, like he did to most other cool people in their late forties, early to mid fifties. He was thrilling, but he was also weird, the only true rock critic this country will ever produce. He was, in many ways, the living, breathing essence of America's music, its dark Baudelaire Rimbaud genius, its Celine, its Brecht, the long crawl from the swamps of Louisiana to the halls of Dadaism and back again, writing with prejudice, but without mercy.

At least I hadn't heard it first from Kurt Loder. But I still wasn't prepared for the news. I'd just seen Pollack at Lollapalooza in Seattle eight months before. He'd been gnawing on a piece of fry bread.

"Neal," I'd said, "you look terrible."

"Grumph," he'd said. "Look who it is. Paul St. Pierre, the world's most pretentious fuck."

"What are you doing here?"

"Shilling for Alice in Chains," he said. "Those ass-eating phonies."

Pollack was standing in front of a yellow tent. A banner over his head read "Anal Piercings. $10."

"This isn't like you," I said.

His eyes teared.

"Whaddya want from me, Paul?" he said. "I needed the money. You don't return my calls anymore. No one does. It's over, don't you know that? They're charging for bottled water, and the kids are paying for it! They like Dinosaur Jr., for god's sake! Back when music was good, Dinosaur Jr. couldn't have wiped me with their set list! I'm done!"

The multiplicity of the market's desire to consume subcultural cornucopia overshadows the integrity of independent scholarship. As a lapsed but hopeful leftist and professor of American culture at three major universities, I understood that. But Pollack did not.

"THEY SHOVED SOUNDGARDEN DOWN OUR THROATS!" he said. "THOSE FUCKING CORPORATE BASTARDS!"

A guy about one-third Pollack's age slapped him across the mouth with a tattooed hand.

"Just collect the money, Grandpa," he said.

I said to Pollack, "I'll call you, Neal. I swear."

Neal Pollack looked at me, his eyes verging on the insane, but also on the wise.

"You never believed in me," he said. "You never understood me. And you don't know shit about rock and roll."

I filed my piece for *Mother Jones*, "Alterna-Capitalism and the New World Disorder," and then I got busy with a feminist monograph for a rock-critic retrospective show at the L.A. County Museum. I cleverly called it *Shirley Manson: American Medusa,* and it was well reviewed in the local weeklies and glossy art quarterlies. But I never called Pollack, never even tried to find his number.

Still, his words had stung me. I'd spent my entire professional life studying the vicissitudes of popular music, and had written about it intelligently, to the point where I never, before this sentence, had used the phrase "vicissitudes of popular music."

So what had Pollack meant? I knew *everything* about rock and roll. Who was he kidding?

In the hours after Wenner called, I sat at the bar of my expensive yet authentically decorated Mexican beachfront hotel, drinking mojitos, each one more vicious than the next. My brain stewed in sugarcoated rum, and my thoughts drifted to Austin, Texas, 1987, where Pollack and I had appeared on a panel at the first South by Southwest music conference. Pollack was living in Washington State at the time, and I'd just purchased my loft home in SoHo. Record producer and Big Black guitarist Steve Albini and the lesser critic Robert Christgau joined us. The topic was "Whither Punk?" My memory picked up the conversation mid-panel:

CHRISTGAU: There are all kinds of hopeful signs. I love R.E.M., and they are straight out of the punk tradition.

POLLACK (belches): Pfft. College boys whining about how their mommies didn't love them.

CHRISTGAU: No. I just think they produce some good songs. I don't know anything about them personally.

POLLACK: They can blow me. And I know, because I'm a goddamn rock critic!

ST. PIERRE: Think about it though. When Chuck Berry was recording *Johnny B. Goode* in 1957, was he making rock music, or was he just practicing enlightenment as mass deception? A group like R.E.M. is just decoding certain innate truths in our culture, whether they're punk or not.

CHRISTGAU: Well, I wouldn't say it quite like that. . . .

POLLACK: But I would say, Paul, that you suck, and your writing sucks, and rock and roll sucks.

ALBINI: Whenever I talk to a band who are about to sign with a major label, I always end up thinking of them in a particular context. I imagine a trench, about four feet wide and five feet deep, maybe sixty yards long, filled with runny, decaying shit. I imagine the band at one end of this trench. I imagine a faceless industry lackey at the other end holding a fountain pen and a contract. Nobody can see what's printed on the contract. It's too far away, and besides, the stench is making everybody's eyes water.

POLLACK: Tell us something we don't know, Steve. Is the moon round, too? Do you have a tiny little indie weenie? This festival is for yuppies, like you, with your one-piece mechanic's jumpsuit and elitist noise. Celebration of music, my ass. Sixth Street is completely gentrified. This ain't the Willie Nelson picnic at Dripping Springs, pal. They're gonna tear down Liberty Lunch and the Armadillo World Headquarters someday. Then The Hole In the Wall won't be able to make its rent, and Austin will be ruined!

The headline in the next issue of the *Austin Chronicle* read: "Pollack Rips St. Pierre, Albini New Ones."

"Fucking Pollack," I said, remembering.

My wife, Ruth, came into the bar. The kids wanted me to tell them a story, she said.

"Only if I can read to them from *Hammer of the Gods*," I said. "It's all I'm in the mood for tonight."

Soon after, the little ones were snug in their bungalow, rocked to electric dreamland by the sounds of the ocean, their heads dancing with visions of Robert Plant sodomizing groupies with moldy tubes of deli meat. Ruth, who is also a professor of cultural studies, slept at peace, her two vacation volumes of Lacan resting quietly, unread, on the rattan nightstand. I cursed her lack of intellectual rigor. Then I rolled and lit a joint and prepared for the calming of my mind. But as is my dark destiny, I just kept thinking.

Someone was going to have to distill Pollack's millions of unpublished words, his vast armada of experiences, into a digestible volume of approximately three hundred pages. Every genius needs a filter, and more than anyone else, I felt qualified. Historians who know the history makers, after all, are the ones who write true history, and by making Pollack's life my own, I figured that maybe I'd get to keep some of his album collection.

In my backpack, I found some pages of Pollack's prose, which I always kept with me in case I ever had to anthologize his work. It was a largely unedited piece he wrote for *Testicle*, a one-issue magazine he published himself in 1976. In those whip-and-chain days of sad ahistorical rock nihilism, no one could have written this but him:

There is no rock-and-roll! Where did you ever really see anyone claiming that there was? On the back of a bus? In some hipster hotel lobby? NO! BECAUSE IT DOES NOT EXIST! A bunch of half-formed pubescent acne-riddled fools thwacking away at their twenty-dollar guitars is not art! You find art uptown, at Lincoln

Center, in George Balanchine's pneumatic tube of a brain! Art is not Dee Dee Ramone shooting speed in the Chelsea Hotel, or some cum-bag wannabe poet twirling around at St. Mark's Church in her long skirts! You can't live like that. Art is slavery, and rock is not redemption. It seems to me that growing up is war and vice versa and you have to react to it like that, and if you have to eat a dog, then eat a dog, and goddamn it, I don't feel like a man anymore, and Frank Zappa sold us out to the Russians, and I am shrieking now, shrieking, can you hear me? AHHHHH! AHH-HHH! My arms are growing horns!

I fell asleep, and dreamt that Neal Pollack visited my SoHo loft while I was on deadline. Downstairs, Ernesto made him sign the sheet. He took the elevator up and there I was at my desk, trying to find traces of Bill Monroe lyrics in the photographs of Walker Evans.

Pollack, unshaven, hair firing in multiple directions like rogue missiles, in his Boy Howdy T-shirt, defecated in my foyer. He said:

"I've been seeing your pieces in the *Times.*"

"What about my column in the *Voice*?"

"I don't read the *Voice*!" he said. "What is this, 1962?"

"I guess not."

"Your stuff's all right, man," he said. "But it's missing something."

"What could it possibly be missing?"

"Oh ho. You poor sucker."

Pollack raised his arms, and was abruptly framed by lightning. Behind him, a simple street sign, flashing above a sea of human color, read BEALE. A storefront window prophesied the Memphis Recording Service. A twang from the hills grew louder and louder until it was heard by the mass and subsequently rendered unrecognizable among a polyglot din. Jerry Lee Lewis threw a piano at my head. I tried to scream, but was drowned out by Dylan gone electric. The lights of Andy Warhol's Factory blinked out into the piss-stained 1966 Manhattan night, and then the world exploded into angry light and noise. I saw guitars flying through windows, angry mounds of barebacked teens grinding in a man-made pit. Streams of blood and puke flowed past my feet like lava.

Pollack threw back his head and coughed. Then he laughed.

"You'll never know, Paul," he said. "You'll never know. . . ."

The phone rang.

I woke in a freezing sweat.

It was Wenner again.

"Kurt Cobain is dead," he said, "and so is rock."

Later, as I composed Cobain's obituary and established phone hookups with local NPR outlets across the country, Pollack's story still vexed me. I was to write two Kurt books and serve as consulting editor for several documentaries, but no one, it seemed, wanted to know about the man who claimed to have made Cobain and then had the misfortune to die three days before him.

No one wanted to know about Neal Pollack anymore.

But something unusual, and perhaps evil, has compelled me to tell you about Pollack. Like all good stories, this one begins at the end. As these words drip from my fingers onto the keyboard like blood from a fresh wound, Neal Pollack's voice cackles at me still.

"You'll never know," he says in my waking nightmare. "You'll never know. . . ."

APRIL 4
WILLIAMSBURG, BROOKLYN

On the morning of the day he died, Neal Pollack woke with a burning pain in his ass unlike any he'd experienced in weeks. He remembered what his father had told him back in Memphis, Tennessee, so many decades before. It was strong advice from a strong man that Pollack, on those days when he still had linear memory, was willing to follow.

"If your ass hurts when you wake up, son," his father said, "sit on some ice."

Pollack felt beside him. No chick. It'd been weeks since he'd met someone in a bar who'd known his name, and months since he'd met someone who'd go to bed with him because she'd known his name, and even then it had only been Patti Smith. She'd lain on her meat-cart bed, swathed in muslin. That pop priestess of Pollack's soul had crossed her arms and said, "We can fuck. But don't you dare touch me."

"How," Pollack said, between slugs, "will that be possible?"

"Figure it out," she said. "Make me come. Then leave."

No, Pollack was alone as usual, lying on something lumpy but also kind of soft. Definitely a futon. An open can of Pringles and a half-drunk bottle of Maker's Mark nestled in the billowing folds. A Richard Hell action figure curled into an alienated ball beside him. He was home.

I own nothing, he thought. His room was all records and needles and crummy furniture, most of which he'd picked up for performing a song at the Johnny Thunders estate sale in 1990. A cat, large enough to be frightening, snored between his feet. Another cat lay to the left of his head, also snoring.

"Max!" Pollack said. "Kansas City! You bitches! Get me some ice!"

The cats didn't move.

"Fat old queens," he said. "Useless dykes."

His ass was on fire and his brain hurt. The previous night was coming back to him. He'd been up until near-dawn, eating beef jerky, listening to Captain Beefheart's *Trout Mask Replica* backward, drinking orange juice laced with nutmeg, working on his novel *The True Story of How Rock and Roll Smacked Me in the Mouth Until I Bled Real Tears*. Had he made progress? A notebook lay nearby, and he picked it up.

"Gang of Four Jimi Hendrix ham salad MIDI Rolling Thunder Viet Cong sonofabitch," he had written. "I'm gonna make you a star!"

Pretty good. A few more years, and the first chapter would be done.

The bile rose, quick and ugly, in his throat. Pollack was used to vomiting on himself; it was often the only way he could begin the day. When it was done, Pollack found himself able to sit up and drink some whiskey.

He stood. Fresh shards of pain streamed toward every sensitive corner of his body.

God! What devil was in his stomach?

He crumpled to the concrete floor.

A few minutes later, he rose again, with agonizing effort, and lurched toward the sink in the corner.

He stared at a hideous goblin, its face a mottled mess of hair patches and dried puke, its worn, emaciated bones poking at skin hanging off joints in loose folds, its belly bloated, legs bowed and arthritic, the last visage of a defeated wretch at the end of a long and lonely ride.

Wait. He was looking at a poster of Iggy Pop.

He vowed to cut out the hard drugs, splashed some water on his face, popped a couple of Xanax, and washed them down with a can of Pabst Blue Ribbon.

Oh! The ass! Ice!

The refrigerator was in another corner of the room. Fifteen minutes passed before Pollack could get there, and then only with the aid of a glass pipe full of White Widow. His cats looked at him with scorn, disdain, and pity, but they always did, because they despised him. When he reached the refrigerator, Pollack found it empty, and also off. Christ! Ever since Giuliani had taken office, it was almost impossible to get electricity in your squat. You couldn't even afford to live in the city for free anymore, Pollack thought bitterly. Bring back the days when you could jaywalk and legally murder a street poet, that's when this place was really good. He was ready to declare the day over, to go back to bed and writhe until sundown. He'd done it before.

"Stinking fascists," he said.

But he had a thought.

"Tussin," he said.

Only Tussin DM could save him. Nothing made Neal Pollack hallucinate and clutch the curtains like a quick shot of dextromethorphan, and it only cost four dollars a bottle with the senior prescription card he'd filched off an elderly Chassid on the outbound L train. But where had he left that bottle? The last time he'd shot up Tussin, either two months previous or the other day, he'd been on the toilet. No. On the couch.

No. There was a stash under his pillow. Bingo, and needles everywhere, some of them from Jim Carroll's personal stash. Now to find a vein. Arms had been out of the question since 1982, and good luck locating something uncollapsed in the thigh. The ass hurt too much, but the middle toe on Pollack's right foot shone out like an emerald in a Brazilian coalfield. It bore a fat juicy vein, never penetrated, much less by the quart-sized needle that Pollack filled with the syrup of syrups, that sweet Tussin DM. He plunged it deep, and felt his tongue grow heavy.

He was down before he could even get up.

In the distance, Neal Pollack saw a man sitting on a stump in a field. The air was bright and the sky crisp. The man was wearing a porkpie hat and playing, on his guitar, some lost inchoate melody that seemed to emerge from the antediluvian swamp of American race memory. He was more than old; he was very old. His face reflected years of not exactly wisdom or experience, but at least hard living and then some.

Pollack walked toward the man, feeling more buoyant and sane than he had for years. His molted synapses were clear for once. He was no longer angry or depressed, self-euphoric or self-loathing. In the back of what seemed to be his mind, Pollack remembered all the petty rivalries and rotgut-fueled midnight expeditions for carbon paper, the long body-slamming nights at CBGB and beyond, and a thousand precoital rejections. But he didn't care anymore. He had found the man.

"Ah've been waiting for you, Neal," said the man. "Waiting a good long time now."

"Then it *is* you," said Pollack. "I knew I'd find you someday. Where are we? Are we dead?"

The man played his guitar, a song that hearkened back to every song Pollack had ever heard. He laughed and coughed and then he laughed again.

"Haw, haw!" he said. "No, Neal, we ain't dead. But we will be soon, if my calculations are correct. I reckon this is a dream!"

"I've been looking for you, on and off, for forty-five years," Pollack said. "Why are you here now?"

"I have come because it's time for you to understand the Message."

"What Message?"

"The Message that is in all music for all eternity but is most easily found in obscure African-American singles of every genre that were released on small, now defunct labels."

The man coughed into a handkerchief that, Pollack somehow knew, he had borrowed from B. B. King.

"Now listen to me very carefully, because our time is limited," the man said.

"OK."

"I want you to go to that record store on Bedford Avenue, the one that's owned by the annoying guy who wears bowling shirts and thick-black-framed glasses, the one who's married to that installation artist you hit on at a party a few months ago."

"Shit!" Pollack said. "I hate that guy!"

"I don't care. You have to buy a record from him. Specifically, you must purchase Eric B. and Rakim's *Follow the Leader*. It contains the lyrics you will need to join me."

"Join you where?"

"At the source of music, of the Message, and your quest will be complete."

"But I'm not on a quest!" Pollack said. "And that record costs eleven bucks! How am I gonna afford that and lunch today?"

The old man sighed.

"Cheap-ass rock critics," he said. "Here, take twenty dollars and go buy yourself the damn record."

The man began to shimmer, and not naturally, either. The Tussin was wearing off. Pollack shouted after the man, but he was fading, fading into the mist of musical time.

"*Woke up this morning,*" the man sang, "*and my boots were full of blood . . .*"

Crap! The cats were making angry noise. They were hungry. It was noon.

A six-pack of Pabst and half a bottle of bourbon later, followed by a line of Peruvian cut with drain cleaner, Pollack was ready to endure the day. He never left the house without making sure he looked cool. It didn't take much: black jeans, black socks, black steel-toed boots, and a black T-shirt with red lettering: "MURDERER." A little water in the hair, a pair of stolen sunglasses, and a mysterious twenty-dollar bill that he'd found by his bedside was all he needed to go out in Williamsburg.

Pollack walked down the middle of Sixth Street. He hummed the melody to "Venus In Furs," the coke and booze and weed and Tussin having filled the day with possibility. He had a mission, a quest, for the Message, and he wasn't going to be stopped.

Coming the other way down Sixth was the number 17 bus, driven by Eric "Little Picker" McGonigle, former substitute bassist for the Asbury Dukes. He'd requested this route specifically, because he knew Pollack lived on the street. The Picker had never forgiven Pollack for his review of *Born in the U.S.A.*, in which Pollack dismissed Bruce Springsteen as "the phony savior from America's bunghole."

Pollack's review had never been published, but that didn't deter the Little Picker, who got hold of it somehow. True Springsteen fans rarely let an obscure slight go unpunished.

"If I ever see Pollack," the Little Picker said in his frequent quiet, lonely moments, "I'm gonna run him down."

On this day, the Picker spotted Pollack swerving dreamily in the road. The opportunity was so easy that he almost honked. But the Picker saw an image of the Boss in his mind. Bruce was weeping, betrayed, on his guitar-shaped cross, and his eyes called for steely revenge. The Picker floored it and his bus hit Pollack square, the chassis smacking him flat in the ribs. Pollack spun sideways and the rearview caught him in the head. He felt something snap in his left arm, something ooze out of his right ear. He fell to the curb, hard.

The Picker drove away.

"You just ran over a man!" a rider shouted.

"That was no man," said the driver. "That was Neal Pollack."

The passengers applauded.

Pollack squirmed in the gutter.

"Fucking hippies!" he shouted, apropos of nothing.

His hair was already matting. A pool of blood had gathered at his head. Everything was blurry, ethereal, beautiful, really. Was he awake or asleep?

"Git up, Neal," said a voice.

Pollack turned his eyes up. On the sidewalk was the old man

from his dream.

"I got hit by a bus," Pollack said.

"Ah know," said the man. "It's all part of the plan."

"What plan?"

"The plan that was written for you long ago, in the Message."

"What is the Message? I have to know."

"You cannot know, for the Message will be told in the telling. It will be known when it is known."

Pollack felt great waves of dread wash upon the shores of his soul. Williamsburg, land of lofts and auto-body, pierogi, calzone, and bodega, held the final secrets to a puzzle that he'd been trying to solve his whole life, a puzzle without pieces and without a name.

"I think my legs are broken," he said.

"They ain't broken," said the man. "They're just bruised."

"I can't stand up."

"Don't be a pussy, boy," said the man. "Think to yourself, W.W.I.D.?"

"Huh?"

"Think, boy. What Would Iggy Do?"

The man had a point. Iggy had endured far worse, daily, and he still had a recording career. Screw this, Pollack thought. I'm alive. In his unconscious consciousness, he raised himself on both forearms.

"That's it, boy," said the man. "You're on the way. The music waits for you."

The man shimmered. He was leaving again, singing his song.

Woke up this morning, and my boots were full of blood . . .

"Clambone . . ." Pollack said, cryptically. "Clambone . . ."

As Pollack lurched down Sixth Street, the children and old people fled in fear from the gore-streaked monster he'd become. He wasn't cute any longer, not like the olive cherub born Norbert Pollackovitz at Cook County Hospital in Chicago, Illinois, on

May 24, 1941, the son of Gladys and Vernon Pollackovitz, themselves wanderers to the music of time.

Vernon came from Ruten, Germany, the son of a son of a butcher. He was a hard man with hard hands and a square humorless face, and he didn't love music. The only record he owned was the Army Marching Band playing "And the Caissons Go Rolling Along." He spun it every night before dinner, and he sang along, *over hill, over dale, we will hit the dusty trail . . .*

Neal Pollack's first act as a rock critic was to throw that record out the window of their apartment building on Lunt Avenue and gather the cracked vinyl in his pockets while Vernon chased him down the street, brandishing a belt, screaming, "Monster! Communist! No son of mine!" Gladys was secretly pleased. She'd hated that damn record, its tuneless clanging and mindless jingoism no match for the Strauss that *her* mother had played for her on the parlor piano in Hamburg, before the soldiers had come and taken the piano away. She was proud of her critic-in-the-making, even if he'd already developed, at eight, a fondness for drinking cough syrup. He had taste, and taste, she imagined, could get you through this impossible life.

A few days later, Vernon Pollackovitz saw that his son's welts had healed sufficiently. Vernon had to go down to Maxwell Street on a Saturday, to see a man about a rug. He took the boy with him.

There, in three city blocks, Halsted from Roosevelt to Maxwell, on the West Side of Chicago, Neal Pollack first saw the true America. The street teemed with vegetable peddlers and half-wits selling ill-fitting contraband. An ancient Greek displayed a wall of watches while his one-armed wife coaxed sad songs of long-forgotten isles from a hand-painted accordion. For two cents, you could stick your head beneath a sheet and see a dancing chicken. A store sold nothing but electric-blue suits with flared collars, and at two hundred feet you could smell the cologne of the hosiery men. Fat Poles in baggy work shirts shoved steaming onion-slathered sausages between their elephantine cheeks, and their jowls quivered with joy. Mexicans and Italians shot dice on tenement stoops in the shadow of where the expressway would someday run. Old ladies padded in their bedroom slippers, little wheel carts full of wares in front. Vernon got into an argument about the authenticity of a leather wallet.

Norbert wandered off. A sound called him.

In a vacant lot on Maxwell, half a block west of Halsted, a few dozen black people were grooving hard next to a rusty Dumpster. There was a drummer, and a man played a guitar that was plugged into an amplifier. The boy had never seen a guitar or an amplifier, much less a black man singing, and he felt destiny in the tuneful air. The singer was about forty-five, but he looked much older. He wore a porkpie hat and a red velvet jacket. A harmonica hung around his neck, and he was sure to use it eventually. He sang:

> *Woke up this morning*
> *And my boots were full of blood*
> *Yeah I woke up this morning*
> *All my boots were full of blood*
> *I shouldn't have stayed*
> *Up all night*
> *Getting nasty in the mud.*
>
> *Well I went down from Chicago*
> *All the way to New Orleans*
> *Yes I went down from Chicago*
> *All the way to New Orleans*
> *I ate a lot of seafood*
> *But I also*
> *Ate some beans.*

I went down to Mississippi
All the way from San Antone
Yeah, I went down to Mississippi
All the way from San Antone
With a demon in my bloodstream
And a devil
In my bone . . .

"Sing it, Clambone!" shouted an old woman.

"You know ah will, you sexy bitch," said the man.

The boy thought, Clambone? Then he thought, Clambone! He knew even then that he'd heard something important, vital. At that moment on Maxwell Street, though he wouldn't realize it for many years, Neal Pollack had been consumed by the essence of rock and roll, a hard twang from the bowels of the wormy earth. For the rest of his life, he would seek to write about a moment as pure, music as true.

The boy felt his father's stern Ashkenazi hand on his neck.

"Get away from these schvartzers!" Vernon said. "They probably have tuberculosis!"

There was no protesting the iron antimusic grip of Vernon Pollackovitz. The moment was over, and the future Neal Pollack never saw Maxwell Street again. On the trolley home, though, he heard the refrain, over and over again, until finally, at the Addison stop, he wept.

Nearly a half century later, Neal Pollack, the ungrateful middle-aged son of Jewish immigrants, stumbled through the hippest neighborhood in America on a bright spring afternoon, singing the blues to himself. In the second gilded era of a fragile empire unaware of its inevitable historical destiny as unwitting destroyer of the world, Pollack was a penurious loser at the end of his line. He was missing a chunk of his scalp, and he was going to buy a record.

Rock and roll is fucked, he thought. We were authentic all those years ago. We were just a bunch of damn hillbilly shitheels with guitars and bad hairstyles, going to see the niggers play the real thing on a Saturday night. We were hayseeds in borrowed cars. They ruined it, the critics did. I remember when it was pure, the music and the writing. Who put the Bomp in my Jew ass? I'd take the Sonics or the Godz over Pearl Jam for breakfast. We didn't need a magazine to make us cool. Don't they get it? We never wanted what they turned us into. I wrote, but I was never a critic. I was rock and roll. I don't care what they claim.

He said, loudly, "Goddamn Fillmore Ballroom Janis Joplin Paul Butterfield Blue Oyster Cult desert-island discs of the seventies Arista Records glitter glam motherfucking Fugazi X-Ray Spex Replacements let it be!"

Oh, god, he thought. I'm not well. Ten years ago, I would never have spoken the words "Blue Oyster Cult" aloud.

Can Records opened on Bedford Avenue in January 1993. Pollack, always watching for signs of gentrification, noticed its appearance. On its first day of business, he used his Swiss Army knife to scratch the word "INSECTICIDE" on the front window. This was the beginning of his friendship with Richard Alvin, the store's owner, a former advertising rep for *Minneapolis Rocker* to whom Pollack referred in private conversation as "the primordial yuppie from the mother ooze." Alvin was behind the counter when Pollack, unshaven and bloody, stumbled in on that desperate spring afternoon.

"Hello, Neal," he said.

"I got twenty dollars!" Pollack said.

"That's nice."

"Gimme a record, you fuck!"

"I've got a lot."

Pollack grabbed Alvin by his Misfits T-shirt.

"Listen," he said, "I got a lot of work to do, and I don't have time. Give me a record."

"Well, I have a very nice copy of *Second Annual Report*."

"I HATE Throbbing Gristle," Pollack said.

Alvin reached behind the counter for his velvet-lined "special box," which he only accessed for discriminating customers. Out came a 1980 Black Flag EP, *Jealous Again*, followed by *Out of Step*, the 1983 Minor Threat EP on Dischord Records that never failed to impress.

"Mint condition," he said.

"I already got those," Pollack said. "And who keeps punk rock records in mint condition, anyway? Show me something new."

"I've got new Archers of Loaf, Velocity Girl, Bunnygrunt, and Tuscadero."

"Pussy bands!" Pollack said.

"Well, there's always *Whip-Smart*."

"That sounds promising," Pollack said.

"It's the new Liz Phair album. Came out yesterday."

Pollack's jaw clenched, his fists tightened.

"I'm getting very angry with you, Richard Alvin," he said.

He took a step toward the record-store owner, and he seemed to grow large and menacing; his shadow filled the room.

"I'VE ALWAYS HATED LIZ PHAIR AND I ALWAYS WILL!" he said.

Alvin shuddered and sighed simultaneously.

"Then what do you want?" he said.

"I want *Follow the Leader*," Pollack said, as he seemed to shrink back to his normal size.

"You want what?"

"Eric. B. and Rakim. Maybe you've heard of them?"

Alvin looked indignant.

"Naturally, I have all their albums here," he said. "Including several bootlegs of which I own the only copies. But they never sell.

The secret tragedy of music is that the races never come together, and Hootie doesn't count. Neither does Clarence Clemons."

"Not in my world!" Pollack said. "I own three Parliament albums, *Fear of a Black Planet, The Chronic,* AND James Brown *Live at the Apollo!*"

"Then you, Neal Pollack, are a better man than I."

"No shit, Phil Spector," Pollack said.

In a remote corner of the store labeled "Black Music" was *Follow the Leader,* alphabetically placed next to *Funkaloop: Wynton Marsalis and the New York Philharmonic Play the Music of Herbie Hancock.* It was a small victory, but Pollack needed one of those, and he wrote an epistle to himself in his head.

"I am a record-store hero," he said.

On the way home, he stopped at a pay phone. He dialed directory assistance and got the number for Coney Island High, on St. Marks.

"HELLO!" he shouted. "THIS IS NEAL POLLACK. CAN I PLEASE SPEAK TO JOEY RAMONE?"

"Neal, you don't have to shout," Joey said.

"Oh, OK," Pollack said.

A long pause.

"So what do you want?" asked Joey.

"Nothin'. Just called to see what was up."

"Well, I'm kind of busy right now. How about I call you later."

"Sure, Joey, sure," Pollack said, "I'll be right here at the pay phone at—"

But Joey Ramone had already hung up on him.

"Sellout," Pollack said.

Stiv Bators was dead, Danny Fields was unlisted, Lydia Lunch was in L.A. Pollack hadn't had a girlfriend since 1986 and didn't remember any of the numbers of his exes. Finally, he called the *Village Voice.* The receptionist answered.

"This is Neal Pollack," he said. "Could you put out a general page in the office to see if anyone wants to talk to me?"

Five minutes passed. Ten minutes. Pollack inserted the rest of his quarters. But the *Village Voice* switchboard was closed to him.

His shoulders drooping, Pollack loped to his building, went down a flight of stairs to the basement, smashed a windowpane, stuck his arm through, and undid the lock. He opened the door.

"Kitties . . ." he said. "Where are you?"

The apartment was dark and quiet. Too quiet. Pollack turned around.

Something was on his head, screaming, and clawing at his eyes. It made a hissing sound, like vapors escaping from hell. It gripped tight.

"Mmmmworrrrw!" it said.

"GODDAMN IT, GET OFF ME!" Pollack said.

He grappled with the thing, which tore at his cheeks and continued its terrible noises.

Another thing, equally vile, attached itself to his right leg and ripped at his pants.

"ARRRRGH! ARRRGH! ARRRGH!" Pollack said. "CATS!"

He kicked his leg up, and shot Max across the room. The extra pain of removing the upper cat would mean little. Enough of his flesh had already been shredded. Shards of skin ripped from Pollack's temples. He threw Kansas City against the door.

They stood on either end of him, hissing, ready to strike again.

"Dinnertime, you fat whores," he said.

The cats rubbed against him. Dinner was the best time of their day. No matter how badly Neal Pollack treated himself, his cats always got dry lamb and rice, and wet salmon with couscous. Ungrateful sluts they may have been, but they were the only family he had left.

Pollack wasn't hungry himself. He popped a couple of Darvon, washed them down with vodka, and collapsed onto the beanbag chair he'd stolen from Allen Ginsberg's apartment.

"I'm so tired," he said to himself. "So very tired. Enough already."

The CD player was nearby. He put on *Follow the Leader* and sparked the bong. The cats, sated, curled on either side of him. The beats began to flow, and the words:

> *What could ya say as the Earth gets further and further away*
> *Planets are small as balls of clay*
> *Astray into the Milky Way—world's outasight*
> *Far as the eye can see—not even a satellite*

Typical pretentious hip-hop bullshit, Pollack thought. All these guys think they're the damn Messiah. Still, after the day he'd had, it felt so good to be relaxing, to be listening. That was all he'd ever really wanted, to kick back with the music he loved. Where had he steered from the truth, the Message? He closed his eyes, for the second-to- last time.

> *In this journey you're the journal I'm the journalist*
> *Am I Eternal? Or an eternalist . . .*

There was something in those words, but what? He'd been somewhere, but where? He'd done something, but how? Why? Where was he going, going, going?

What was this, Yom Kippur?

Then he heard, in the music, a distant echo of the past. Were Eric B. and Rakim really sampling Clambone?

Woke up this morning, and my boots were full of blood . . .

Pollack closed his eyes and saw Memphis.

Woke up this morning, all my boots were full of blood . . .

He saw the University of Michigan student center, its floor covered with broken glass. Man, that was a great show!

I shouldn't have stayed up all night . . .

He saw the sweet filthy Bowery in 1974.

Getting nasty in the mud...

Forty-five years had passed, and the music was still there. Neal Pollack saw his father, Vernon Pollackovitz, waving the finger of disapproval, but the music had finally drowned his voice. Pollack was following the leader now, back into the recesses of rock-and-roll time, and he remembered. Remembered. Remembered.

PART ONE
COME ON OVER TONIGHT

1952–1959

What a wonderful morning. I'd just finished reviewing the galleys of my book *The Threepenny Hip-Hopera,* which compares the sociopolitical roots of Chuck D's work with those of Kurt Weill's. It serves as an excellent companion piece to my oft-studied book *From Bauhaus to Compton: Sixty Years of Revolution in Western Popular Music.*

Then my editor from the *Times* arts section e-mailed.

"We haven't interviewed Sam Phillips in nearly two years," he wrote. "Our readers demand roots-music coverage."

It was the perfect research opportunity. I needed to seek verification for my still-nascent Pollack biography, to summon my remarkable powers of research, drive into that Delta dawn, and never blink at the truth. I knew that Pollack had spent part of his youth in Memphis, because I possessed this protean gem from the secret diaries he'd kept at age twelve. It was dated July 3, 1953:

I think Rocket 88 is neat/It really makes me tap my feet/They'll be dancing in the street/When Ike Turner brings the heat.

Brilliant. But I needed more.

My wife was home because her New School seminar, Rapacious Global Corporations: Imperialist Mind Control in the So-Called Third World, didn't meet on Thursdays.

"Honey," I said, "I'm gonna get an apartment in Memphis for a few months. It's for work."

"OK," she said.

"Are you gonna miss me, baby sugar?"

"Eh," Ruth said. "Not really."

"Oh," said I.

I've often written, at *Harper's* folio length, about Sam Phillips, spoken about him on panels, composed tribute songs to him in my mind, but I'd never had the opportunity to meet him in person. While I felt this was the insulting equivalent of Boswell never meeting Johnson, or David McCullough not meeting John Adams, I was still grateful for the assignment and the resulting paycheck.

When I encountered Phillips on a balmy Memphis night a few days later, the father of Sun Records, the grandfather of all records, really, the original benefactor of Elvis Presley and Johnny Cash, stood on the front lawn of his Memphis home in his bathrobe, his longish hair and reddish beard appearing just as they had on that recent *CBS Sunday Morning* feature.

"Who the hell are you?" he said.

"Paul St. Pierre," I said. "I'm here for the interview."

He looked confused.

"Someone interviews me every day," he said. "I can't keep you damn people straight."

Every room of the house was full of memorabilia from a life in rock. There were gold records, and platinum ones, and records with no color at all but black, the presence of all musical color. Lyric sheets, both framed and unframed, adorned the walls. A life-size copper statue of Roy Orbison stood in one corner, across from a wax model of Howlin' Wolf. And everywhere, photos, of men fresh from the cotton fields, hillbillies hitchhiking into town, people recording, picking, playing, laughing, self-promoting, shouting into microphones and sitting on the laps of pretty girls. It was a house to be envied indeed, filled with haunting music from the dawn and twilight of the real America.

Without any prompting from me, Phillips began to talk, in a relaxed, folksy, intelligent drawl, about the birth of rock 'n' roll. As he spoke, I realized that he'd channeled, in his life, an American ethos about which I'd only dreamed, or occasionally seen in movies made in the 1970s. I realized my rock archivist's fantasy. Phillips had stood at the center of popular history. Fifty years later, he sat beside me, recounting:

"You see, the motto of my Memphis Recording Service was 'We Record Anything, Anytime, Anywhere.' Well, actually, the original motto was 'Don't Be Afraid To Record With Me Just Because I'm White,' but nobody came in off that one, so I changed it. In any case, I opened my shop at 706 Union Avenue in 1949. I wanted to bring together what I saw going on in Memphis at the time, these black and white music scenes that had more in common than even the musicians knew. All along, my mission was to bring out of a person what was in him, to recognize that individual's unique quality and then to find the key to unlock it. And one person, to me, embodied all the hopes and dreams I'd ever had for American music."

"Of course," I said.

"I'm talking," said Sam Phillips, "about Neal Pollack."

Pollack had come barging out of the shadows yet again, and my imagination veered into places at once horrible and hopeful.

"Pollack?" I said.

"Oh, yes," Phillips said. "I knew him from very early on. Why, I remember—"

"Damn Neal Pollack," I said aloud. "Damn him!"

"Neal Pollack," Phillips said, "Neal Pollack. Now there's a name I haven't heard in many years."

"But you just mentioned him."

He slapped his forehead.

"Why, that's right!" he said. "I did. Well, let me tell you the story about how Neal Pollack and I met."

My notebook and tape recorder snapped to attention. He began:

"It was early fall, 1951. I'd driven up to Chicago with my dear friend Kemmons Wilson, who was getting ready to open the first Holiday Inn. I'd made the trip to squeeze some money out of Leonard Chess, that parsimonious bastard, and Kemmons was looking for investors in his enterprise. One evening, after retiring our respective alms cups, we met at a bar on Roosevelt, just west of State. It was your typical Chicago bar, tin ceiling, autographed photos of Hack Wilson and Jack Dempsey, bitter anarchists mumbling over their pamphlets at a corner table, fat-fingered city employees ogling the working girls. We sat down. I ordered a draft beer with the density of sausage. Kemmons had sour mash straight.

"Next to us was a thick-shouldered fellow who smelled like beets. I noticed him right away because he was wearing a very nice coat, and I always said you could trust a man in a nice coat. He was with a skinny little boy, maybe ten years old, with a bad haircut. That boy's eyes radiated a clear intelligence. It's rare that you notice that kind of perspicacity in a man of fifty, much less a child before puberty. I had to look down into my beer, the kid's eyes were so bright. Kemmons, always the friendliest sort, started talking to this fellow about this and that and the weather. The man said his name was Vernon Pollackovitz, and the boy was his son, Norbert. The boy just gazed shyly into his ginger ale.

" 'Say, Pollackovitz sure is a funny name!' Kemmons said.

" 'It's German.'

" 'Hey! An immigrant! Well, I've always said, if an American works hard, an immigrant works twice as hard!'

" 'That is true.'

" 'What line of work are you in, anyway, Vernon?'

" 'I am employed in an executive position at a prominent rug company.'

" 'Rugs! Well, I've always said that rugs are a good business, because people will always need rugs. But at the same time, rugs aren't really growing. I mean, you can't go wrong with rugs, but they're not moving forward, if you know what I'm saying. Now the hotel business, on the other hand . . .'

"At this point, I had to tune out the conversation. I'd heard Kemmons make that pitch a thousand times.

"I talked to the boy instead.

" 'Hello, Norbert,' I said. 'My name is Sam Phillips.'

" 'Hello,' he said. 'I'm in the fifth grade.'

" 'Well, I'm in the music business. Do you like music?'

" 'Oh, yes,' he said. 'It's my favorite thing in the whole world. But my dad won't let me listen to it. He says it gives people too many ideas, especially jazz.'

" 'Well,' I said, 'that's not very enlightened, is it?'

" 'No sir,' said the boy, 'especially because if you listen to black music, in my opinion, you can hear, like Walt Whitman kind of said, the real America singing.'

"Well, you could have hit me on the head with a Studebaker when that boy uttered those words. It was the most extraordinary piece of criticism I'd ever heard come out of anyone's mouth.

" 'Where'd you get an idea like that, boy?' I said.

" 'I dunno,' he said, sipping his soda, 'I just made it up, I guess.'

" 'That's not the kind of idea a boy just makes up.'

"He looked at me, his eyes confessional.

" 'Sometimes,' he said. 'after my parents go to sleep, I drink cough syrup and then I write secret stories.'

" 'You do?'

" 'Yes. They're about musicians. Last night, I wrote a story about how Billie Holliday took me to an ice cream shop.'

" 'Say!'

" 'Then she overdosed on pills, so I got to have all the ice cream

I wanted.'

"I sat there, near-stunned, and then I said, 'Well, son, how'd you like to meet the real Billie Holliday, in person? I think I could make some phone calls . . .'"

" 'Oh my goodness gee!' said the boy.

"The thrill in his voice reminded me of myself as a cotton-picking boy with imagination.

" 'Let me tell you a story, young fellow,' I said. 'It takes place back in northeast Alabama, a long time ago, in the 1930s.'

" 'All the way back then?' he said.

" 'Yes. Many, many years ago. See, we were poor, very poor, but not too poor that we didn't have a Negro manservant. We called him Cousin Brutus. Now, Cousin Brutus was blind. He was missing one leg and one arm. Also, he was seventy-five years old, really too old to be much good around the house, but he was fine company, and a fine musician. He would rock on the porch, hold his harmonica with his one hand, tap his one foot, and sing us sad, strange songs that none of us had ever heard before. One day, Cousin Brutus sat me down on his only knee and said, "Sammy, ah'm not gone live a very long time now. I hear the Lord callin' mah name, and I don't see fit wah I shouldn't answer him. But ah'm not afraid of dyin'. 'Cause I know that when I get to heaven, there are gonna be these wonderful trees, and ah'm gonna climb them. But you know what? Instead of leaves and flowers, those trees are gonna have fried eggs, and delicious Virginia ham, and big heaping bowls of biscuits and sausage gravy. And one day, Sammy, you're gonna meet me there, and we're gonna climb those breakfast trees together, and it's gonna be delicious and we're gonna be happy until the end of time."

" 'That's what I'm saying to you, young Norbert. One day, we're going to climb those breakfast trees, with Cousin Brutus, and the music we love is gonna be there, and we'll be happy. That's what life is all about.'

" 'Gee!' said the boy.

"Vernon turned to me and said, 'Mr. Phillips, my son is not allowed to talk to black people.'

" 'Well, why the hell not?'

" 'They carry disease.'

" 'No, they don't!'

" 'Please, Daddy . . .' the boy begged.

" 'Son,' said Vernon. 'be quiet or I will lock you in the pantry when we get home.'

"I'd never heard such cruelty expressed, and you could just see the tears well up in that poor boy's eyes. Spotting brilliance was, and always has been, my specialty. Somehow, I thought, I have to give that boy a chance to express himself through popular-music criticism.

" 'Don't worry, son,' I said softly. 'We'll figure something out. I promise.'

"Meanwhile, Kemmons had finished his pitch to Vernon, and Vernon had bit hard.

" 'Sam,' he said. 'I'd like you to meet my new assistant vice-president in charge of something or other.'

"Vernon put his change on the bar.

" 'Come, Norbert,' he said. 'We have news for your mother. We are going to move to Memphis, Tennessee.'

"I winked at the boy.

" 'Hasta luego,' I said. 'That's Mexican for see you later . . .' "

Near 9 P.M. one night in February 1952, the Pollackovitz family first appeared inside the Memphis city limits. Vernon drove a car whose make and model have been lost in the junkyard of time, but accounts indicate that it was large and sensible enough to hold a family of three and all their vital possessions.

Young Norbert was in the backseat, fidgeting.

"I'm bored," he said.

"Be quiet," said Vernon.

"Darling," said Gladys, "why don't you read your *David Copper-field*?"

"I finished that before we got to Indianapolis," he said. "And I read *Dombey and Son*, too."

"A smart guy, eh?" Vernon said.

"He is my little genius," said Gladys.

"Can we listen to the radio?" Norbert asked.

"No," said Vernon.

"Please?"

"No."

Norbert started to cry.

Gladys turned on the radio.

"Now, Vernie. It's been a long drive," she said. "And he's been such a good boy. Let him listen to the radio for just a little while."

"Dee-gaw!" the radio shrieked.

"Ach!" Vernon said.

"Dee-gaw! Broadcasting from right downtown Memphis from the magazine—I mean mezzanine—floor of the Chisca Hotel, this is the Dew with Red Hot and Blue. Dee-gaw-a-roonie! Wuzzat? Wuzzat? I hear a Martian talking into my ear. You better talk louder, Martian, because old Dewey's gone deaf! Hello, Mr. Dewey Phillips, the people of Mars would like to tell you that this broadcast is being brought to you by Falstaff Beer. If you can't drink beer, eat it with a fork or put it in your stew. Pour it right through the hole in your neck, just like they do on Mars!"

"What the hell is this?" Vernon said.

In the backseat, Norbert was giggling like he'd never giggled.

"Now here's one from Coogie Mitchell, for all those people down at Lansky's Department Store. A little bitty number called 'Big Pair of Jugs.' Dee-gaw!"

From the radio came a raw and dirty song. Norbert Pollack-ovitz listened, gape-mouthed, as the horns, guitar, piano, and call-

and-response double entendre chorus swept across his brain like a
street-cleaning machine at dawn.

> *Now, I love my little baby*
> *Love to give her special hugs*
> *But nothin' says I love you*
> *Like a whopping pair of jugs.*
> *My mama always said to me,*
> *Son you can buy them drugs*
> *But nothing makes a lady scream*
> *Like the special gift of jugs*
> *So if you're buying poodles*
> *Or if you're buying pugs*
> *Remember you can trade them in*
> *And give your woman jugs.*

> *It's a big pair of jugs*
> *It's a big pair of jugs*
> *It's a big pair of jugs*
> *It's a big pair of jugs*
> *Yes, you can buy a picture frame*
> *For framing both your mugs*
> *But your woman's gonna scream your name*
> *For a big old pair of jugs.*

"Oh, dear god!" Vernon said.

He turned off the radio.

"Darn it!" Norbert said.

"Shut your mouth," Vernon said. "That music is poison."

Vernon had long ago lost the battle for his son's soul, but now
the music had distracted him as well, and they were lost. The car
was moving down Fourth Street. Vernon turned left the first
chance he could.

Beale.

"Oh my goodness gee!" said the boy.

He rolled down his window to behold an establishment of sorts. Its sign read: "RESTAURANT—DANCE HALL—CRAP HOUSE—WE NEVER CLOSE." Next door, another said "DINER—BOARDING HOUSE—BURLESQUE—NOTARY PUBLIC." For blocks along the sidewalk, in front of many other storefronts of similar repute, men and women played craps, dealt cards, beat on each other, ate hot dogs, laughed, danced, spat, jumped up and down, and kissed in public.

"Zoot suits!" shouted a tall, bearded black man, who was wearing a zoot suit and holding a sign that read "ZOOT SUITS $25." "Get your zoot suits here!"

There were all kinds of people. Field hands still covered in the day's mud abutted the dandiest swells. Gawking teenagers and eye-patched pimps, bookies and sharps and lawyers and aldermen and prostitutes and soda-foundation clerks and secretaries, the wise and the naïve, the penny cowboys and dime-store Indians, everyone was welcome on Beale Street, even German Jewish immigrants in stolid cars. You went down to Beale, and you were part of the show.

Across the street, in W.C. Handy Park, a man in a porkpie hat played a mournful blues that Norbert knew well . . .

> Woke up this morning, with the grease up on my pole
> Yeah I woke up this morning, you were greasing up my pole
> Baby climb aboard my chassis
> We can do the rock and roll . . .

"Sing it, Clambone!" shouted a woman, nearly falling out of her red velvet blouse.

"You know ah will, you sexy bitch!" said the man.

"Rock and roll," the boy repeated to himself. His soul awakened. In his short pants, he felt the bulbous stirrings of his first erection.

Vernon was nearly choking with panic.

"Close the damn window! This Memphis is crawling with schvartzers! I can't believe white people are going anywhere near them!"

"Oh, Vernon," Gladys said. "Don't be ignorant."

Vernon slammed the car into park. He raised his hand, and slapped Gladys hard across the jaw.

"Well," said Gladys, "that's a fine welcome to our new home."

Years later, an adult Neal Pollack wrote, in *Crawdaddy*, of that day:

Well, hellbroth and damnation, oh, mama, could that really have been the beginning, if my little eleven-year-old rod had the power it would have ripped right through my slacks, because I saw it, the music, and don't you tell me that Gene Vincent was the leader of any pack because Memphis was it before I saw Elvis or Jerry Lee or Warren Smith, before I met the Prisonaires before I had even heard of acetate, when cough syrup was the only thing I was on, and I grabbed my daddy hard around the neck, and I pulled and tugged and said, "don't you fucking touch her, you fucking bastard!" and outside the Black Boy played an electric blues and I never needed "Hound Dog" or some "Love Me Tender" shit because I was there at the source. I had no time for adolescent rebellion or that Blackboard Jungle greaser imitative second-tier crap because when you're live from the phonograph department at W. T. Grant's in downtown Memphis, when Saturday night is Willie Mitchell and the Four Kings at the Arkansas Plantation Inn, you realize that rock-and-roll is not born, and it does not die. I see the continuum with my own two eyes, suckers, and when my dearest daddy smacked me with a closed fist in that car and my mother scratched at him with her sharp lacquered nails and he bled from the cheek and someone tried to sell him a fifty-cent chicken pie through the window and he said "fuck your nigger food," and smashed it back in that man's face, well, then, it wasn't much of a choice between my family and the blues. It was one and the same. I was in Memphis, boy.

On that day, as his father bled and his mother sobbed in that car on Beale Street, the boy said, "This is the Southern dream of freedom. Where black and white play music together."

"What are you talking about?" Vernon said.

"I see things in my mind," said the boy.

"You are an idiot and insane."

"No, Vernon!" Gladys cried. "Can't you see how brilliant he is?"

The family moved into a two-story, three-bedroom Victorian on Alabama Street, which Gladys decorated in dark wood, brass and mostly imitation velvet. She needed a comfortable home, because she could not think of a more repulsive place than Memphis, Tennessee; you were sopping wet as soon as you stepped outside. There were no Jews to speak of, no opera, no activities at all for a woman of refinement, particularly one so refined as she. Better to stay inside and not be infected by the vermin and their vulgar mass culture. Vernon, meanwhile, happily drove the South looking for men like him, joiners with the desire to work for a company on the rise. "Imagine staying at a hotel wherever you go," he'd say, "and every room the same! It is the future!"

They enrolled young Norbert at Henry Clay Junior High. The boy was tan and skinny, quiet, and a mediocre student. Most class hours, he drew cartoons of ghostly men playing the blues, of a breakfast tree in the sky, of a better world that he'd seen in short anecdotal snippets throughout his life. On his way to and from school every day, he'd hear strains of music, from houses or passing cars, and his little heart longed for something different.

I wish I were black, Norbert thought. Then all my troubles would be over.

One afternoon in October 1952, Vernon returned from a business trip to Macon, Georgia. It was already close to dinnertime, and he was hungry. Vernon said, "Norbert, I want you to run over to that butcher at 704 Union Street. Get me some pig's knuckles. Be a good boy. Don't stop anywhere else."

Gladys slipped Norbert an extra quarter.

"Buy yourself something nice," she said.

Oh boy, Norbert thought. Now he could afford the latest issue of *Weird Tales of Batman.*

But he never got to the comic store. Because next to the butcher shop, at 706 Union, was the Memphis Recording Service, soon to be the home of Sun Records. In the doorway, Sam Phillips stood.

"Hello, Mr. Phillips," said Norbert.

Phillips grinned, like in his archival photographs.

"Well, young Norbert," he said. "Are you ready to hear some music?"

"Oh my goodness gee," said the boy.

As his parents listened politely, Norbert ran around the living room in circles, frenzied and happy.

"And then he showed me his Presto five-input portable mixer board and its PT 900 companion piece, and then he let me play with his collection of Crestwood tape recorders, and then we used his Presto 6-N lathe to cut acetates, and then he let me help him mount an Ampex recorder in a rack behind his head so he could create a slapback bass echo, and then, and then, oh boy oh boy oh boy!"

He collapsed on the rug, humming to himself.

"Were there any black people there?" Vernon said.

"No."

"You're lying."

"No, I'm not. Anyway, they weren't there very long."

"How many?"

"Only four."

Vernon took a puff from his pipe, folded his newspaper in his lap, sipped his tea, crossed and uncrossed his legs, ran a hand through his thinning hair, and performed several other gestures that indicated he was about to speak.

"Norbert," he said, "Mr. Phillips is a foolish and frivolous man. I forbid you from ever seeing him again."

Norbert stood up. He was twelve years old and growing, still no match for his father physically. But he did possess a mighty pair of lungs and a gift for language.

"FUCK YOU, MOTHERFUCKER!" he said. "I HATE YOU! I HATE YOU!"

Vernon shot from the chair and smacked his son hard three times in the gut, and once in the small of the back. The boy dropped, gasping. An archipelago of bruises took shape in his midsection.

"Never defy me," Vernon said.

Gladys jumped on Vernon's back and clawed at his eyes. A shriek emerged from her prim throat: "Leave him alone! You common monster!"

His parents slapped and scratched and wrestled on the ground. Norbert crawled down the hall, sobbing. It was the same scene every night, with little variation, but he could no longer look upon their battles uncritically. Tonight he realized, for the first time, that his parents didn't have a good marriage.

As it did every night, the mad, bloody scrum gradually turned passionate. Vernon pinned Gladys by the shoulders and kissed her, full and hard, smearing her mouth into a mush. She slid her knee into his groin, and he began to grind. He tore at her blouse with one hand and plunged his other below her skirt.

Norbert stared sadly. Vernon saw him.

"Do not watch us," he said.

Norbert went to his room, curled into a fetal position on his bed, and read the latest issue of *True Boy Detective Digest.*

Minutes later, Vernon and Gladys finished their death tango of love.

As they lay gasping, Vernon said, "That boy will never be involved in the music business. Not as long as I am alive."

The next afternoon, an awkward, shy teenager appeared at the front door. He slouched with a hangdog sneer. His eyes were cloudy with adolescent confusion and dreams of stardom.

"Flour," he said.

"I can't understand you, son," Gladys said. "Stop mumbling."

"Um um flour."

The kid had a look and an attitude that impressed her, even if she didn't immediately realize how or why. She felt a stirring below, in her private heart, but she later attributed it to the fact that she'd just finished rereading *The Sorrows of Young Werther* in the original German. Goethe always got her going.

"You want to borrow some flour?" she said.

"Yeah," he said. "Momma's fryin' up some okra."

"Do you live next door?" Gladys said, hopefully.

"Um yeah."

"What's your name?"

The young man shuffled his feet, shook his greasy head once or twice, and leaned toward Gladys sweetly.

"My name is Elvis, ma'am," he said with perfect clarity. "Elvis Presley."

The stirring below became a flood.

"Norbert!" Gladys said.

In his room, Norbert was reading the latest *Haunted Soldier* comic.

"What?"

"Come here and meet the new neighbor!"

Norbert shuffled to the front room, where he beheld Elvis.

"Hey," Elvis said.

"Hey," said Norbert.

Gladys crossed her legs and squirmed.

"Why don't you go over to Elvis's house for a while? Momma has some work to do around here."

"But he's too old for me to play with," Norbert said.

"JUST GO!" she said.

"OK," he said.

"But . . ." Elvis said.

Gladys looked at Elvis with a longing and lust that he would soon experience hourly, but had not yet seen until that day.

"Take him," she moaned, "before I do something sinful."

"Yes ma'am," Elvis said.

Next door, inside 462 Alabama Street, a large and merry woman was puttering in the kitchen.

"This is my momma, Gladys," Elvis said. "Momma, this is Norbert."

"My momma's also named Gladys," Norbert said.

"Well, isn't that something!" Gladys Presley said.

"She's not as happy as you, though."

They went upstairs to Elvis's bedroom. Norbert found it deadly dull. Elvis didn't have any comic books or baseball cards or posters of Jennifer Jones, all the things that made life worth living.

"You go to Clay?" Elvis asked.

"Yeah."

"I'm graduating from Humes in two weeks. Then I'm going to work at M. B. Parker's Machinists' Shop."

Norbert was so bored that he contemplated suicide.

"But what I really wanna do is play guitar."

"Really?" Norbert said.

"Yeah," said Elvis.

"Are you inspired by the music in the air in Memphis?"

"I dunno," said Elvis.

"Do you feel the soul of the South traveling up the delta, settling in the place where modernity meets the old, weird America?"

"What?"

"Can you play me a song?"

"Well, sure," Elvis said.

He got his guitar out of the closet.

"This here's one I've been working on that I heard on Dewey Phillips's show."

"Dee-gaw!" said Norbert.

Elvis sat on the end of his bed and sang, *You ain't nothin' but a Bear Cat/Scratchin' at my door . . .*

The future Neal Pollack heard something that day, which he later described in his unpublished book of prose poetry, *Elvis, Elvis,* as "Elvis, pure Elvis."

"Elvis," he said, "there's somewhere I must take you."

"Huh?" Elvis said.

On a Saturday afternoon in the summer of 1953, Elvis and the future Neal Pollack walked into the Memphis Recording Service. That day, as his many chroniclers have chronicled, Elvis recorded two popular ballads: "My Happiness" and "That's When Your Heartaches Begin." Neither of them was very good. Sam Phillips sat behind the mixer board, filing his nails and drinking a soda.

"Well, this is simply not interesting," he said.

"I disagree," said Norbert. "That boy has something inside him, a fullness of spirit that barely begins to reveal his true intentions."

Phillips sighed.

"Norbert," he said, "if I could find a black man who criticized music as well as you, I'd make a million dollars."

"Gee!" said the boy.

Elvis was done.

"That's the end," he said.

"Well, we might give you a call sometime," said Sam Phillips.

What happened next had been lost in time except for an account in the *Memphis Commerical Shopper's Gazette*, a small newspaper that the young Neal Pollack published himself but never showed to anyone.

"We got one more song," Elvis said.

"We?" said Sam Phillips.

"Me and the boy. He wrote these lyrics that I like."

"Well, I've got nothing else to do today except promote about a dozen records," Phillips said. "Let's get this over with."

The boy went into the booth with Elvis. Sam Phillips took a deep, meditative breath, which he always needed during recording sessions so he could channel the true sound of music being born.

"Let's begin," he said.

Elvis strummed his guitar, tentatively at first. But as the lyrics took hold, he took control of his material, and then he plunged toward the piano, and played that, too. His dumb gawk became a confident swagger. They sang the first song that Neal Pollack had ever written, an up-tempo number called "Come on Over Tonight":

> *Well, a whoppa whoppa woo*
> *I got the boogie in my shoes*
> *Well, a whoppa whoppa wee*
> *I got a shakin' in my knees*
> *So come on*
> *Come on over tonight!*

Come on over tonight
If you have to drive a car,
If you have to take a flight
If you haven't got a cigarette,
I haven't got a light,
So come on
Come on over tonight!

The song went on for a couple of verses. When they finished, Sam Phillips said to Elvis, "Son, I think we might be able to work together."

"What about me?" said Norbert.

Sam Phillips laughed, and so did Elvis.

"You'd better stick to criticism," Phillips said. "There's no room in the music business for songwriters who can't sing."

Norbert thought that someday he'd meet someone who couldn't sing. That person would then become famous. He'd prove the founder of Sun Records wrong.

Such a god might walk the earth even now. But where could the boy find this tuneless wonder?

Where?

On June 20, 1954, as he did every morning, Vernon Pollackovitz woke at 6 A.M. did fifteen minutes of vigorous calisthenics, smoked a cigarette, gargled with salt water, took a shower, read a couple pages of Norman Vincent Peale, ate a boiled egg with a slice of country ham and sourdough toast, went to the toilet, where he surreptitiously looked at a Betty Page flipbook, and put on a natty gray suit and a stylish Kangol hat. He wore comfortable shoes, because he walked the five miles to and from work just about every day.

"Cars make people lazy," he said.

Gladys liked to look out the window because she wanted to

know the exact daily moment when she'd be free. On this day, she saw Vernon stroll down the sidewalk, whistling "And the Caissons Go Rolling Along." She also saw Elvis Presley in his Crown Electric service truck, windows closed, singing along to some unknown boogie-woogie. The truck backed down the driveway and ran Vernon over.

Elvis shouted, "Oh, my god, Mama!"

Gladys Pollackovitz rushed from the house. Her husband's brains dribbled into the gutter.

Norbert ran out after her.

"He's dead!" Gladys said.

"Oh thank god," Norbert thought.

"I wasn't looking," Elvis said. "Oh, mercy!"

Gladys acted with wit and speed.

"Norbert, Elvis, grab his legs," she said.

"Huh?" Elvis said.

"Drag him into our driveway," she said.

They were too shocked to do anything else. Gladys ran into the garage, started the car, and drove it down the driveway over her now lifeless husband, taking care not to flatten him with the tires. She got out of the car. With a screwdriver, she punched a hole in the oil pan. Thick black goo gushed over Vernon's mangled corpse.

"Holy shit," Norbert said.

Gladys said: "Here's the story. Vernon was working on an oil leak, the parking brake slipped, and the car ran him over. I'm going to tell the police that I saw the whole thing from the kitchen window, but nobody else did. Elvis is not going to jail. Not for accidentally killing that bastard."

"God bless you," said Elvis. "But what do we do about the brains on my curb?"

"Norbert," said his mother, "go start the hose."

"Wait," Elvis said. "Why would he wear a suit to work on the car?"

"And bring me a garbage bag!"

Vernon Pollackovitz's funeral, held a week later, was attended by his wife, his son, the Presley family, Kemmons Wilson, twenty-seven employees of the Holiday Inn company, and two traveling rug salesmen based in the South. Everyone was late for the service except Gladys and Norbert, neither of whom wore black. The rabbi read the eulogy, which Gladys had written: "He was a prompt man, and in above-average physical shape. His work made him happy, much happier than his family, who he often called 'his greatest disappointment in life.' He thought his son was gay, or at least mentally lame, and he could only sexually please his wife if she worked him into a homicidal frenzy. Music was his enemy, everything he ate seemed to be covered with a gelatinous layer of fat, and his farts smelled like death. But he did own several life-insurance policies, and has left his son Norbert with a substantial fortune that the boy could never possibly squander."

Afterward, as the funeral party enjoyed a delicious dinner at a riverfront seafood house, Gladys Presley said to Gladys Pollack-ovitz, "How can I possibly repay you for saving my son from jail?"

"I can think of one small favor," Gladys said.

Norbert got to plan his own Bar Mitzvah party. He invited all of Memphis through separate ads in black- and white-owned news-papers. Gladys set no restrictions on money, so Norbert rented out the Eagle's Nest. He hired Earl's Drive-In to do the catering, with an all-ages open bar. Through Sam Phillips, he signed Dewey Phillips to play records between acts. Little Milton did an opening set, and James Cotton stopped by to play "Cotton Crop Blues." Everyone was drunk within fifteen minutes.

At 10 P.M. on September 10, 1954, Elvis, Scotty, and Bill took the stage. The girls rushed the band, desperate pilgrims seeking baptism. They screamed and cried like harpies on the mount, swaying rapturously, their ponytails loosening in unholy surrender. As they pressed their rippling breasts against the pounding stage, they felt rock 'n' roll slathering their dawn-thighs, and they were women born. The men felt the empty pit of jealousy down in a primal place, a slow grind of envy that could only emerge in a Cro-Magnon shout toward the musicians who'd upended their cheap and easy scores. Something was happening in America, but no one knew exactly what.

Elvis sang "That's All Right" and "Blue Moon of Kentucky," then he sang them again. At that point in his career, he didn't know too many songs. Sam Phillips was by the stage, recording everything, nodding sagely, knowingly.

"Ah wanna call the Bar Mitzvah boy onto the stage," Elvis said. "Where is that Norbert Pollackovitz?"

"Norbert, Norbert!" all of Memphis said.

Norbert went up on stage.

"How you doin', little man?" said Elvis.

"I'm wasted!" said Norbert.

"Man, we gotta get you a new name."

"OK. I hate my name anyway."

"How about Pollack? That's shorter."

"OK."

"Nick Pollack?"

"Too many k's."

"Ned Pollack?"

"Naw."

"Well then," said Elvis, "I'm just gonna have to call you Neal Pollack."

Sam Phillips felt a familiar tear on his cheek.

"Neal Pollack," he said. "What a beautiful, beautiful name."

That night, Elvis anointed Neal Pollack. His band played a familiar song that became somehow unfamiliar and then familiar again after a while. It was "Hava Nagila."

The crowd lifted Neal Pollack onto a chair, and Gladys onto

another. They bobbed about the room. Gladys was drunk for the first time in her life, and it felt damn good. She whooped and ripped open her blouse. Three men simultaneously kissed her breasts.

"Mein Gott!" she said. "I feel alive!"

Dewey Phillips threw himself onto the stage.

"Neal Pollack!" he said. "Today you are a man!"

Pollack dropped out of high school and got on the bus with Elvis, Scotty, and Bill, riding that Mystery Train over the Blue Moon of Kentucky, on assignment for a little mimeographed magazine called *Hillbilly Hot Rag!* He followed that Hank Snow package tour through New Mexico and Mississippi, to the Grand Ole Opry, sneaking a peek at Mother Maybelle in the altogether, pinching the Carter Sisters' collective Carter ass, and then up to Cleveland, where he met Alan Freed, another one just like him. "Let me tell you, Neal," Freed said. "Jews who love rock 'n' roll are born to run this country!" They listened to Jimmie Rodgers *and* Fats Domino all across Texas, Elvis blowing flies off his lips, Scotty and Bill becoming progressively less famous, Neal chugging the cough syrup, staring bug-eyed out the window, singing "Baby Let's Play House" as they steamed into New Orleans and Jacksonville and all roads leading to stardom.

On stage one night in Texarkana, late summer 1955, a girl appeared in a ruffled blue dress, guitar slung across her chest, her mouth wider than the American highway, her skin perfect, her eyes full of hellfire. Neal Pollack watched her move her hips and he fell in love. She saw him from the stage.

"There's a boy I can use," she said to herself.

Soon, Neal Pollack found himself mending Wanda Jackson's dresses on the bus while Wanda played for hundreds. She was a pitcher of delicious sugary cream. She was his bad, bad girl, and he was her good little boy.

"I love you, Wanda," he said one night as they lay beneath the stars because they couldn't afford a hotel.

"I know you do, baby," she said. "Could you pass me the bourbon?"

He did, and she slugged it. Then she kissed his little face, which he was shaving nearly every day now. Her tongue wandered to unforeseen places. Neal Pollack tasted the sour mash that to him would always mean love.

"God have mercy, Wanda Jackson!" he said. "You are my forever!"

One morning in early December 1956, Neal came home. Wanda had gone to visit her uncle in New York City, leaving him with a bunch of her clothes to take to the cleaners.

"You have an uncle in New York City?" Pollack had said.

"Honey," she'd said, "I have an uncle in *every* city."

Neal opened the front door and beheld ruin. His mother's velvet curtains were torn and stained. Stuffing billowed from the couches. The kitchen teemed with dirty dishes and piles of festering rat turds. Paint peeled off the walls in long lacquered sheets. A great, horrific, if somewhat metaphorical beast lurked in the dark hallways, breathing hateful fire from its blazing nostrils. The house stank of death and sex.

In the foyer, Gladys lay naked, surrounded by candles. A sandy-haired drunk was fucking her wild, pounding her against the floor.

"Yeeeeeeee-hooooooooo!" he said.

"Mom," Pollack said, "what the hell are you doing?"

"Hello, honey," said Gladys, between moans. "Meet your new daddy, Jerry Lee Lewis."

"Jesus Christ!" Pollack said.

Jerry Lee dismounted. He extended a hand.

"Hello, kid," he said.

"Fuck you," said Pollack.

Jerry Lee pounded him on the jaw.

"Don't talk to your daddy that way," he said.

Pollack pounded him back.

"I'm not your son," he said.

"Like hell you ain't," he said. "I married your mother one month ago today!"

Pollack looked at Gladys, who shrugged through a daze of pills.

"I was lonely," she said.

Jerry Lee hitched up his pants.

"I like your spirit, son," he said to Neal. "Have some whiskey."

"Nah," said Pollack. "Too early."

To Gladys, Jerry Lee said, "Your men are hungry. Put on some damn clothes and make us some eggs!"

She jumped on his back and bit his ear.

"Arrrrrrgh!" he said.

"Make your own eggs!" she said.

"I'll take some of that whiskey now," Pollack said.

Later that day, after Gladys had passed out, the Killer and Pollack drove over to Sun, where Jerry Lee was booked to play piano for a Carl Perkins session. On the way, they hit a pedestrian, and didn't stop.

"He could be hurt," Pollack said.

"Who cares?" said Jerry Lee.

"I've gotta take Wanda's clothes to the cleaners."

"Kid," said Jerry Lee, "that woman is making a woman of you."

"But I love her!"

Jerry Lee busted Pollack in the chops with a full bottle of gin.

"Ow!" Pollack said.

"Love is for weaklings!" Jerry Lee said. "And you're the weakest of them all!"

Neal next returned home a year later. He found his mother wallowing in a pile of shredded British tabloids. She was drinking gin and weeping.

"Jerry Lee married his thirteen-year-old cousin," she said.

"When?"

"Four months ago."

"Wanda left me for a preacher," Neal said.

"When?"

"Today."

They had long misunderstood the region in which they lived.

"Fucking Tennessee!" they said together.

The fall of 1958 found Neal and Gladys heartbroken, rich, and bored. Neither of them felt much like doing anything. They cleaned the house, and had a contractor come repair the damage from the Jerry Lee years. Gladys put her hair back up and started dressing like she had before the wild times, went back to reading Goethe and staring out the window, listening to Bach records, cooking schnitzel and cholent for dinner. Neal started working on a novel that he called *Long River of Tomorrow*. Its protagonist was a young man with a guitar, misunderstood by a cruel world, who sold his soul to the devil so he could appear on *American Bandstand*. He'd written about seventy-five pages and was very pleased with himself. His mom seemed to like it, too, and they talked about where they'd go eat in New York when it was published.

Dewey Phillips called one night. He wasn't on the radio much anymore because he'd gotten all hopped up on pills.

"Come pick me up," he said. "Elvis just called. He wants us to visit him at Graceland. Bring some friends."

That was exciting. Elvis had stopped taking visitors months before. Neal put on a shirt and told Gladys he was going out. She just stared out the window onto Alabama Street, her eyes empty.

"Go, son," she said. "Go into the world and be young."

Neal loved his mama. She was all he lived for, with Wanda gone. When no one else believed in his writing, which was most of the time, she told him to keep going, because he was her little genius superstar.

He kissed her cheek.

"You'll be all right," she said.

Neal picked up some friends and drove to Dewey's house. Dewey was definitely on pills, because his pupils were like bowling balls, and he'd been drinking, too. They could smell it on his breath. He said "Dee-Gaw" to them, but very quietly, not like the Dewey Phillips Neal remembered from his first day in Memphis.

"Thanks for setting this up, Dewey," Neal said.

"It's nothing, boys," he said. "Say, why don't we stop by the Manhattan Club first and catch some of the house band?"

"Aw, I dunno."

"Drinks are on me," he said. "As long as you don't have more than one apiece."

So they went to the Manhattan Club. Willie Mitchell and the Four Kings were playing, and people were dancing, and it kind of felt like the old Memphis again. Dewey bought a round and Neal bought two more. Soon Neal was grinding up against a big black girl and he felt alive.

"Elvis is sending a Cadillac for us," Dewey said.

"Sure he is."

"No, really. The Cadillac is gonna pick us up right out in front. Let's go wait in the car."

Two hours passed, then three. No Cadillac came. Dewey really began to fume.

"Where's that goddamn Cadillac? Fucking Elvis Presley has a few hit records and he thinks he's too big for the Dewster, huh? Well, I'm gonna show him! Boys, drive me all the way to Grace-land!"

"I don't think so, Dewey," Neal said.

"Do it!"

They drove the four miles to Graceland. The security guard stopped them at the gates. It was about 2 A.M.

"Tell Mr. Presley that Dewey Phillips is here to see him."

"Elvis is not taking any visitors."

"Well, he'll see me."

"No, he won't."

Dewey got out of the car.

"You tell Elvis Presley that I made him, goddamn it, and he had better see me because there are some boys here who love his music and they know that he would never sell them out!"

"No, sir."

"Neal Pollack is in the car!"

The guard picked up his house phone.

"Is it really Neal Pollack?" he said.

"Yes, goddamn it!"

"Because Elvis said that he wasn't taking any visitors except Colonel Parker or Neal Pollack."

A few minutes later, a sad, lonely Elvis Presley loped down the drive. Neal had heard that his mother's death had beaten the King down, but wasn't prepared for the grief that overwhelmed Elvis's face. He looked wise, but also lost.

"I only want to talk to Neal," he said.

"Aw!" Dewey said. "Aw shit."

"Go," said the King.

Neal's friends drove a few yards down the road and left him to talk to Elvis alone. They spoke through the gate. An eerie whistling wind blew through the Graceland elms. Some distant owl hooted twice. The night was cool with fear.

"I'm going into the army," Elvis said.

"I know," Neal said. "I read about it in *Life*."

"I don't wanna go, but they say I have to."

"Yeah."

"My momma died."

"I know."

"It's no fun being famous."

"Yeah."

"Not what I expected. So. How's your momma?"

"She's OK."

"Be good to your momma, Neal. No one understands a boy like his momma."

"OK, Elvis," Neal said. "I will."

"And keep the spirit of rock 'n' roll alive. I won't be able to from here on out."

"Aw, you'll get back to the old music," Neal said.

"I don't think so," he said. "Do me a favor."

"What?"

"Tell people what it was really like. Let them know the truth."

"I intend to, Elvis."

"Now I have to go. The photographers lurk in the woods. They can smell me."

"OK."

"Remember your momma," said the King.

He faded back toward his mansion, America drifting into its endless tomorrow.

They dropped Neal off at his house around 3 A.M. There was a lot of blood in the bathtub. Neal found a note attached to a fresh meat loaf in the kitchen:

"My darling boy," it read. "This is lunch for the next week. Put it on toasted bread with mustard. I also cleaned your room. Make me proud. Someday you'll understand why I had to do this. I love you. Mama."

A darkness enveloped Neal Pollack's heart then, and he knew it would never completely lift. He was no longer a boy. He was alone in the world.

On February 3, 1959, Neal Pollack drove his Chevy to the levee. It was dry, but that didn't matter to him. All his affairs were in order, the house sold, half his money in a blind trust for blind people who wanted to be musicians, the other half in his pockets or his knapsack. He looked upon the city of his boyhood and felt no sadness. Then he realized that a true American hobo didn't drive a brand-new car.

He left the Chevy, still running, for someone who might need it more. It was about a ten-mile walk to Sun Studios, but he had all day and he was capable. He got there around sundown.

"I'm skipping town, Sam," he said.

Sam Phillips got teary.

"They always leave," he said. "It's my fate as a man."

"Memphis is finished," Pollack said. "American music is dead."

"Oh no, son," Sam said. "You're wrong. It will rise again. And you'll come back to me. They all will, whether they're in a Cadillac limousine or on the bus or crawling on their hands and knees. They'll all come back to old Sam Phillips, and then, like Cousin Brutus said, we'll be climbing those breakfast trees and eating country ham in heaven."

Neal Pollack, mature well beyond age eighteen, looked at his mentor sadly.

"Sam," he said, "I hate to tell you. There ain't no breakfast in heaven. And there ain't no trees."

Sam Phillips sighed for the ideals Neal had lost.

"Where are you going to go, Neal?" he said.

"I don't know," said Pollack. "Wherever the road takes me, into the real America, where real people sing real songs."

"Well, then, son, I wish you all the luck. Remember that you have a gift and that someday there will be publications devoted solely to music criticism. Don't miss that particular boat when it docks."

"Sure, Sam," Pollack said. "Sure."

With that, Neal Pollack wandered off with nothing more than a change of clothes, some trail mix, $500,000, and dog-eared copies of *On the Road*, *Journey to the End of the Night*, and *Butterfield 8*. The last one he wasn't going to show to anyone else, but he couldn't help it. He had a secret thing for John O'Hara.

Soon he'd write about his experiences, hundreds and hundreds of pages, probably without punctuation, pouring out all his grief and joy and frustration, as well as his hatred and love for those elusive things called America and rock 'n' roll, all the while thinking, knowing, understanding, telling himself the sad singular truths he had learned during all his hard years in Memphis and now beyond.

There ain't no breakfast.

And there ain't no trees.

PART TWO
THIS STATE HOUSE OF DETENTION

1961–1965

I returned home from Memphis early one stale evening in July. The loft was silent save the hum of the central air. In her office space, Ruth worked on an essay for *Cultural Studies Today* in which she wittily deployed found quotations from the scenarios of Ashley Judd movies to comment on cable-television coverage of the Robert Blake trial.

"Hi," I said.

"Hey," she said.

I had a bag full of Elvis presents from Graceland, barbecue from B. B. King's restaurant, and a plush Robert Johnson doll from the Clarksdale, Mississippi, historical society. I couldn't wait to give them to the children. After all, I hadn't seen my kids in six months, and I had to make good.

Their rooms were pristine, untouched. The beds were made and the GameCube had been put away. Looking in the refrigerator, I saw only vegetables, yogurt, and Italian soda.

"My god, Ruth!" I said. "The children! Where are the children! What have you done with the children?"

I sat on the sofa, turned on MSNBC, and started to sob. I'd been away so long, and now the children were gone!

"My babies!"

"Paul," Ruth said, "it's summer. They're at camp."

"Oh," I said. "Thank god. Music appreciation camp, right?"

"No. Zoe is at horse camp, and Paul Jr. is at Derek Jeter camp."

"Then let's go get some dinner."

Over a delicious bowl of basil-infused miso corn soup, I said, "So are you teaching next year?"

"Mmm-hmm."

"How's your book going?"

"Pretty well. And yours?"

"Not bad."

We didn't speak for the next two courses. When we got home, we turned on the TV and sat on opposite ends of the couch.

"Do you wanna have sex?" I said.

"OK."

Ten minutes later, Ruth was asleep, but I was restless. I took a long bath, because the slate tub and massage jets usually relax me. Not this time. My book wasn't really going that well, I admitted to myself. After all those hours in Memphis, I felt that I barely knew Neal Pollack. If the story ended here, Pollack would be a sweet, sad, but incomplete kid, a footnote to a footnote to a parenthetical citation. There was little connection between the Pollack I'd researched thus far and the grizzled monster he became at the end of his life. What about the world could wear a man down so? What in his own time had drawn Pollack away from himself, made him seek veracity in a country—a country, if you were honest, both old and new, barely a country in name alone, more like an *Übermensch* skulking out of the Bible—when before him lay nothing but the future? Why was rock 'n' roll destined to destroy us all?

Neal Pollack's ghost lingered above me. This was not what I needed to see in the tub. I got out and blow-dried my hair, which was still full and handsome, and slapped some Lotrimin on my loins.

Only one man had the answers I needed, and he was more legend than man. It was nearly midnight. If I started driving now, I figured, I'd be in Woodstock by dawn.

I knelt next to Ruth. She was still attractive to me, but barely. I whispered, "Honey, I'm going away for a while."

"Mmm-hmm," she said.

"I have to talk to Dylan," I said. "It's been too long."

There's an old man who lives in your neighborhood, or maybe the next neighborhood over, who spends his days smoking cheroots as if they were cigarettes, then tosses them in the bushes, which catch on fire, so he has to put out the fires with big pitchers of homemade iced tea, spiked with whiskey, but the booze makes the flame burn ever higher, so you have to call the fire department, and the neighborhood gets noisy and the trucks wake everyone up and you're pissed off at the man, who doesn't seem to care.

A strange character, this man, and if he asks you into his house, you're not sure if you should accept, because he passes his time singing you songs or playing you old records, and sometimes you're not sure if it's him singing, or if it's the record. He's that kind of man. There are hundreds of CDs in his parlor, an actual parlor by most standards except there are posters of the man everywhere. Many of those CDs are bootlegs of a fellow named Lyman Mathis, who was a prison preacher in Alabama in the 1920s, the man will tell you. The strange man, who has a weird, wispy mustache, plays a song, either on his guitar, a piano, the CD player, or all three at once. *Jesus murdered my wife,* you think the lyrics go, but they sound vague, indistinct, apocryphal, lost words from a lost era. There is menace in the words, and myth in the woods, but you can imagine the lyrics being sung on a street corner or in a swamp-bound tar shack. *Jesus murdered my wife, and I'm gonna take his life, come on down to the church, 'cause the flood is rising higher . . .*

I arrived in Woodstock around 7:30 A.M., with an offering bag of Krispy Kreme. There was no answer at the main house, so I went around back, to the barn. An old hound dog lay tethered to a post. Chickens pecked freely around the rusty remains of a vintage tractor. A raccoon, stuffed, leered at me, perched on a vintage anvil. There were poplars in bloom and plump tomatoes on high vines that crawled up a wooden fence. The air brimmed with fecundity and low-lying summer dew; the ground was festooned with auto parts and rusted tools. It was like I had stepped onto the set of a movie based on a murder ballad.

The barn doors were bolted. I knocked. The bolt came undone, automatically, and the doors swung open without my touching them. Bob Dylan sat inside, atop a purple velvet cushion, which itself nestled in a broad-framed oak chair, big enough for a king, all perched on stilts eight feet off the ground. Dylan's head rested contemplatively in his right hand, and his guitar lay beside him. He wore a black suit, white shirt, black tie with yellow spots, and bowler hat. He always chose interesting headgear. You could say that about him.

I bowed.

"Hey," he said, cryptically. "How've you been, Paul?"

"You remembered me!" I said.

"Of course. Man doesn't forget a guy who's written three books about him, now, does he?"

"Do you like me?" I said. "I mean my books? Do you like my books?"

"Yeah," he said. "They're pretty good. I see what you're getting at when you talk about me. Hey. Wanna hear a song I just wrote five minutes ago?"

"Oh, yes. Please," I said.

I thought to myself, "Bob Dylan wants to be my friend!"

He played his guitar, focused intensely on the chords, and from his mouth came words infused with tradition and historical allusion. Yet they were also stamped with his unique poetry. As always with Dylan, meaning was subordinate to art, making it somehow stranger and more meaningful, and also more artful. Listen, now:

People say I'm old, but are you old, Mrs. Watkins?
My sugar baby's lonely by the side of the road
Love is an animal, a humpbacked spiny monster,
Somewhere down the line you're gonna lick the toad.

The Serpent king is livin' on the wrong side of the tracks,
Followin' the ward boss for a cup of powdered soup
We were carryin' the mayor on the workin' people's backs,
There we went, here we go loop de loop de loop.
All down the line.

All down the line
Down the line,
Mrs. Watkins.
My dear sweet lonely spinster girl
Lookin' out the window
Give this ugly man a whirl.
All down the line
Down the line,
Mrs. Watkins.
Dancin' by the side of the ditch.
Come on over and rest a while
'Cause loving is injustice
And living is a sonofabitch.

People say I'm young, but are you young, Mrs. Watkins?
My lovelorn lovely's near the back of the plane.
Passion is illusion, abrasion, and contusion,
Somewhere down the line, you're gonna feel my pain.

Pancho Villa ridin' ponies to traverse the dusty land
Followin' the border for a money train to rob
Carryin' our freedom to El Paso across the Rio Grande

There we went, here we go, lookin' for a job.
All down the line.

All down the line
Down the line,
Mrs. Watkins.
My dear sweet lonely spinster girl
Lookin' out the window
Give this ugly man a whirl.
All down the line
Down the line,
Mrs. Watkins.
Dancin' by the side of the ditch.
Come on over and rest a while
'Cause loving is injustice
and living is a sonofabitch.

People say I'm dying. Are you dying, Mrs. Watkins?
My darlin' darlin's at the edge of the field.
The dawn is yellow, the corn is ripe and mellow
Somewhere down the line, get a dollar on the yield.

Cesar Chavez was always boycottin' the vines
Lookin' for his followers and lookin' for a home
All the handsome people must drink their handsome wines
So they can pay their tithes to the Emperor of Rome
All down the line.

All down the line
Down the line,
Mrs. Watkins.
My dear sweet lonely spinster girl
Lookin' out the window

Give this ugly man a whirl.
All down the line

Down the line,
Mrs. Watkins.
Dancin' by the side of the ditch.
Come on over and rest a while
'Cause loving is injustice
and living is a sonofabitch.

"My god," I said. "That is beautiful. It emerges from the lost murk of Americana like a clear diamond."

"I didn't choose the song," he said. "It chose me. I'm just channeling something in the air. But who cares about me anyway?"

"I do," I said.

"I know," said Bob Dylan.

"I'm working on a project."

"Hmm."

"It's about music, but also not about music."

"Hmm."

"It's about a man."

"Neal Pollack," said Bob Dylan.

"Yes," I said. "How did you know?"

"I know," he said. "Because I knew Neal Pollack. Oh yes, I did."

"I thought so," I said. "But I wasn't sure. There aren't any pictures of you two together."

"I had them destroyed," Dylan said, "to protect my reputation."

I was overcome, and I genuflected.

"Now, then," Bob Dylan said. "If you're willing, I'll tell you about Pollack."

One morning in January 1961, a bus pulled up in front of the Greystone Park Psychiatric Facility, an ordinary building in an ordinary northeast New Jersey suburb. A young man, handsome in a hairy, unwashed way, got off the bus, which he'd ridden all the way from Salt Lake City. He wore a royal-blue cowboy shirt with a light blue fringe, decorative flowers adorning the collar and sleeve, as well as fading work dungarees, a fisherman's cap jaunted to the side, and a bloodstained pea coat. When asked about it later by a female reporter who was in love with him because she thought he was someone else, the young man said he'd retrieved the coat off a dead sailor during "the siege of Cyprus."

He'd slung a banjo over one shoulder and a guitar over the other. In his knapsack he carried a washboard, a fiddle, some powdered eggs, a fraying copy of Gregory Corso's poetry collection *The Happy Birthday of Death,* and several harmonicas that he'd stolen from dying hobos in and around Bakersfield, California. The temperature outside was twelve degrees Fahrenheit, which froze the lice that had burrowed into the young man's clothes. He hummed a coolie work song that he'd learned from a ninety-five-year-old Chinese tailor in San Francisco. Opening the doors to the hospital, he went inside.

"Mornin', sweetheart," he said to the desk nurse.

"What do you want?" she said.

"I'm here to see Woody Guthrie," he said.

The nurse sighed, and picked up the phone.

"Betty," she said, "another one for Woody."

Another one? the young man thought. Why, he'd found a copy of Woody Guthrie's 1943 autobiography, *Bound for Glory,* at City Lights Bookstore. Reading it, he was sure he'd stumbled onto a forgotten American treasure. He'd memorized vast passages of the book, though he'd forgotten most of them during an unfortunate cough syrup binge with some merchant marines in El Cajon, and then even more of them in that Tijuana jail cell. Nonetheless, the image of Woody Guthrie, hobo, poet, patriot, two-fisted troubadour fighting fascists across America, stuck like an old work shirt to the young man's skin after a day's hard labor.

The nurse broke his sublime waking Woody Guthrie dream.

"Go on up," she said. "Can I have your name?"

"I'm Neal Pollack," he said. "But they call me the Fishin' Cowboy. They used to call me the Singin' Fishin' Cowboy, but that was hard to fit on a record jacket."

"You have a record?"

"Not yet. But my day is coming. I know a lot of songs. Learned 'em out there, on the open road. Also, I write really good music criticism."

Pollack took the elevator to the third floor, to his hero's room.

Bob Dylan, just as young, was already in there. He had one hand on Woody Guthrie's throat, another on his sternum, and he was slamming Guthrie down on the bed, hard.

"Stop it!" Pollack said. "Stop trying to kill Woody Guthrie!"

He leapt for Dylan, grabbed Dylan's arms, and kicked at his shins. Dylan wrenched away, both hands plunging for Guthrie's midsection. Guthrie was turning blue.

"Goddamn it!" Pollack said. "Nurse! Nurse!"

"You fucking idiot!" Dylan said.

Woody Guthrie spit up a chicken bone.

"Urrrrgh!" he said. "That's one tough chicken."

"Holy god," Pollack said.

"You almost killed him," said Dylan.

"He didn't mean it, Bob," Guthrie said.

This Bob, Pollack noticed, was also wearing a fisherman's cap, and denim clothes filthier than his own. Still, compared to Pollack, whose skin had been leathered by months of scorching Southern California dock work, and whose arms were covered in cigarette burn scars from rumbles in train yards half across Texas, the kid was a pallid, sour glass of milk.

"I came all this way to see Woody, you damn rubbernecker,"

Pollack said.

Woody Guthrie rubbed his sore sternum.

"They all come to see me," he said.

They did, indeed. Guthrie was pretty sick of them, in truth. He just wanted to watch a Yankees game on TV, or to read a novel, or go down to the pond and watch the ducks. A hot bath in a claw-foot tub would be nice, he thought. Or maybe a blow job.

"I'm a songwriter," Pollack said.

"Of course you are," Guthrie said.

Bob Dylan had turned to the window. He stared out, almost sulked, silently. Pollack thought, Is he ignoring me? Suddenly, Pollack really wanted Bob Dylan to like him.

He unslung the guitar and sang, improvising his own words to an old miner's melody he'd picked up at a rest stop in West Virginia.

> *Hey, hey, Woody Guthrie, chokin' on a chicken bone*
> *Dyin' in the hospital while the nurse is on the phone*
> *I came a ways out east, a hobo all alone*
> *To see this Jersey loony bin or wherever you call home.*

"I can't remember the rest of the tune," Pollack said.

"Oh, thank god," Guthrie said.

"Hey, man," said Bob Dylan to Pollack, "I like your song."

"The music is old," said Pollack. "Older than I am. I write lyrics. I'm a writer."

Dylan studied Pollack, his eyes steady and considerate.

"Mind if I play that song tonight at the Café Wha?" he said.

"Hell, no," Pollack said. "It's a folk song."

Guthrie, pretending to sleep, rolled his eyes under his lids.

"It's the singer, not the song," he mumbled. "Folk, my ass."

Neal Pollack had arrived in New York. From then on, a Friday, or a Monday, or a Sunday, or any day at all, really, you could find him in Washington Square Park in his blue cowboy shirt, playing one of his instruments, impressing Columbia sophomores with his rope tricks, talking up women, passing around packets of brownish-white seeds that he said he'd smuggled from Mexico. He told people to grow them in damp soil, under good light, and to never smoke the stems. Bob Dylan joined Pollack from time to time, and they passed Pollack's hat, which he called Old Cecil, for money. Pollack had a patter that went like this, "I'm the Fishin' Cowboy. They used to call me the Singin' Fishin' Cowboy. Now this here is the music of the people, coming up the mighty Mississip to the

mouth of the Columbia River Gorge. Lots of blood and sweat went into these songs, many of which are about murder. Donations would be appreciated. . . ."

One afternoon Pollack walked over to Washington Square Park. There was Bob Dylan, sitting on a bench, a woman on either side of him.

The women listened as though Dylan's words meant something to them, and his words did, because they were the essence of meaning distilled into words. It was the dawn of the morning of a new afternoon in America. From the suburban earth came these men and women in their work pants and thick-black-framed glasses and serious gazes. Soon they would sing and march and transform the social and political consciousness of the entire world.

I'm gonna get laid tonight, Pollack thought, and these broads are gonna make me dinner, and I'll probably have a place to crash.

"Hey, Bob," he said. "Introduce me to your friends."

"This is Susan," he said, "and this is Evelyn. They're from New Jersey, and they love folk music."

"Well," Pollack said. "We can't deny them."

They sang together, and the women listened:

Hey, hey, Woody Guthrie, chokin' on a chicken bone . . .

The magazine *Sing Out!* sent Pollack to cover an April 9, 1961, protest against restrictions on folksinging in Washington Square. Pollack got drunk at the Cedar Tavern, passed out, and missed the whole event, but he filed the article anyway, calling it a "real righteous hootenanny." The next night, April 10, everyone got together at Gerde's Folk City to celebrate a successful protest. A rested Pollack brought his guitar and his notebook.

The mainstays of the folk scene each sang a couple of songs—Dave Van Ronk ("subpar," Pollack wrote in his notebook), Doc Watson ("half a man, no staying power"), Gil Turner ("sucks big ass"), Bob Dylan ("superhuman prodigy"), and, at the white-hot center of the evening, Ms. Joan Baez herself ("the luminescent paragon of perfect, a beauty unmatched on this continent, a voice like that of Circe, but with good intentions").

Pollack gazed upon Baez as she sang "Silver Dagger" and "El Preso Numero Nueve," songs that, when sung by others, he later dismissed as the work of "pre-Cambrian Eurofags." But on that night, as he later wrote on a bar napkin, "My heart thundered like the hooves of a thousand rhinos. I was Zorba the Greek drunk on ouzo afire, hovering over a moonlit bog of unrequited desperate love. Joan was the shimmering *luz de mi corazon.*"

Afterward, Pollack and Dylan sat together at Gerde's, eating peanuts and grinding the shells under their authentic work boots.

"Hey, man," Dylan said. "I want Joanie to hear our Woody Guthrie song."

"Naw," said Pollack, his stomach boiling with love. "She wouldn't have time for us."

It was nearly 2 A.M., and a friend was hustling Baez out the door, along with her sister Mimi. Dylan made for the exit, but Pollack, unusually shy, could barely stand to follow him.

"Joan, hey, Joan!" Dylan said. "I'm Bob Dylan! Mind if I play you a song?"

He sang for her.

"That was very nice, thank you," she said.

Behind Dylan, Pollack wept softly into his fisherman's cap. Joan Baez noticed him for the first time.

"Who's your sad and sensitive friend?" she said.

"My name is Neal Pollack," he said. "My life for you!"

Pollack covered his mouth.

What's the matter with me? he thought.

"Are you a folksinger, Neal?" Joan asked.

"Yes, ma'am," he said.

"Can I hear something?"

Pollack sighed, his belly full of hungry love rodents that gnawed at his soul.

"Yes," he said. "This here's a song that I wrote after I saw something terrible in Kentucky, something so terrible that I had to write a song about it."

What he sang next had been lost until the lyrics and music were recently found in the basement of a Long Island lighthouse. No one knows how the document got there, but it bears Pollack's authentic scrawl. In a voice from the past, yet very much in the present, he played ...

THE BALLAD OF EMMETT O'DONNELL

Poor Emmett O'Donnell shot the Boone County sheriff
With an old Remlinger that he perched on his shoulder
At his family's farmhouse way out in the country.
And the cops were called in and they shot up his barn
And they brought the dogs in to nuzzle his corpse
And they hacked up his body all riddled with bullets.

But you who don't understand the story of Emmett O'Donnell,
We do not need your attention.

Your sympathies are quite worthless in
This state House of detention.

Emmett O'Donnell, who at twenty-four years
Farmed six hundred acres of corn and of carrots
With no one around but his simpleton sister
And a hulking manservant, left over from slavery,
Could not tolerate the banks' sternest warning
All the notes of foreclosure went straight into the garbage
With the leftover fruit and the cheese and the wrappings.

But you who don't understand the story of Emmett O'Donnell,
We do not need your attention.
Your sympathies are quite worthless in
This state House of detention.

Marcellus Kincaid was the Boone County sheriff
He was fifty-five years and had fathered twelve children
By six different women who he never married
Who he never looked at while he was impregnating.
He planned and completed more than sixty-two lynchings
He laughed and he laughed at the drunks in the gutter
And burned down the taverns when they didn't make payments
To his election fund, which he used to throw parties
In a brothel with guests like the mayor and governor
Who passed bill after bill to hurt the cursed farmers
Like Emmett O'Donnell, who was dead on his birthday.

But you who don't understand the story of Emmett O'Donnell,
We do not need your attention.
Your sympathies are quite worthless in
This state House of detention.

In the courtroom of honor, the judge pounded his gavel
To let the people know that dead Emmett O'Donnell
Would hang for the murder of the Boone County Sheriff.
And that Emmett's corpse, it would twist from the galleys
For one hundred long weeks before heading to prison
Where an outfitted cell would be specially curated,
For the remains of the man who'd shot up the sheriff.
For a most dire warning for the other poor prisoners
That until their death, the state owned all their bodies
And would hold them in jail until eternal heaven
For their baseless desire to smoke marijuana.
Oh, but you who don't understand the story of Emmett O'Donnell,
We do not need your attention.
Your sympathies are quite worthless in
This state House of detention.

As Baez later recalled in her memoir *Fly, Tender Butterfly,* "his singing was abysmal and his playing was worse, but something about Neal made me fall like I'd never fallen before. I melted."

"Come home with me tonight," she said.

"Yes," Pollack said. "I must."

"Can I come, too?" Dylan said.

"No," said Joan Baez.

"Can I go home with your sister, then?"

"No," she said.

Joan extended her hand to Pollack, and he took it in an exulted trance. Their flesh seemed to ripple at the touch. They laughed together instantly; no one could understand their love, borne on wings to heaven by the tragedies of folk and the triumph of future hope.

A cab took them into the night. Neal Pollack eased his head onto Joan Baez's lap and began to cry.

"It's been so hard," he said. "I miss my mommy."

"I know, sweetie," she said. "I know."

Back in front of Gerde's, Bob Dylan picked the nits out of his hair and stared at the bills. Pollack was a big fucking phony. He wasn't no hobo, no fishin' cowboy. And he'd stolen Joan Baez.

"Jesus Christ," he said to himself. "This just won't do."

In the summer of 1961, Pollack and Baez moved into a one-room pine saltbox house in the Carmel Highlands of California. Joan did all the cleaning and made all the meals on a wood-burning stove. She also tended to the lawn and the gravel driveway and cleared away the pine needles to make a path leading to a stone chapel in the woods, which she built herself. Sometimes she stole an hour to practice her guitar, but she also had to feed the ten chickens that Neal, on a whim, had purchased at the farmer's market in Monterey. Twice a day, at Neal's command, they made love, and then, also at his command, she wrote song lyrics about him, which he promptly made her discard.

"Now that I think about it," she said later, "it wasn't an entirely equal relationship."

They lived this way for months. Pollack spent the day working on a novel, which he said was about "an abandoned child in America," as well as occasional folk songs, and various other untitled projects. At night, they would eat dinner and drink wine. Joan would sing for a while, she would draw his bath, and then they would tumble about. In bed, they shared as lovers do.

"We must have a civil rights bill in this country," she said. "It's a moral imperative."

"Yes," he said. "I know a black man."

"Josh White?"

"No. There is another."

Pollack began to weep.

"What is it?" Joan said.

"Every time I think of this man, it reminds me of something

true, yet also false. He's the source of everything, but also nothing. All my life, I search for him, find him, and then lose him again. To me, he's nothing but a loosely disconnected series of glimpses, yet also the raw hard truth of the primeval."

"What are you talking about?"

"Joan," said Neal, "I've kept this from you all these months, because I didn't want to hurt you. But I'm not who you think I am."

"Who are you?"

Pollack seemed to grow in size, and stature. He also seemed to radiate glory. Like Persephone returning to the underworld after an overripe summer, Baez absorbed his words, feeling her soul grow darker.

"I'm a rock critic," Pollack said. "Since I was eight, I've known that I bear a critical mind so shrewd that it may someday tragically lead me to damnation. And it's all because of this man. When I first heard his music in a Chicago alley, I knew that I had to find the source. But that was fifteen years ago, and I'm no closer now than I was then. Everything I've done, whether I've known it or not, has been a search for this man. They call him Clambone Jefferson. He is the horrible essence of American music. He is my god."

"Tell me about him."

"I'm scared."

She stroked his hair, soft from months of her careful conditioning. He cried softly.

"There, there, little bird," she said. "Let it all out. Tell your Joan about your Clambone."

And so he did:

William Arugula Clambone Jefferson was born in South Carolina to a recently immigrated Afro-Cuban Jew named Carmela Goldfarb. When Clambone was four, his mother accidentally mailed herself to Omaha, Nebraska. A judge sent Clambone to live with his only known relative, a vicious bootlegger and killer by the name of Pee Wee Wilson, in a three-room outhouse in the very depths of Louisiana Bayou country. Clambone spent his days locked in a four-by-six cedar crate, listening to his uncle play the accordion, plotting murder. In 1917, the judge sent Clambone to the Louisiana Boys' State Reformatory Home for the crime of disemboweling his uncle with a tuning fork. Clambone quickly amazed his fellow inmates with his easy mastery of a number of instruments, including the saxophone, drums, slide trombone, and hurdy-gurdy.

One of Jefferson's fellow inmates was a young man named Louis Armstrong. He heard Jefferson playing in the prison courtyard one day and never forgot that sound. "It sounded like a clam," Satchmo said, "only with a bone in it."

At the age of seventeen, Clambone Jefferson broke out of prison. He began a journey deep into the heart of the South, descending into a seamy world of clinging vines and thick, viscous swamps and broken-down old juke shacks populated by big-hipped rough-skinned women, down, down, down into the depths, into the dirty stanky hungry maw.

Rather than making a deal with the devil, which was popular in those days, he moved in with a white farmer and hillbilly guitarist named Doc Thompson, who lived just outside Natchez, Mississippi. All day, they would beat each other senseless with hoes and then play out on Thompson's front porch, a keg of moonshine between their legs, songs like "Shrimps in My Shoe," "If I Had One More Minute I'd Pass This Stone," "The Devil Bit My Ass In Two," and "Won't Stop Drinkin' Till I Start Drinkin' at Dawn," which went like this:

> *Won't stop drinkin'*
> *Till I start drinkin' at dawn.*
> *Yeah, I won't stop drinkin'*
> *Still I start drinkin' at dawn*

Well, the devil bit my ass in two
And now my baby
Is long gone.

Musicologist Alan Lomax ran out of gas in front of Thompson's farm one night. He heard the music and got out his gear. The next day, Jefferson beat Lomax up and took his recordings. He and Thompson sold their collected songs to a company in New York for more than one thousand dollars.

In 1930 Jefferson shot Thompson dead, stole his car and his prize sheep, Tootie, and lighted out for Chicago, where jazz was hot and jazz was cool. For a time Clambone owned a nightclub called the Wet Grotto, which was closed by the health and revenue departments simultaneously, and he played piano with Cab Calloway, but, unfortunately, it wasn't *that* Cab Calloway. The 1940s came along soon enough. Clambone spent much of the decade in a coma. On December 6, 1941, after attending a meeting of the American Nazi Party, he injected a quart of sugar water into his left leg.

He awoke in 1949, staggered down to Maxwell Street, played a full set, kissed a mysterious woman who he only knew as "sexy bitch," and collapsed again.

Then it was 1951, and a beautiful nurse was hovering over him. "Where am I?" he said.

"Why, Memphis, Tennessee," she said.

She held his hand.

"You're going to be OK," she said. "I'm going to take care of you. Forever."

Clambone ripped out his IV. He slugged the nurse in the face, pinched her wallet, and fled the hospital into the street. For blocks and blocks, he ran like he had nowhere to go. Then he realized that he really did have nowhere to go, and he collapsed on a park bench, panting to himself, "That's all right, Mama, that's all right."

He started saying it louder and louder, and then singing it, until his voice became a quivering, plaintive wail that fused together the blues and country yodeling, with a distinct, rhythmic backbeat.

The legend goes that Clambone's voice was heard all throughout Memphis that spring morning. As he moaned away on the park bench, a tall, handsome man wearing a cowboy hat approached him.

"Hello," the man said. "My name is Sam Phillips."

Clambone never saw the man again.

The story ended, incomplete. Dawn shivered over the trees, and bathed an exhausted Neal Pollack and Joan Baez in redemptive light. The ocean heaved a half mile in the distance, and he slept. Joan looked at the strange, hairy man lying next to her, and her eyes trembled with tendrils of love. What an authentic person he was!

The doorbell rang. Neal didn't stir. Joan put on a flowered housedress.

Lo and behold! It was Bob Dylan. He kissed Joan's hand.

"Hey hey," he said. "Come to stay a while. And I brought very cheap wine."

During the day, while Pollack wrote, Dylan and Baez took long walks by the sea and in the woods. Dylan told her things that, at first, she didn't believe.

"Neal says that he's just with you because he wants to become famous."

"Neal believes that we should resegregate the schools, and he voted for Nixon in 1960."

"He doesn't like your singing or your cooking."

"He had syphilis."

The effects accumulated. At night, Pollack and Dylan worked on songs and smoked cigarettes while Joan cooked them dinner.

When Dylan was around, Pollack tended to ignore Joan, only taking her into his lap after the second bottle of wine.

"I love this woman!" he said.

Meanwhile, Dylan filled Joan's head with sinister whispers.

"Pollack has other girlfriends."

"He told me you're a lesbian."

"His family sent money to McCarthy in 1953."

Baez began sleeping outside, because she said it was good for her skin. Pollack joined her in the sleeping bag often, but she no longer stroked his hair or talked to him after sex. Her eyes gazed at the moon, but not at him.

Late one night, a wolf moaned, causing the elk to flee. A vague frost formed on the ground, and Pollack felt his body chill. Next to him in the sleeping bag, Joan was stirring.

"Neal," she said, "we can't do this anymore."

"You're right," he said. "It's almost winter. We should sleep inside."

"No. I'm leaving you."

"You are not."

"I am. We can't see each other anymore."

"But I love you!"

"You may think it's love, she said, "but it's not. It's become something sick and terrible."

"Come on, baby," Pollack said. "Don't be such a drag."

"I don't need you, Neal," she said.

"I am your deflowerer!"

"Neal," she said, "I wasn't a virgin when I met you. Not even close."

Neal Pollack yowled into the darkness. He scrambled from the sleeping bag, mad with heartbreak and shattered ego. Plunging naked into the woods, he tore at his cheek flesh with long nails.

"ARRRRRRRRGH!" he said.

It was unimaginable out there.

The moon threw off shards of glinty light. Pollack's bare feet touched a patch of stone slathered with slimy moss. He spilled to the pine-needle floor, his head slamming to the rocky earth. His chin cracked and bled. He crawled toward wood's end, where the ocean slammed the cliff with tidal inevitability.

There, on a stump, sat Clambone.

"Ah've been waiting for you, Neal," he said.

"You!"

"Yes, you done found me."

"What . . ."

"Hush," Clambone said. "My time is limited. Now listen. This folk that you've been listening to is a false music. It is not the answer. It does not represent the true spirit."

"But the songs!"

"No. I was there when the songs were written. They weren't like that. These white folks have changed the music."

"What do you mean?"

"They've made it boring, but it won't always be this way. You must find the ones who do not sing well, and do not care about their bodies. They are coming soon, and they are many."

"But Dylan can't sing!"

Clambone sighed, and began to shimmer in the dawn.

"Damn it, Dylan is not the one," he said.

"Yes, he is," said Pollack.

"OK, OK," Clambone said. "I'll give you Dylan. Follow him if you must, for he will become well connected very soon. But you must seek the other prophets of rock 'n' roll."

"Where?" Pollack said. "Where?"

"Start in England . . ." Clambone said, vanishing. "But beware Asbury Park. It is a distraction and a curse. . . ."

"Clambone!" Pollack shouted into the dawn. "Clambone!"

At that moment, Pollack's heart calcified. There were no more women, only receptacles on the way to his final destiny. Only the quest, the truth, and rock criticism remained.

He emerged from the woods a madman. Dylan was packing his duffel as Pollack banged on the back door of the house. Pollack was slathered in mud, skin ravaged, a crown of brambles in his hair.

"Man," Dylan said. "What happened to you?"

Pollack grabbed Dylan's shirt and spat in his face.

"I need a shower!" he said.

"You sure do."

"Where's Joan?"

"She went to the store. She wants you out by sundown."

"Good! She's a goddamn phony anyway!"

He sat on Dylan's duffel.

"Where you going?"

"Gotta get to London," Dylan said. "Be on a TV show, playing myself. Maybe record an album."

London, eh?

Neal Pollack walked into a bar.

Two guys with guitars, one bassist, and a big-lipped lead singer were onstage. The singer was writhing around like a monkey, doing his best to murder "Sweet Little Sixteen."

Maybe fifteen people sat in the audience, guys in white shirts and zoot suits and their well-dressed dates.

"You're a tosser!" one of them shouted. "Get off the stage!"

"Cool," Pollack said.

Pollack looked at the band, in their black work shirts and ruined jeans with Scotch tape across the rips, their hair as mangled and dirty as their sound.

"Rock 'n' roll," he said. "I've found you again."

After the show, Pollack hung around.

"We don't want you," the manager told the lead singer.

"Why not?"

"No room for your kind of music."

One guy, one of the guitar players, was scruffier than the rest, much scruffier. He looked like a rat that had been tumbling in his own filth for weeks.

"Need a gig," he said. "It's winter and I gotta buy myself a coat, man."

"Not my problem," said the manager.

Pollack got in the manager's face.

"Give these guys a job!" he said. "They're the best band I've heard since I got to England!"

"Sod off, Yank," said the manager.

Pollack reached around for a bar stool. Fluidly, almost professionally, he swung it around and smacked the manager in the face. The manager buckled.

"Christ!" said the scruffy guy.

The manager moaned, on his knees. Blood pooled into his cupped hands.

"Police!" he shouted. "They bloody broke my bloody nose."

The band and Pollack scrambled into the street. The sky was bright and cold. They sprinted and squinted. It started to snow.

The whistles erupted. Pollack tried to keep up with the Rolling Stones as they ran.

"I'm Neal Pollack, and I'm a rock critic," he said, in an alley, as they panted.

"So?" said the lead singer.

"I came here with Bob Dylan, but he's boring. If I have to hear 'Poor Miner's Lament' one more time, I'm gonna plotz."

"You know Bob Dylan?" said the scruffiest and handsomest one of all.

"Yep. And I'm rich, too."

"My name's Brian," he said. "Buy me a coat. Also, I need a new guitar."

The next day, Pollack and his knapsack moved into the second floor of a three-story house in Ealing. With him were Brian, Mick, and Keith from the band, a couple of students from the London School of Economics, and a mysterious Norwegian who refused to tell anyone his name. The Norwegian sat in a corner of the living room and read the same three pages of Kierkegaard day and night, his lips shaking with each repeated sentence.

It was the dead of winter. No one had any money but Neal.

"Give us some for the gas bill, wouldja?" Mick said.

Neal did, without complaining, because this was the greatest band he'd ever seen.

"Right, then," said Keith. "Let's go get some hamburgers."

The burger place was a few blocks away.

"I'm cold," said Keith. "Give me your sweater."

"Sure," Neal said.

"And give Mick your boots."

"Sure."

"Now give us ten quid."

"OK."

They went in the hamburger place.

"Wait outside for us," Keith said.

"Can't I come in? I'm hungry!"

"You want to see us play in West London or what?"

The show that night was unreal. Nearly a hundred people, many of them women, rubbed deep grooves into the floor. Under the hot dingy lights, Mick emanated menace. Pollack saw and felt the living power. The band, he knew, was a cut of prime beef that the public would devour whole. They played:

> *Where you going*
> *Where you going*
> *My little gasoline girl?*
> *In your upstairs two-room flat*

Petting your mangy orange cat
Blowing your gas-streaked hair
Letting it grow and curl?
All right.

Where you going
'cause I'm coming
My little gasoline girl
On a private gassed-up jet
In the ocean, getting wet
Gas me up
My little gasoline girl.
All right.

Are you coming
Are you coming
My little gasoline girl
In the fancy foreign car
In the honky-tonky bar
In New Orleans
At King's Cross
Or in Queens
I means what I says
And I says what I means!
All right
My sweet
Little gasoline girl.

One night, in February 1963, they were lazing around the apartment on moldy pillows, drinking expensive booze that Pollack had bought, and listening to Big Bill Broonzy records. Keith wailed along on the harmonica.

"Hey," Neal said, "I got an idea. Let's go to Liverpool. Check it out."

"Eh?" said Keith. "There's nothing going on in Liverpool."

"Oh. OK."

From the kitchen came moaning. Brian was shagging a girl. This should have been disgusting; the kitchen stank of months of unwashed dishes and rotting trash. They had placed it under quarantine. But the women just loved it when Brian treated them bad. Pollack watched, listened, and learned.

"If you can play a guitar," he wrote in his journal, "girls will let you do whatever you want."

Mick turned up the record.

"This is the *real* stuff," he said.

"I *met* Big Bill Broonzy once," Neal said.

"Sod off."

"No, I really did. And I know Clambone Jefferson, too!"

"Who's Clambone Jefferson?"

"Who's *Clambone Jefferson*? Oh, man! Someone give me that guitar. He wrote this song. You must have heard it, because it's the most important . . . *Woke up this morning, and my boots were full of blood . . .*"

"Nope," Mick said.

"*Yeah, I woke up this morning, all my boots were full of blood . . .*"

"Quit the racket!" Brian said. "I'm shagging over here!"

"*Shouldn't have stayed up all night . . .*"

Brian burst from the kitchen, leaving his girl in the ruins.

"You can't bloody sing, Pollack!" he said.

Brian pounced on him. Pollack dropped the guitar.

"What're you doing?" Pollack said.

Brian pushed him down, cackling madly. Mick and Keith unbuttoned and unzipped his jeans, then pulled them off. They started going through the pockets.

"Oh," Mick said, "a credit card!"

"Stop it!"

Keith held down Pollack's arms, and Mick his legs. Pollack squirmed, in his underwear, but he couldn't cut loose. The girl, out of the kitchen, rubbed her breasts in his face, for torment's sake. Pollack began to weep.

Brian produced a wire cable, which was connected to an amplifier. It gave off sharp electric sparks. He waved the wire in Pollack's face.

"You must confess," he said.

Mick and Keith cackled madly.

"Confess to what?" Pollack said.

"Confess!"

The wire sizzled. Pollack's eyebrows singed.

"But I was just playing the blues!" Neal said.

"Stick the blues!" Mick said.

Brian touched the wire to Pollack's testicles.

An unholy scream filled the Ealing night.

Pollack kicked loose, shot up, and limped toward the door.

"You bastards!" he said, sobbing. "You goddamn bastards!"

He ran out into the street, in his underwear.

Two days later, Pollack showed up again. He was covered in all kinds of filth. Ungodly. He was naked, except for his dung-crusted underpants, which he wore on his head. Somewhere along the line, he'd taken the plunge into deep madness.

Brian smacked him in the face with a tambourine.

Pollack broke the tambourine's skin with his fist.

"You won't hurt me anymore, Brian," said Pollack.

"I need a hundred quid," Brian said.

Pollack pushed him against the wall.

"I mean it. You touch me again and I'll break your hands."

The future Sir Mick appeared.

"Right then," he said. "Who's up for bridge?"

DON'T LOOK BACK: THE BASEMENT REEL

Hotel suite, London, England. Present are Neal Pollack, Bob Dylan, Albert Grossman (Bob Dylan's manager), Twiggy, and an interviewer from Life *magazine.*

DYLAN: Did you see my concert last night?

INTERVIEWER: Yes.

DYLAN: Did you like it?

INTERVIEWER: Oh, yes. Very much.

DYLAN: Phew! That's a relief. I was worried that you weren't going to like it and

write something bad about me.

INTERVIEWER: No, I'd never do that.

POLLACK, *sits down next to Dylan, addresses interviewer:* Why not? Are you afraid to say what you think? Are you afraid, man? Because I know your magazine, and how your magazine works. I've read your magazine, I've seen what you do, with your words and your pictures. You're just gonna say what your readers want you to say. Because your readers are sheep and so are you. You're just a sheep. You can't understand Bob Dylan and his genius. No way!

DYLAN: Hey, Neal. Relax.

POLLACK: How can I relax? This guy doesn't care about you! You think the people who listen to your records read *Life* magazine?

INTERVIEWER: I just wanted to ask Mr. Dylan about what kinds of messages he's trying to impart through his lyrics.

DYLAN: Well, gosh, there's not one specific message, but if young people come away with anything from my music, I'd like it to be—

POLLACK: Why does music have to have a message, huh? Why does it have to *mean* anything? You journalists are very interested in meaning, but not very interested in just being. You

know? Just people being people. You only care about rich people anyway, not poor people who are vomiting in the gutter.
You think they're gonna read your article? Or care about a
message?

INTERVIEWER: What kind of people do you want me to write
about, then?

POLLACK: I don't know, man. Just people. Like some bum wiping
his ass with a newspaper or Mr. Thompson wanting to kill
himself on the 5:13 train back to his soulless house in the sub-
urbs. Why don't you ever write about them?

DYLAN: Listen, I think I have something to say . . .

POLLACK: Sure you do. But you don't have to tell this guy! This
guy represents Lyndon Johnson and Rockefeller and all the
billionaires who are sending kids off to fight in Vietnam! He
writes for a magazine, man, but all magazines are shit!

DYLAN: Yeah. I'd never thought about it that way before. I hate
you, Mr. *Life* magazine!

In a trailer behind the stage, Pollack and Dylan drained the last
puffs from a roach.

"I'm gonna do it tonight," Dylan said. "I'm gonna go electric."

"Seriously?" Pollack said.

"Yep. This is it."

"Oh, man!"

Folk music was about to die, and Pollack was going to be
there.

They sauntered backstage, wearing identical black leather
jackets and motorcycle boots, each packing a Fender Stratocaster.

"Bloomfield!" Dylan said.

"What?" said Mike Bloomfield.

"I want you, and Arnold, and Lay. Get me that Goldberg guy
on piano."

"Bob, they don't know the songs."

"Who cares if they don't know the songs?" he said. "I ain't Dizzy Gillespie! This is goddamn rock 'n' roll!"

"What am I gonna play?" Pollack said.

"You're not in the band," Dylan said.

"Whaddya mean?"

"I mean I don't want you onstage."

"Fuck you!"

"No, fuck you!"

While Pollack sulked on the sidelines, Peter Yarrow, of Peter, Paul and Mary, introduced the band: "Coming up now is a person who in a sense has changed the face of folk music to the large American public, because he has brought to it a point of view of a poet. Ladies and gentlemen, the person that's gonna come up now has a limited amount of time. His name is Bob Dylan!"

Yarrow came backstage.

Pollack punched him in the face.

"Puff this, pansy," he said.

The band broke into "Maggie's Farm." It was terrible, a discordant buzzsaw of noise. Pollack saw the future.

"Fuckin' rock 'n' roll!" he shouted.

Next to him, Alan Lomax and Pete Seeger were not happy.

"Augh!" Seeger said. "That song has a socialist message, but you can't hear it! The instruments are too loud!"

From somewhere, Seeger produced an ax, and charged the power cord. He swung the ax over his head. Pollack tackled Seeger from behind.

"My generation grew up with the rock, old man," he said. "You can't stop the rock!"

"Heresy!" said Lomax.

Lomax threw his bloated self on the dog pile. Pollack scratched and spat. Seeger had a fat lip. Pollack kicked Lomax in the nuts.

From the audience, he heard booing. They were booing Bob

Dylan. Or were they cheering, or maybe hooting? He couldn't tell. The guitars produced a horrible screeching noise, a cacophony of chaos. It was horrible. It was heaven. The young crowd outnumbered these old men with their sour egalitarian breath. Dylan merely needed to summon revolt from the stage, and they would be history.

Pollack whipped off his leather jacket, tore his collared shirt, and squirted out of his jeans. He burst onto the stage while the band played "It Takes a Lot to Laugh, It Takes a Train to Cry" and began to dance in rhythm to the music. But there wasn't much rhythm, so he jumped madly, there, in his underwear, twitching, stinky, borne on the wings of rock madness.

"Get lost, Neal," Dylan hissed.

"WAHHHHHHHHHHGH!" Pollack said, and he launched himself into the crowd.

He landed among ten friends from Cambridge, Massachusetts. In their early twenties, like him, they were looking for something new. They didn't know exactly what to do when a mostly-naked man in motorcycle boots fell on them from the sky like a stoned dervish. But Pollack had ideas.

Dylan finished his set and went backstage. Seeger, Lomax, Yarrow, and Bikel were waiting for him.

"Bob," Seeger said, "people are very upset with you."

"I am one of those upset people," said Lomax.

"There's no place for rock music in a folk festival. You have to go out there and play something to calm the crowd down."

"I only have my electric guitar," Dylan said.

He began to cry.

"I didn't mean to upset anyone," he said.

"I know, Bob," Seeger said, "I know. Be a good boy. Someone will get you an acoustic guitar."

Theodore Bikel, to Dylan's surprise, said, "Pete, you can't stop the future."

"Yes, I can," Seeger said. "Now get out there, Bob, and play some folk music."

In the crowd, Pollack was leading a stomping chant: "Dylan! Dylan! Dylan! Dylan!"

Pollack grabbed the girl next to him and kissed her, sliding his hand beneath her gingham dress. She melted to his sweaty touch.

"Dylan! Dylan! Dylan!"

In garages across America, the motor was starting to rev. Boys were plugging in their guitars and pounding on their drum sets. Factory loft spaces were getting ready to host parties centered around blotters and monster joints. The sound barrier was about to be broken, and Neal Pollack was getting a hand job from a drunken stranger in front of the stage at the Newport Folk Festival, where it all began. His eyes bugged, his hair slicked back in ecstasy, as the rain soaked him in almighty transformation.

Peter Yarrow took the stage.

"Aw shit!" Pollack said.

"He's coming," Yarrow said. "Bobby's going to get an *acoustic* guitar. . . ."

"Boo!" Pollack said.

"Hey, Neal," the girl said. "Pay attention to me."

Dylan returned, tears streaming down. He played "It's All Over Now, Baby Blue," all the time glancing backstage, as if for approval.

"Anyone have an E harmonica?" he asked. "An E harmonica, anyone? Just throw 'em on up!"

Pollack pulled a harmonica out of his underwear and tossed it on stage. He knew Dylan had a plan. He knew that this was the moment he would kick folk music out of the world forever.

Dylan blew into the harp.

"Ew," said the girl.

Dylan began to sing "Mr. Tambourine Man."

No, Pollack thought. *Not* "Mr. Tambourine Man." That was

what they *wanted* to hear, wanted him to sound like. What they wanted him to play. It was wrong, wrong, wrong, and he suddenly knew exactly why. Neal Pollack's dominant aesthetic formed that moment. As he later wrote in *Crawdaddy*:

> Rock has to be bad. What's the point of playing rock if it's good? You have to push people to the brink. You have to make them want to kill you. Good musicians have no place playing rock 'n' roll.

Dylan played, and sang, and gazed tearily over his multitudes of fans. We are a generation of obnoxious, self-absorbed bourgeois sheep, Pollack thought. We will be immolated in the fires of history.

The rain came. Pollack opened his mouth, filling it with acidic water. He spat a broad stream of it onto the stage. It caught Dylan between the eyes.

"Judas!" Pollack cried. "Judas!"

PART THREE
GYPSY TIGER IN MY SOUP

1965–1970

In 1965, I graduated from Northwestern University's Medill School of Journalism, with a minor in American history, and moved to New York City. I immediately began to wield a "generational" cultural authority. The editors of the *New York Times*, *Esquire*, the *Village Voice*, *Life*, *Reader's Digest*, and other publications for which I wrote and still write didn't know what to do with me, a longhaired weirdo in his torn jeans and hooded Mexican sweatshirt who had much to say about a "new" kind of "music" that was "going on" in the "streets." But though I lived on the Lower East Side, within easy walking distance of Max's Kansas City, CBGB, and, much later, the Mudd Club, I never felt entirely at home there. I was a reporter, not a homesteader.

Soon after arriving in New York, I met my first wife, who wore a leopard-print eye patch and referred to herself, in her *East Village Other* column, as "Commie Girl." It was a dark two-month marriage, marred by deadlines on my end and tranquilizer addiction on hers. But in our brief time together, she transformed my aesthetic.

One day, Commie Girl shot heroin on our fire escape, which overlooked a bleak lot where, every day, Chinese butchers slaughtered anemic hogs.

"You look like a hobo, Paul," she said. "Get yourself some black leather. We live downtown, for Christ's sake."

On that particular day, I had to finish a profile of Ricky Nelson for *Time*. But the next, I went out and bought two leather jackets, which I continue to wear casually today. I was no longer from the suburb of Chicago in which I was raised, but of the real city. That night I listened to my Chuck Berry records with a fresh mind, while drinking a beer. I'd become a true rock critic.

Now, as I appear on various symposia, speak on my book tours, or lecture at one of the three major American universities where I hold tenure, I think of those wild days that were also rife with responsibility. Do I miss it? Does a dead bird miss the wind? But I also think about my then-naïve and still-developing "revolutionary" aesthetics. Today, I'm glad to have the maturity and perspective truly necessary to understand cultural crosscurrents, which are always current, and crossing.

"I'm sorry, what were you talking about?" Ruth asked.

We were at a present-day party in a Chelsea loft, thrown by a dear friend of mine who's in charge of artist development marketing for a major record label.

"My intellectual evolution," I said. "How I'm glad it happened."

"Oh yes," she said.

"I've really come a long way."

"Mmm."

Ruth and I met in 1974. She was a junior at New York University, taking my class on the Rolling Stones and the Birth of the New Hedonism. I barely noticed her among the five hundred other students, until the day she flashed a tantalizing leg from under her long jeans skirt while presenting her brilliant paper "Mick Jagger: Dionysus in Spangles."

We were married four years later, on Cape Cod.

"Remember our wedding day?" I said.

"Not really," she said.

"Oh," said I.

To the left of the catering table, I spotted an enigmatic figure in black T-shirt, black jeans, and wire-rim glasses. He was jotting notes into a well-loved copy of Frantz Fanon's *The Wretched of the Earth.*

"Hey," I said. "Is that Lou Reed?"

"Yes," said Ruth.

"Excuse me," I said. "Lou, Lou!"

"Oh, shit," he said.

Lou Reed dropped his book and his chicken satay and ran for the door.

"Wait," I said. "I need to talk to you!"

He fled the party and burst into the hall. I gained on him quickly. The elevator wasn't coming. He got to the exit door and started running down the stairs. I pride myself on my aerobic fitness. But Lou Reed was fast and sleek.

Lou Reed! Poet of my heart! Intemperate fickle lecher of my loins! Are you a god, or dappled tragic figure from mythos? Do you dare fly too close to the sun, or do you gaze at yourself in the pond? Or are you Hippocrates, oathless, the sickness or the cure? From whence you came you shall never return. Because what is a little S&M and cross-dressing to a glam god with shiny boots of leather? Nothing, as we are to you, even though you birthed us all; ultimately, we are powerless children of Zeus. We sprang from your head. The Velvet Underground, the greatest band that no one ever heard, lives on in dorm rooms up and down the eastern seaboard, but especially in New England, and your attitude has inspired a thousand aborted road trips. Banal? Yes! You don't care about us, and that's why we love you, Lou Reed. You are the bard of no bullshit, which in itself is the ultimate bullshit! See how we run. See how we run toward you, alongside you, Lou Reed, as you break the mold that made us all.

Lou! Reed! Lou Reed!

You are running from me now, through the streets of lost New York, and I feel you in my heart, you are panting in the streets, knocking over falafel carts, and I want to talk to you, my Lou, I am waiting for your words, have research that needs to be done, and I'm getting very old, and you're working on an opera with Peter Sellars about the Armenian genocide, another step in your evolution as an artist, and you are the god of cool, and you think that I'm a fool, and we're in a weed-strewn lot, former tenement that's now home to a former dot-com head who is starting his own magazine about how to start a magazine. We've forgotten how to breathe. You are wheezing and afraid. Oh, Lou Reed.

"What do you want?" he said.

"I'm writing a book."

"Another one?"

"Yes, but this one is different."

"Why?"

"It's about Pollack."

Lou Reed grabbed my shirt and singed my mind with hot poet's fire. He said:

"Don't ever mention that name in my presence again."

A dew-eyed curly haired kid walked into the offices of Pickwick Records on Staten Island.

"I'm looking for a job," he said. "I'm a songwriter."

The receptionist directed him to a back office. He opened the door to find a guy maybe three years older than him sitting behind a desk, talking on the phone. The floor was spilling over with stacks of newspapers, magazines, coffee cups, paperback pulp novels, album covers, half-eaten donuts and hamburgers, windup toys, bad cheesecake photocopies of Betty Page doing unspeakable things to pommel horses and bearskin rugs, and many other things.

The guy swung around. His shirt was covered in grease and bits of moldy meat. He simultaneously shouted into the phone and a tape recorder.

"Screw you, Grossman!" he said. "Who needs your goddamn

touring schedule anyway?"

He hung up.

"Who are you?" he said.

"I'm Lou Reed," the kid said. "I want to be a songwriter."

The guy gave a long laugh. His belly buckled.

"Is that right?" he said. "Well, I'm Neal Pollack, and I want to be a goddamn astronaut."

Reed was confused.

"Lemme play you a record," Pollack said.

He had a turntable. He put on the Byrds's *Turn! Turn! Turn!*

"You like this?" he said.

"No," said Lou Reed. "I hate folk rock."

"Goddamn right," Pollack said. "It's shit."

He handed Reed the record.

"Break it," he said.

"Right here?"

"Right now."

Reed found a free corner of floor and smashed the record.

"Did that feel good?" Pollack asked.

"Yeah."

"Good! You're hired! Where you from?"

"I just graduated from Syracuse University."

"Hmm."

"I studied English with Delmore Schwartz."

"He's not a writer."

"Yes he is."

"No," Pollack said. "I AM A WRITER! The living incarnation. There is no one else."

"OK," said Lou Reed.

"I need you to work on a song for me," said Pollack. "We do surf and hot-rod music here. Nothing but crap. But all real music is crap. Remember that. Anyway. This radio station in California says the kids need a new dance. I came up with something called the Ostrich. So far, I've got this:

> *Well put your head in the sand!*
> *Ostrich!*
> *Shake your tail in the air!*
> *Ostrich!*
> *Do the BRAAAAWK BRAAAAWK BRAAAAWK!*
> *BRAAAAWK BRAAAAWK BRAAAAWK!*
> *Ostrich! Oh Yeah!*

Can't seem to finish it though."

"Let me think about that for a second," Reed said.

He thought about it for a second, and then sang, in perfect monotone:

> *Well put your head in the sand.*
> *I said put your head in the sand, sand.*
> *Yeah put your head in the sand.*
> *You wanna be my man.*
> *Just put your head in the sand.*
> *I'm just waiting for my man*
> *To put his head in the cold cold sand.*

"That's perfect!" Pollack said. "You're hired!"

"You already hired me."

"Right!"

Reed looked at his shoes.

"You should form a band, record this shit!" Pollack said.

"OK," said Reed.

Pollack stood on the desk, unzipped his pants, and urinated at Reed's feet.

"I had to do that," he said.

"No problem."

"Reed? You Jewish?"

"Yes."

"Good! You a junkie?"

"No."

"You look like a junkie. You're a good-looking guy."

"Thanks," Reed said.

"Let's go to the bathroom," said Pollack.

Neal Pollack stuffed a towel under the door of the stall. He tied off with a rubber tube, and he showed Reed how. Their arms swelled and purpled, tensed and relaxed.

"Stole this needle from Mount Sinai," Pollack said. "The hospital, that is."

They both felt the cool rush of almighty heroin in their blood. Suddenly the Ostrich wasn't much of a worry for them anymore. Pollack looked at Reed, tender, lithe, breathing softly, smiling on the bathroom floor, slender, beautiful and challenging.

"Man," Pollack said, "I do this every day."

"Cool," said Reed.

"You know what else I do every day?"

"What?"

"Remove your pants," said Pollack.

"OK," said Lou Reed.

Neal Pollack offered his loft apartment on Clinton Street to Lou for rehearsal space. The loft was eight thousand square feet and very expensive. It had quickly become a center of neighborhood social life. Freaks, weirdos, and street hustlers stopped by at all times of the day to score, and sometimes stayed for days.

"Holy shit, Neal," Reed said. "How can you afford this?"

"Elvis ran over my father," Pollack said. "I got the insurance money."

Lou laughed.

"No," Neal said. "Seriously."

Lou brought his friends Sterling Morrison and John Cale. Other musicians rotated in and out, including for a time the director John Cassavettes, who made a movie about those days that he refuses to screen. There was always someone having sex in front of the band while they practiced, but they didn't care, because the space was free. They would sometimes play for forty-eight hours straight without stopping. It was minimalistic music that sounded like nothing you could hear on the radio. Cale played viola and bass and sometimes guitar. Lou did most of the singing. Neal sometimes joined in, but mostly he just smoked pot and sat in a papasan, masturbating.

One night, Pollack got up from the chair and started to moan a song. He said he'd written it with Lou, but Lou swore he'd never heard a word. Halfway through, the band put down their instruments to go drink some beer. Pollack didn't notice. He went on for many hours, repeating the lyrics over and over again. That song was, technically, the Velvet Underground's first. It's been called "Never Get Emotionally Involved With Man, Woman, Beast, or Child," or "Vein," and it went like this:

> *In the mornings I get lost*
> *Near an alley with no name*
> *And I wish I could escape*
> *To a place beyond the world*
> *Where the pirates drink their tears*
> *Where the wenches like to slap*
> *My pathetic drooping face*
> *And I'm so so so alone.*
> *Can't you see me on TV?*
>
> *Oh,*
> *My vein.*

Shining mistress in the dark
Where you been since I was born?
Feel the fat and angry crush
Of your boots against my chest
When my skin begins to leak
Bearded streets begin to bleed
There is nothing on TV
And the radio is blank
And the Negroes roam the streets

Oh,
My vein.

Johnny's parties are so dull
They don't start 'til 2 AM
Want to burn Chelsea Hotel
All the hippies need to die
The black leather needs to fade
The mad monster in my shorts
Feels a hunger with no face
And there's nothing on TV
And there's nothing on TV

Oh,
My vein.

Feel the vein run through my arm
Feel the blood run through my vein
Silky platelets in the blood
What are platelets anyway?
And I'm jonesing for some weed
It is not a gateway drug
Gypsy tiger in my soup

With a needle in his arm.
And I'm dying every day.

When Pollack stopped singing, it was noon. His hands trembled; little pools of bloody sweat formed on his arms. He was exhausted.

"Lou?" he said. "Where are you, Lou?"

The Velvet Underground had left. After that night, they rented their own place on Ludlow.

They were the greatest band of all time.

Neal Pollack got the Velvet Underground a gig playing R&B covers at the Café Bizarre, a tourist trap in Greenwich Village. One night Polack came into Café Bizarre shaking and twittering some nonsense about "dumping Allen Ginsberg in the East River." He'd been on a five-day amphetamine binge. He was also completely hairless, both on his body and his head.

"I gave myself a wax treatment," he said. "I've become a sleek warrior."

Pollack had heard that Andy Warhol was looking for a hairless androgyne for a film he was working on called *Andy Warhol Presents a Hairless Androgyne*. He went to the Factory and had a screen test.

"I AM A HAIRLESS ANDROGYNE!" he shouted, while a Martha and the Vandellas record played in the background. "The police can whip my wrists!"

"Hey, Neal," Warhol said to him, "you're a superstar."

Pollack popped a couple pills and trembled on the sofa.

"So can I be in your movie?" he said.

"Gee, I dunno," Warhol said. Turning to his assistant, he said, "Paul, can Neal be in my movie?"

"No," said Paul Morrissey.

"Sorry, Neal," Warhol said. "You can't be in my movie."

"Let me take you to see this band," Pollack said.

"Gee, I dunno," Andy said. "Rock 'n' roll makes me nervous."

Wrapped only in a leather towel, a mystery entered the room, a sleek brown-eyed blonde who wore weirdness like other women wore thigh-high boots.

"Wubba wubba woo!" Pollack said.

Pollack was wearing black leather pants, a black leather shirt, and a black leather jacket, along with black leather sunglasses and leather socks. He lit a joint and offered Nico a puff.

"I'm Neal Pollack," he said.

"Yeah, I heard about you from the Rolling Stones," Nico said. "What are you doing in New York?"

"Nothing much," said Pollack. "Just working on my novel and living the bisexual drug addict's dream."

"Andy," Nico said, "I'm SO bored. When do I get to sing?"

January 1966. Pollack took a bottle of whiskey from the bathroom sink, slugged it, and squatted. It was 3 A.M. His house was empty. He braced himself on the toilet and saw his reflection in the shimmering water. The cold porcelain and the even colder air made him shiver. His stomach hitched and erupted, his spine arched into the air. After a few minutes, it was over. He collapsed by the bowl, his breaths coming in heavy, bearlike sighs.

He'd been drinking cough syrup since he was eight, whiskey since he was fourteen, smoking marijuana since he was nineteen, and, for the last two years, popping pills, shooting heroin, and snorting drain cleaner off back issues of the *Saturday Evening Post*. At first he'd been insatiable and wild, able to wake at dawn with little aftereffect. But of late, he'd found himself stirring at noon, and then unstirring, then waking up again just before dusk, hungry and alone. At times he withdrew into the damned sanctums of his brain, cursing the abomination that he'd become, wondering how to get an invitation to that party he'd heard about, trying to figure out who would publish him next. A dog with two heads named ambition and desperation gnawed at his mind, and a jungle cat named confusion roared alongside. His muscles ached. His bones throbbed. He'd lost his way. He wasn't quite yet twenty-five.

The buzzer rang.

"What?" Pollack said into the speaker. "What?"

"It's Nico," said the voice. "And I've brought twenty-five friends."

So the cycle began again.

Andy Warhol began to curate shows at the Dom Theater on St. Marks Place. Pollack told him no one would pay attention, but Warhol ignored him. He called his show the Exploding Plastic Inevitable and charged five dollars. The Velvets played with their backs to the audience. Warhol showed films. On another wall, he showed slides. On a third wall was a kinescope of animals being tortured. Gerard Malanga wore leather pants and danced rhythmically. Beautiful women in leather bustiers cracked whips at one another, relishing the streaky blood that squirted from their welts.

Wearing only an executioner's mask, Pollack sat centerstage, grinding on a broom.

"I AM THE ANGEL OF DEATH!" he said.

The dancers ran through the audience, shining flashlights in people's faces. They dry-humped one another in a winding mass. The audience was shocked, shocked.

Nico, standing next to Warhol, gazed on the scene from the balcony.

"It's like the Red Sea," she said, "paaaaaaarting."

"This is my happening!" Warhol said. "And it's freaking me out!"

"WHOOOO!" Pollack screeched from the stage. "WHOOOO! S and M! S and M!"

"He must be stopped," Warhol said.

But against Andy Warhol's wishes, Pollack went on tour with the Exploding Plastic Inevitable. One night in Ann Arbor, Michigan, he and Nico spent hours pacing their hotel room, staring each other down, mad, poetic, and desperate.

"Come on, Nico," he said. "Let's get outta here."

"Not until you give me my pills back," she said.

"I need those pills!" he said. "I need them to live!"

"Leave me alone!" she said.

Pollack grabbed her hair.

"You wanna cross the Nealster?" he said.

Nico wrenched away, dove for the door, and ran downstairs to the bus. Lou Reed was simultaneously giving and receiving a blow job.

"He's trying to kill me!" she said. "Oh, please help! Neal's going to kill me!"

Pollack sunk his head in his hands.

"I'm a monster!" he said. "Oh, dear god!"

It was time for an aesthetic and personal reckoning. Pollack was wracked with boundless guilt. Was this what he sought? Whips and art films in college auditoriums? Fistfights with German hipster succubi? Quiet, secret betrayals and noisy, anonymous group sex? Well, yes. But how far could he go by partying and making art with the coolest, most intelligent people of his generation? In his diaries, Pollack wrote, "As I sat there on that motel room bed with my cock hanging out and Lou Reed pounding on the door, I took the needle from my arm and I knew it was time to move on."

He went to a bar called Mother's and wrote this archetypal garage-rock song:

You can smoke my cigar
You can ride in my car

You can buy me a bar
You can play the sitar
But I won't be . . .
Happy.

You can piss in my bed
You can spray-paint me red
Pound my brains till I'm dead
You can Flintstone my Fred
But I won't be . . .
Friendly.

You can strap me sidesaddle
In a hotel room
Or split open my ass
With an extra-thick broom
You can suck on my monkey
From Beijing to Khartoum
But I won't love you.
(one, two three, four)
'Cause I'm a seeker.
Yeah, oh yeah
I'm a seeker.

I can cut off your hair
Take you to the state fair
Win a big teddy bear
I can be your au pair
But I'll never . . .
Kiss you.

I can make you a pie
I can find you a guy

I can spit in your eye
I can laugh while you die
But I'll never . . .
Want you . . .

Pollack drank a Pabst Blue Ribbon and a shot of Maker's Mark, and then another, and another, while he worked on the song. It was a perfect expression of what he felt, a guttural shout of rage against hypocrisy. But it wasn't right for Lou Reed. Lou didn't have the vision to bring these words to life. Who could do it, then?

A band took the stage. They were the grimiest, scuzziest degenerates Pollack had ever seen. Oh, they were disgusting. They called themselves the Prime Movers. During the first number, the bass player set himself on fire.

"Put that out!" Mother said.

"Bite me, Mother," said Ron Asheton. "I'm a dirtbag!"

But no one rocked harder than the drummer, a little pimple-faced kid in a white shirt and tie. Between numbers, he sat there shyly, head bowed, sticks hanging limply by his arms, but as each song kicked up, he flailed like a demon, pounding, grinding, evil, dying.

A stool came out of the crowd and hit the drummer in the head.

"Ow!" he said. "Gee! That hurt! Don't do that again!"

Out flew a bottle. It got him on the chin.

"Golly!" the drummer said. "That wasn't nice!"

And then he just kept playing.

Pollack downed another shot. He looked at his lyrics.

I'm a seeker, he said to himself. He felt alive. The drummer soldiered on.

"I have found him," Pollack said. "I have found the one."

James Osterberg lived in a trailer camp in the middle of a farm off US Highway 23 between Ypsilanti and Ann Arbor, Michigan.

"I don't usually take people home with me," James said. "I'm ashamed."

"I've lived in worse," said Pollack. "I respect the workingman, because only the workingman can create true rock 'n' roll."

Inside, a middle-aged couple was watching *Get Smart*.

"Mom, Dad," James said. "This is Neal Pollack. He's a writer from New York."

"You need a bath, young man," said Mrs. Osterberg.

"It's true, ma'am," Pollack said.

"I wanna show you my room," James said.

The room wasn't much, a few Rolling Stones records, a baseball glove, a poster of Mickey Mantle, clothes strewn everywhere, just another sad lair of a dirtball teenage slob.

Pollack sat on the bed.

"Lemme tell you a secret," James said.

"OK," said Pollack.

"I'm telling you because of all those nice things you said to me at the bar about me being the savior of rock music."

"I meant every word."

"So listen, you see that shoebox on the windowsill?"

"Yes."

"I shit in it."

"You shit in a box?"

"Yeah. And then I put it on the windowsill, because I like to watch the birds eat my shit."

Pollack stared at the kid.

"Damn," he said. "You *are* weird."

"Gee," said James.

They went outside. Two big jocks in overalls came up to them.

"Hey, Osterberg," said one of them. "You still playin' with dollies?"

James withered visibly.

"No," he said.

"You still have your teddy bear?"

"Yes."

They pushed him, and he fell, crying.

"I wouldn't touch him, boys," Pollack said, his eyes filling with wild menace. "I'm from New York City and I could slit your wrists with my teeth."

The jocks backed off.

"We'll get you, Osterberg," one of them said. "Your friend has to go back to New York sometime."

James drove Pollack back to the motel in Detroit. It took them forty-five minutes.

"You need a drink," Pollack said.

"Aw, I don't drink much," said James.

"You need something. Come up to my room."

Nico was there in bed. Lou was in bed next to her. Gerard Malanga was in bed next to Lou. Someone else was moving around under the covers. They were smoking joints and shooting up and also doing acid.

"Gosh!" said James.

"Hello, handsome," Nico said.

James woke at noon. Outside the Algiers Motel, trucks were roaring. No. That was his head. Oh, god. The sheets were sticky, and where they weren't sticky, they were crusty. He looked around. The room was festooned with discarded needles, beer cans, pizza boxes, roaches, empty packs of cigarettes, and blood-soaked towels.

"Ohhhhhh," he said. "I'm late for school."

The tour bus was gone. They all were gone. He thought about the night and smiled. Then he thought about what had happened later in the night and wept.

On the motel dresser was a note.

"Dear James," it read. "What we did to you last night was unforgivable, but we aren't sorry. We all agree that you are the true spirit of rock, and we can't apologize for your debasement. It had to come eventually, at someone's hands, and at least we knew what we were doing. With proper lubricant, it will be less painful the next time. Remember, be loud, be strong, be a man, and never let anyone tell you how to live your life. You are a golden god and owe nothing to anyone. Your starter kit is in the top drawer. Good luck. See you in heaven. Love, Neal."

In the drawer were a fat joint, a bottle of Tuinals, gilded pants, some eyeliner, and a silver tube of lipstick with the engraving "THIS BELONGS TO NICO."

"Nico," James sighed. "Nico . . .."

He took off his T-shirt. His chest was young and raw and sleek. He removed his jeans and slipped on the gilded pants. Slowly, he applied the eyeliner and the lipstick, and gazed at himself in the mirror.

"I am a beautiful man," he said.

He went out on the highway. A carful of girls picked him up.

"Ladies," he said, "do me. And then take me home."

As he walked toward his trailer, a jock approached.

"Oh, look, Osterberg's wearing makeup!" he said.

He stared at the jock, his hands on hips.

"Oh, you little turd," he said.

"What's the matter, Osterberg? Boyfriend dump you?"

Iggy Pop leapt upon the jock and buried his teeth in his neck. He howled and ripped, emerging covered in gore. The jock howled in agony and struck out. Iggy dodged him and kicked him in the nuts. The jock limped away, sobbing. Iggy raised his hands to the sky, triumphant. He said:

"I'm a streetwalking cheetah with a heart full of napalm!"

Pollack got kicked off the Velvets tour one night in San Francisco. He celebrated by falling asleep on the sidewalk at the corner of Haight and Asbury. In the morning, a boot was kicking him.

"Hey, man," a voice said. "You're blocking my motorcycle."

"Whuhhhh?" Pollack said.

"Come on, you bum. I've got to get to work."

"I'm not a bum," said Pollack. "I'm a rock critic."

The guy looked at him.

"You need a bath," he said.

Pollack looked up. The guy wasn't bad looking, in a Berkeley dropout kind of way.

"Well then," Pollack said. "Why don't you give me a scrub, big boy?"

An hour later, Jann Wenner rode to the office on his motorcycle. Pollack held on behind him, trying not to vomit. Wenner said he was starting a new magazine about rock music that would "revolutionize" the "youth culture" but also be "professionally reported and edited."

"Pfft," Pollack said.

The *Rolling Stone* offices were two rooms, a few typewriters, a couple of phones, some Moby Grape posters, and records piled everywhere. But it was clean overall, too clean for Pollack, who made a mental note to piss in a corner when no one was looking. Two guys were sitting around listening to Jimi Hendrix, smoking a joint.

"This record is quite interesting," one of them said.

"It's shit!" Pollack said.

He ripped the record off the turntable and smashed it.

"That's what I think of this record," he said.

Wenner's employees were stunned. One of them started to cry.

"Quit your whining," Wenner said. "Call the record company. Tell them the Hendrix they sent us is warped, and we need a free copy. Emphasis on free."

Pollack sat on a couch, picking his nose.

"Why not write a review for us?" Wenner said. "A real review on a typewriter. Pick any record you want."

"OK," Pollack said. "I need some whiskey."

Wenner went looking for booze. Pollack sat down and wrote this:

"Loo0ks']ojkdp908-,lk'][ki 90-90ej spj99j mknsoidnnl IOIOI-Jisnn oisoihjhsoijipwmpjghooueornaovi ######~*********!!!! joatrjopgjif9ptkudjgkn0awefk;jpknjpi   OPiJuilJhjiPoNIP oeaweipfargaiojit."

He handed the paper to Wenner.

"Here's my review," he said.

"I don't think this is what we're looking for," Wenner said.

"You're an industry whore," Pollack said.

"Get out," said Wenner.

Pollack kicked open the door and went down the stairs.

To one of his assistants, Wenner said, "follow him and make sure he doesn't steal my motorcycle."

This is beneath my scholarly abilities, thought the assistant, who was me, Paul St. Pierre. I endured Wenner's bossiness because I knew that rock 'n' roll was the future, both of the American intellect and the soul of the world. I wanted to write for as wide an audience as possible. In Wenner, I saw a like-minded individual who also epitomized entrepreneurship. Even today, I respect Wenner beyond all other figures in rock journalism and appreciate the fact that he continues to give me work.

At that moment, though, I wanted to talk to Neal Pollack, who was fuming and cursing on the sidewalk.

"Hey!" I said.

"What?" said Pollack.

"I saw you at the Velvet Underground show last night."

"Yeah?" said Pollack. "So?"

"You really made quite a ruckus."

Pollack sneered.

"What'd *you* think of the show?" he said.

"I thought it was brilliant. Lou Reed is like Tristan Tzara with a guitar."

"Like who?"

"Tristan Tzara. He was a European artist—"

"Bullshit," Pollack said. "Lou Reed is a fucking phony!"

"I disagree."

Pollack sat on the curb.

"My head hurts," he said.

He vomited on my shoes.

"Shit," he said. "Sorry."

"It's OK," I said. "That's rock 'n' roll."

"No it's not! It's just an asshole puking on your shoes!"

"But . . ."

Pollack stood.

"You ever in New York?" he said.

"I live in New York," I said. "My name's Paul St. Pierre. I'm just out here for a couple months."

"Look me up," said Pollack. "Buy me dinner."

"Where . . ."

"I'm at Max's Kansas City every night," Pollack said.

With that, Pollack walked into the street, where a car promptly hit him.

Mother was baking hamentashen. Norbert smelled it from his room. The apartment in Rogers Park filled with the sweet doughy smell and Gladys's tuneless humming. Outside his window, the trees budded and the birds warbled. He could hear the quiet rush of Lake Michigan a block away, and the jingle of the knife-man's cart.

"It's Purim!" he said. "It's Purim!"

He bounded out of bed. Running through the living room, still redolent of Vernon's morning pipe, there was Gladys in the kitchen in her apron. She was in the full blooming flush of beauty.

"I made you some treats," she said.

"Mommy!" said Norbert. "I love you, Mommy!"

She nudged his ribs.

"Who's my little man?" she said.

"I am! I am!"

"Who's my little genius?"

"Me! Me!"

"Hey, buddy, wake up."

"Whuh?"

A cop was standing over Pollack, poking him with a night-stick. Shit. Still laid out at the Detroit bus terminal. His mouth caked with dried puke. Someone had taken his shoes. Goddamn it, he stank.

"You can't sleep here."

Pollack sat up. His spine lacked fluid.

"When's the next bus to New York?"

"Tomorrow morning. Go get a room."

"No shoes."

"Not my problem."

Pollack emerged into the late June evening. He heard sirens and smelled smoke. The newsstand guy had a radio. He heard, "Reports are that troopers shot and killed three men at the Algiers Hotel in downtown Detroit. The mayor has declared a state of emergency . . ."

"Great," Pollack said.

He walked a few blocks, dazed, toward the smoke. A rock flew by his head.

"Die, whitey!" he heard.

A baton thudded the backs of his knees.

"Get outta here!" said a cop.

Two bricks flew out of a fourth-story apartment. The cops

raised their Plexiglas. The rocks bounced away harmlessly, smacked Pollack in the chest.

"Ow," he said.

"Goddamn sniper," said the cop.

He cocked a rifle, aiming toward the window, and fired. Pollack saw a young black man clutch his chest, teeter, tip out the window, and fall, his body splattering the concrete on contact, an unholy tableau of death. A car exploded. The cops launched a tear-gas canister. A gang of four young black men busted a department-store window with baseball bats. A great dome of unwanted smoke engulfed them all.

"Jesus Christ," Pollack said.

Through the streets of a Detroit he didn't know, Pollack ran, past marching lockstep phalanxes of armored law, black knife-wielding rebels and cowering mothers. He was maddened by fear and hunger, making mental notes the whole time, thinking that this would make a great feature, or scene in a novel.

The police advanced in great crawling columns. Three blocks away, toward them, moved black Detroit, slightly less organized but no less in number. Clubs versus bullets, but no one would win. Pollack felt a twinge in his knee. He collapsed in the middle of the street and couldn't stand. Bullets popped and whizzed. He was going to die.

Rough-hewn middle-aged hands hooked his armpits and lifted him.

"Git up, you idiot," said a voice.

Pollack couldn't make out the man's face in the smoke, but his arms were strong. He lifted Pollack up, flung him over his back, and carried him down a side street while the city raged.

"Dang, boy, you got to take care of yourself," said the man.

Pollack next remembered sitting on an enclosed porch in a two-story graystone. The radio and TV spewed reports of property damage, death, and injury. Behind him, in a shadowy doorway, the man held a glass of whiskey.

"You need this," he said.

He came into the light.

"Clambone," Pollack said.

"I got me a job at the Ford Motor River Rouge plant," Clambone said. "On the assembly line."

"But you're a musician!"

Clambone laughed. "Boy, you should know better. Ain't no way for a black man to make a living as a musician in this country! We've got to work."

Clambone sat in a porch chair next to Pollack. He shouted into the house.

"Lois!" he said. "We got company! Bring us some hot dogs!"

A long-suffering woman appeared.

"We're outta hot dogs, Willie," she said.

"Damn it, woman. Then go to the store and get me some!"

"Radio says they burned down the store."

"Shit," said Clambone. "Just bring us some whiskey then."

Pollack pressed a damp cloth, dabbed the dirt and clotted blood off his forehead.

"I don't understand," he said. "What's happened to America?"

Down the street, a group of teenagers ran in terror. An armored tank followed, firing volleys, making deep pits in the street.

"City's never gonna fix those potholes now," said Clambone.

"Let me ask you a question," Pollack said. "Where've you been all these years?"

"Philly," said Clambone. "Philadelphia, PA."

"Ew," Pollack said. "Why'd you live *there*?"

"That's what all the white people say. But they don't understand that Philly has the *vibe*.

"I moved to Philly in 1963. The south had banned me pretty much; they wanted me in Tennessee, Alabama and Mississippi, I

had illegitimate children in Kentucky and Arkansas, and a trail of
bad debts down Atlanta way. My cousin opened up a barbershop
on Girard Avenue, so I had me a job, an apartment up in German-
town, and a woman within a week. And I cut hair but good."

"Wait a second," Pollack said. "You were a barber?"

"Well, sorta," said Clambone. "We didn't really have too many
customers, since my cousin made the mistake of opening up next
to another barbershop that'd been there for thirty-five years. We
had to spend the time somehow, so we started singing, me, my
cousin Terry and these other barbers. I brought in my neighbor,
this tall skinny guy named John Holland, he was a garbageman
who believed in Jesus. A lotta harmony come out of that barbershop at night, I'm telling you. We called ourselves the Soul Cut-
ters, but John objected because that wasn't very Christian, so we
changed it to the Soul Barbers."

"I thought you were a bluesman!"

"Boy, it's all black music from the mouth of the Nile. Now listen up. We got our first paid gig at this big old crate of a boxing
gym called the Blue Horizon up on Broad Street, which has been
there, I think, since the 1920s, maybe before. It's got all these rows
of wooden chairs hanging down over the ring. Retired fighters sit
up in the balcony keeping score every night. You're always afraid
they're gonna drop their cigar ash on your head. They serve beer
for a quarter out of big kegs, white man beer, from the Schmidt's
Brewery on Girard, and it tastes sweet during the undercard. You
got the finest-looking women in their furs and they're with men
who are fat as moose, with sweat soaking their shirt collars. Quite
a scene.

"The ring girls in their slinky dresses were circling, and the ring
announcer says, 'Ladies and gentlemen, to honor America with our
national anthem, please welcome the Soul Barbers of German-
town.' And the crowd went crazy for us, because we'd filled the
cheap seats up with all our friends. When we'd finished that 'Star

Spangled Banner,' we sang a beautiful song that I had written for just this occasion. It went like this . . ."

Clambone rose from his porch seat. Pollack imagined the lights low in Blue Horizon with a sweet coating of soul in the air as the Clam and his Soul Barbers in their gilded shirts made the blues into something deeper. Clambone sang:

> She's my sweeeeeeet love
> She sings a lovely song
> She's my sweeeet love
> She sings a lovely song.
> I come home from the factory
> And the rain falls all night long.
>
> I'm a poor man
> And I work hard all day long
> I'm a poor man
> And I work hard all day long.
> My sweet wife takes my loneliness
> And nothing can go wrong.
>
> I was a haaaaard man
> And I sang a sad, sad song
> I was a haaaard man
> And I sang a sad, sad song
> Until my wife done saved my life
> I was crying all night long.
>
> Men
> Let me tell you something.
> If you've got yourself a woman
> And you love her.
> Don't let nothing lead you astray.

You have to take that woman in your arms
Every night
And squeeze her tight
And tell her,
Baby, I love you more than anyone alive
Because it's a cruel world out there,
And a woman is the only thing
That can set the bad things right.
So if you see yourself a sexy lady on the street
Or you feel yourself straying after that
Last whiskey you shouldn't have had
Just remember what you've got back home
And never, ever do something bad.
Because you know her
And you love her
She will never leave you
She believes in you
And you work hard
And you love hard
And you live with your woman until you die
Because when they lay you in the ground
What do you want them to say?
He was a good man
And he loved his woman
And she will cry real tears.

She's my sweeeeeeet love
She sings a lovely song
She's my sweeeet love
She sings a lovely song.
I come home from the factory
And the rain falls all night long.

Clambone eased himself back into his porch seat. Pollack wept.

"That's the most beautiful song I ever heard," he said.

"Why, thank you," said Clambone. "But it's not the end of the story. We finished the song, and the whole place was bawling. The ring announcer came up and said, 'Ladies and gentlemen, there will not be any fights tonight. All our boxers have gone home to their women, because they know that real lovin' is good lovin'. We will refund your money. Now go home and love each other.'

"A bottle of Wild Turkey flew out of the crowd and hit the announcer in the head. Someone shouted, 'Shaddup! I wanna see da fights!' This was Philly, after all.

"So after the main event, the place was clearing out, and a man came up to me and said he was from Detroit and he wanted to fly us out and record that song for Revilot Records, which was his label. Well, we weren't doing anything much at the barbershop, so we said yes, and that's how we came to record our hit 'Sweet Love (Love Your Woman).' But as soon as the profits started coming in, the label renegotiated our contract without asking us, and we didn't get a dime."

"Same old story," Pollack said, "wherever you go."

Lois came on the porch and sat on Clambone's lap. She was a good woman. The helicopters flew overhead, searchlights strafing the projects for survivors. The sounds of gunfire and breaking glass continued to echo into the night.

"So me and Lois were in Detroit without any money and any prospects. I'd been working at a barbershop for years, but didn't have the money to start my own shop. Thank god for the auto industry, which will always provide me with a stable income. I got that job at the Ford plant and started playing nights on Hastings Street for a little extra money. Looked like I was gonna be a part-time bluesman until the day the good Lord called me home."

"So that's it?" Pollack said.

Clambone broke out into a long, loud laugh, which grew louder and longer as it stretched out into the night.

"Lois, he wants to know if that's it," Clambone said. "Hell no, that ain't it. Tell this boy what happened as soon as we moved into this house."

"We saw the spaceship," Lois said.

Willie and Lois Jefferson were sitting on their front porch at 3727 Cass Avenue in Detroit one night in September 1966. They'd just watched the premiere of *Julia* on ABC, and were feeling flush with race pride. "At long last, one of our own is being accurately represented on network television," Lois said. "This should go a long way toward removing black stereotypes from popular culture."

The sky above them flooded with great beams of colored light. The air shimmered with a sonic roar. The porch door flew open. A shiny disc topped with spikes descended.

"Sweet Jesus!" said Clambone.

The ship touched down. No one else on the block came out to look. Clambone knew, somehow, that this ship was meant for him, and him alone.

A ramp opened. In a wash of white light, a man emerged. He was eight feet tall, his skin deep brown. He wore a red spangled top hat, and a spangled tuxedo in an American flag pattern. Behind him, a music played unlike any Clambone had ever heard, a great cacophony of instruments, horns, guitars, percussion, electric sounds from another galaxy. Somehow all the instruments stayed on the same beat. Clambone felt himself compelled to rise and move to the one.

"Damn!" he said.

Behind the man, a backup band danced out of the spaceship. They wore the coolest costumes imaginable, an array of spangles, rags, and wide-bottomed pants, long rubber noses and feathered hats. They played their instruments in time.

"Willie Clambone Jefferson?" said the ambassador from space. "That's me."

"Well, glory be! And this is your lovely wife?"

"Oh, yes!" Lois said.

"Please permit me to introduce myself," the man said. "I am P. Amazing Frankenbooty, the Cosmic Ambassador of Style. I have flown all this way from the far reaches of the Groove Galaxy to trace the nappy smell of funk to its roots here on Planet Earth."

"Nice to meet you," Clambone said. "But what does that have to do with me?"

P. Amazing Frankenbooty sang:

> *Underwater Dog*
> *Number One in The United States*
> *Of Underwater America*
> *Making that doggy noise*
> *Let me drool all over your booty!*
> *Get my muzzle wet.*
> *Doggypaddle*
> *Doggystyle*
> *In my doghouse*
> *It's all right.*
> *P. Amazing Frankenbooty here*
> *Cosmic Ambassador*
> *Of the eternal chocolate boogie*
> *20,000 Leagues*
> *Under the chocolate sea*
>
> *We are living*
> *In Underwater America*
> *California!*
> *Underwater!*
> *New York City!*

Underwater.
Can you hear me, Ohio?
You are swimming
Underwater.
Glowing nuclear fishy dogs
Swim on by
Your open swimming hole
Come on.
Wind it up.
Let me hear you now, my cosmic knights!

All the musicians, together, sang a very catchy chorus:

Underwater son and daughter to the slaughter well you oughter get
*   with me.*
Undercover be my lover I'm a rock star cosmic cock star chicken of
*   the sea.*

P. Amazing Frankenbooty brandished his spangled cane, cir-
cled it in the air. An array of cartoon stars sprayed forth from its
tip, swirled in the air into a funnel shape, and enveloped Clambone, who felt a warm tingle deep in his guts. He opened his eyes
to the stars. The rhythm of the one flowed through his veins.

There were ten-inch white platform shoes on his feet. A shaggy
suit of white synthetic fur had replaced his overalls. On his head
was a turban of fabulous colors, and he held a bright blue guitar.

"Hallelujah!" he shouted. "I am Clamzilla!"

He played.

I Am Clamzilla!
Not the friendly clam
But the holy clam
And I'm here

To fill your days and nights
With funky creamy delights!
Because glory be!
The cosmic light I see!
I'm gonna hitcha now
With everything I got
Get ready,
Git up and dance with me
Because the party has begun.
We're gonna have some
Interstellar
Cosmic fun
Whooooooo!

Another wave of the wand. The stars formed into an enormous pair of cartoon lips that planted themselves on Lois Jefferson's mouth. She found herself transformed into a beautiful starchild in an electric-green one-piece pants suit, slitted at the neck into a V. Suddenly, she found herself at a keyboard, playing with both hands.

"Hit me, boys!" she shouted.

Well, back in 1955
Me and my girls were barely alive
But it's no lie
I do not occupy
the back of the bus no more
I'm a chocolate sister,
Mister
So bow before me
When I get you on the dance floor!

"Willie Clambone Jefferson," said P. Amazing Frankebooty, "I appoint you the ambassador of my message here on Earth."

"I'll do it!" said the Clam.

"You have the power. Just shout 'Hallelujah!' and you'll feel it in your bones."

With that, the cosmic god retreated to his ship, swallowing the light up with him. Then the craft was gone, with no sign it had ever arrived. Clambone and Lois sat on their porch again in their civilian clothes. They were spent.

"It was an extraordinary dream," Clambone told Neal Pollack almost a year later. "But it was very real."

For some reason, Pollack believed him.

Down the street, a pickup truck crawled. In the back were the dirtiest greaseballs Pollack had ever seen. They were murdering their instruments in a gory symphony of screeching, idiotic noise. Ahead of the truck walked a white man, hair shaggy as jungle brush. His beard went down to his chest. Small round glasses accentuated his wily, beady eyes. The man held a joint in one hand and a megaphone in another.

"Attention, brothers and sisters!" said John Sinclair. "These riots show that a peaceful solution to the world's problems is not upon us! The methods of Dr. King have been rendered meaningless in the burning hellfire instigated on our city by the vile pigs of our police force! Join me now in violent revolution against the class system and those who oppress us! Join the MC5, the ultimate band, feel their Trans-Love Energies burst through the dissonant mainstream in the final overthrow of the square! Undo your shackles and commit total assault on the culture by any means necessary, including rock 'n' roll, dope, and fucking in the streets! If you're a woman, you don't need to wear underwear!"

Pollack rose.

"I must follow this man," he said to Clambone. "And write about him."

Into the street, Neal Pollack marched, joining the unholy blaze of revolt. His respite in the arms of the Clam had ended. Rock would soon become his void.

In the summer of 1967, Neal Pollack and Wayne Kramer from the MC5 entered Cobb's Corner, a bar on the edge of Ann Arbor where all the revolutionaries went to drink cheap. Pollack wore a T-shirt that proudly read "DETROIT: THE MURDER CITY," and Kramer wore an ammo belt, a hunting rifle strapped across his back. The lumpen revolt could break out any minute, John Sinclair had told them, and what good would rock 'n' roll be against the pigs? They needed guns, especially in bars.

At a table was a longhaired sleaze in a leather jacket. He looked like he'd just stepped out of a Camaro.

"This is my cousin Barry," said Wayne Kramer.

"Hi, motherfucker," said Barry Kramer. "You're an asshole!"

"Barry has a magazine called *Creem*," Wayne said.

"Screw your magazine!" Pollack said. "Let's get loaded!"

Twenty whiskies later, Pollack and the Kramers had locked arms, and were singing "Sweet Caroline." Pollack unzipped his pants. Through his open fly, he pulled a document. It was a fifteen-thousand-word essay called "Jefferson Airplane Through the Meat Grinder and Onto the Grill." Barry Kramer read the opening sentence: "One song made me nauseous; another made me puke."

"I wanna publish this as my cover story," he said. "We'll get R. Crumb to do the cover art."

Pollack stood on the table.

"You may publish my story!" he said. "But I need five thousand dollars immediately! To build a bomb!"

"I'll give you twenty-five bucks," Kramer said.

They loaded into Barry's Chevy and headed off to the Frutcellar in downtown Detroit where the MC5 was scheduled to do a show in front of the same hundred people who always came to see them when they were unannounced. Pollack stumbled in to find

John Sinclair standing in the middle of a crowd of black guys, telling them about the upcoming "race war."

"You must arm yourselves," he said. "It's gonna be the biggest race war yet."

Wayne took the stage.

"Brothers and sisters!" he shouted. "Are you ready to blow up the world?"

The crowd, half black and half white, retreated to opposite sides of the room, eyeing one another suspiciously. From the stage, Kramer shrieked: "Get ready for the race war!"

John Sinclair shot his gun, once in the white direction, once in the black. The two sides charged each other, snarling, fists pumping, chains brandished. The MC5 thwacked away, providing the soundtrack for the end of the world.

Pollack inhaled the smoke and the blood and the urine and the sweat, and excitement shot through his bones.

"Twenty-five bucks for a *magazine article?*" he said.

A large black man grabbed his ankles and flipped him onto the floor. A white guy looped a bicycle chain around his neck and yanked. Cartilage popped. Pollack was in agony. John Sinclair whacked his attackers with a gun butt.

Shit, Pollack thought. I'd do this for free.

The next day, a Sunday afternoon, a dozen people including Pollack and Danny Fields from Elektra Records straggled into the University of Michigan student union to see a rock show. Three dirtballs took the stage and started slogging through an incomprehensible chordless flood plain of noise. Pollack snored standing up. Then a note of clarity sounded in the sludge, followed by a sharp guitar rip. Onto the scene bounded a lithe mad thing of beauty, a man-boy, teeth bared. An atomic viper blast of dervish, he twisted his body in ways not known to man. From his throat came a dumb roar of pure anguish.

"My god," said Fields. "He's beautiful."

Pollack stood his ground, trembling with fear and joy.

"James Osterberg!" he shouted.

The lead singer gave a quick karate chop, and the music froze. He stared coldly into the audience. Sweat dripped from his every pore.

"No, man," he said, "I'm Iggy Stooge."

Iggy whirled the microphone in a broad loop, and smacked himself in the head. The music began again, just where it had paused. Danny Fields started to dance, but Pollack stayed still, awash in love.

Afterward, they approached Iggy, warily, deferent. Iggy picked lice out of his hair and scratched his balls.

"I'm from Elektra Records," Fields said.

"Yeah," Iggy said. "You some kind of janitor?"

"No, I'm a talent scout."

"I got no talent."

Pollack dropped to his knees.

"You have risen," he said.

Pollack got back to New York about six months after he'd planned. Detroit had a way of sucking you in. The cab dropped him off. His loft building was gone, replaced by public housing, a parking lot, and a highway overpass.

"Goddamn you, Robert Moses!" he said.

He went to the bank.

"Your account is empty," said the teller.

"That's not possible," Pollack said. "I have a trust fund because Elvis killed my father."

"Our records show that you've spent three hundred thousand dollars in the last two years."

Pollack smacked his forehead.

"Fuck! I'm so stupid! I should never have bought that bar in Phoenix and given it to Waylon Jennings!"

He looked at the teller as sweetly as possible.

"Can I borrow a twenty?" he said. "I'll get you into the Fillmore East tonight. . . ."

Well, now he really needed some money. Where was he going to get it? The *Voice* paid, but not enough. *Rolling Stone* paid, but not enough. *Creem* didn't pay enough either. Plus, he didn't have a typewriter.

Pollack walked the streets of Manhattan that were no longer his streets; he was broke and desperate and alone. Vast waves of steam rose from the sewers and enveloped him in waves of gaseous filth. A hard neon glow tore at the bags under his eyes. He dreamed of a hot shower and a feather bed. Sleeping in the park may be glamorous when you're twenty-one, he thought, but when you're twenty-seven, it's just another stop on the road to hellfire.

He stopped at Fifty-third Street and Third Avenue, where he found an unusual concentration of teenage boys in seductively tight jeans and cowboy shirts. They were smoking cigarettes, leaning against lampposts, squatting on newspaper boxes. Cigarettes hung from every mouth, packs bulged from every back pocket. Pollack stood on the street corner, not sure what to do.

Iggy sure would like it here, he thought.

A limousine pulled up and the window rolled down. A porcine businessman with a bad toupee peered out. He wagged a fifty-dollar bill.

"Let's go around the block," he said.

Pollack held the bill. He studied it, and it seemed real. One of the boys in tight jeans nudged him.

"If you don't want this trick, I'll take it," he said.

The businessman furrowed and began to look frustrated. The limo driver stepped on the gas. Pollack fixed him with a gaze of pure seduction.

"For seventy-five dollars, I'm yours for the night," he said.

He got in the limo, which drove away. A buzz rose up on the

corner about the competition. Who's the new slut, the boys wondered. He sure is cute.

Pollack made so much money as a male prostitute that he was
able to take Iggy to Woodstock.

"You'll love it," Pollack said. "This will be the greatest music
festival of all time."

And so they came into the fields and through the hills, along
the mighty highway strip, trudging through an epic of mud in
their boots and their sandals, lined two by two by four, sleek
naked bodies romping in the ditches of freedom, arms locked
around the lake. By the campfire, they sang the song of their age:

> *We are the Woodstock Generation*
> *We love the sun and rain and cloud*
> *We take our drugs for recreation*
> *We like to play our music loud.*
>
> *We are the happy, happy people*
> *We love our Crosby, Stills and Nash*
> *We'll have our coitus unprotected*
> *No fear of fluid, itch or rash.*
>
> *We smoke our pot, we drop our acid*
> *We think the world's so brave and new*
> *Our youthful gaze is bright and placid*
> *No one can tell us what to do.*
>
> *We are the Woodstock Generation*
> *We love the stars and sky and earth*
> *We are God's loveliest creation*
> *The world is ours by dint of birth . . .*

"Fuck this," Pollack said. "We're walkin'."

Pollack had freelance assignments to write about the festival from eight different publications. None of the magazines printed them because they were afraid of the truth, Pollack said later. Still, on that hopeful Friday morning, he and Iggy traveled eight miles through the summer haze from the spot where the car they'd stolen had broken down.

"Man," Iggy said on the fourth mile, "I'm thirsty."

He grabbed the nearest woman and began licking her. Other women gathered around Iggy and began licking him. He gyrated from woman to woman like a dynamo. Moving in a swirl of sex, they all disappeared behind a copse of poplars. Pollack watched, followed, took notes.

How did Iggy get all those chicks?

Later, they came upon a circle of albinos sitting around a kitten. "Rise, kitty, rise," the albinos chanted. A man was wrapping himself in plastic, because, he said, he was Plastic Man. A beautiful girl dressed in frontier-era clothes handed out apples from a basket. The rain came then, and the girl seemed to melt away. Enormous purple dragons swooped from the sky and crisped the crowd with their nostril flames. The moss on the rocks was alive. Sometimes great droves of people trampled by, and other times, the earth was still. From below, a sonorous voice called Neal Pollack's name, called him home to Hades. These mushrooms are really strong, Pollack thought. Was that dwarf really wearing a Richard Nixon mask?

They were actually close to the stage. Iggy chewed on a mouthful of grass. Pollack smeared mud on his chest. A folk warbling filled the air . . .

> *Swing low, sweet chariot*
> *Comin' forth to carry me home . . .*

"God," Iggy said. "That is *horrible!*"

"I know that voice," said Pollack.

There she was on stage: Joan Baez, slightly older, always wiser, wearing that same white cable-knit sweater, still impervious to playing in front of four hundred thousand people. Neal Pollack felt his heart bloom again with love, like it had that first night in the Village so many years ago.

Iggy was shaking him.

"Neal, man," he said. "Hey, Neal. You were singing along!"

"I'm in love," Pollack said.

"Love is for idiots," said Iggy. "Folk music is for fools. Take this brown acid."

As the LSD pickaxed his brain, Pollack made his way through the crowd. He slid under the fence and past security. In the performers' area, Joan sat on a quilt, knees drawn up to her chin, pensively regarding the sky.

"Joan," Neal said.

"Hello, Neal," said Joan.

"How are you, baby?"

Their eyes met and they felt the idyllic hopes of 1961. Their hearts briefly filled. Joan exhaled.

"I'm good," she said. "What's that on your head?"

"It's a top hat," said Neal. "With flowers on it!"

"Yes, but why?"

"Because," Pollack said, "I AM A HIPPIE!"

He and Iggy began a mad war dance.

"Whoop! Whoop! Whoop! Whoop!" they said. "Whoop! Whoop! Whoop! Whoop!"

Joan shook her head.

"Good-bye, Neal," she said.

She put a hand on Iggy's face and kissed him, hard, on the lips. Then she shouted: "Guards!"

Security moved toward them. Pollack and Iggy ran. The heavens exploded with great zags of lightning, wild peals of thunder, and raindrops the size of grapes. Pollack and Iggy threw themselves into the opening of a white plastic tent. Inside, eight kids were gorging themselves on a great buffet of gourmet salami, cheese, fruit, bottled water, and chocolate cookies.

"Where'd you get all this stuff?" Pollack said.

"Never underestimate the power of a Connecticut trust fund," one of them said.

They smoked hash but soon they slept, because morning was coming. When they woke, it was nearly noon. They saw that the stage was empty, but the field was more crowded than before. The air felt like the inside of a washing machine on rinse. Army helicopters hovered, dropping supplies.

"Forget this," Pollack said.

Three hours later, they were at the house of J. Douglas Finch in Greenwich, Connecticut. His parents were at the beach for a month, and he had the place all to himself. Pollack and Iggy had their pick of high school graduates, and they slurped on the girls merrily. The air was full of high-grade pot. They all smoked and laughed and listened to Kinks records.

There were highlights of Woodstock on television.

Some hippie babe said, "It was all so beautiful."

"What a bunch of assholes," Pollack said.

On New Year's Day, 1970, I, now a firmly established and respected critic of American popular culture, went to Max's Kansas City to pick up a press kit from Lou Reed's publicist. Neal Pollack was spread across the stoop, naked except for a party hat, passed out in a puddle of vomit. I nudged him with my foot.

"Neal," I said. "Wake up. It's the seventies."

Pollack stirred.

"Already?" he said.

"Why don't you go home?" I said. "You look terrible."

"Don't have a home," said Pollack. "I'm broke."

A short cab ride, two pots of coffee, and a hot shower later, Pollack was at my loft in SoHo, wearing a velvet smoking jacket, sitting on the couch, listening to a Flying Burrito Brothers album.

"This is OK," he said. "But it ain't George Jones."

Through the front door came a woman. She had long dark hair down to her waist and soothing, soulful almond eyes. She wore a black turtleneck and flared jeans, and carried a bag of books from the Strand.

"Sorry," she said. "I decided to stop at a Visconti retrospective on my way home."

Pollack reclined on the couch in his most seductive posture. A thin purring sound emanated from his gut.

"We have a houseguest, darling," I said. "Just until we can get him a couple checks from the *Voice*. Neal Pollack, my second wife, Barbara."

Pollack moved to kiss her hand.

"Charmed," he said.

"She's an editor at *Film Comment*."

"Ah! Well, I auditioned for an Andy Warhol movie once. Perhaps you saw the finished product?"

"No," Barbara said. "I despise Warhol."

In the kitchen, we unpacked our Dean and DeLuca bags. Pollack was in the living room. "Midnight Rambler" played very loud. Barbara peeked out. Pollack was masturbating.

"Paul, I don't like having this man here," she said. "He scares me."

I took a can of salt-packed Apulian sardines from the bag and put them in the cabinet where Barbara and I kept our Italian canned goods.

"It's just for a few weeks until he gets himself together," I said. "You don't understand. Neal is the dark genius prince of rock criticism."

From the living room, we heard "OOOOOOOOOH, BABY!"

We looked out. Pollack was spread-eagled on the couch, naked, snoring. Barbara bit her lower lip. I later realized she was feeling vague stirrings of lust.

She could fight it all she wanted. She could protest and beg me to get rid of the interloper. At night, in bed, she could be a feral panther. But on those nights when I shrugged her off to read my Foucault and my Dada art books, she twitched in the sheets wretchedly. Pollack was the most disgusting person she'd ever met. But, damn him, he had a way of insinuating himself sexually into any situation. He stripped the reproductive dance of any pretense, reduced it to the barest elements of noise and flesh. It was all fluid exchange and bald sensation. As he wrote once, "Fucking should be a raw sock in the guts." From the abyss of her heart and a hidden corner of her loins, my wife knew she wanted him.

The weeks passed like months. Pollack would just be coming home when we left for work. When we'd return from dinner in the Village, he'd be sitting at the kitchen table, bottle of Jack Daniel's in front of him, listening to Zombies LPs at full volume, making rough pen sketches of Ornette Coleman in his notebooks. He called them "meta words in picture form." He sent them to various newspapers, wiped himself on the rejection letters, and left the soiled papers sitting around.

"You disgust me," Barbara said one morning as Pollack climbed through the kitchen window from the fire escape.

Pollack wagged his tongue at her.

"Aw, baby," he said. "You just wanna feel the hot lizard on your thighs."

She blushed.

"Why do you waste your brilliant mind on such depravity?" she said.

February 24 came along soon enough, and the Stooges were playing a show at Ungano's. Pollack showed up backstage and opened his coat.

"Daddy went to the drugstore!" he said.

Out spilled quantities of weed, booze, coke, heroin, blues, reds, Romilar, Robitussin, nutmeg, shrooms, acid, and the magic substance known as STD.

"Whoa!" Iggy said.

Pollack took them all. He smoked and snorted and licked and injected. Swallowed and ingested. Iggy took it easy, just going for the coke and heroin and pot. He had a show to do, after all. Pollack broke a bottle, slashed it across Iggy's chest.

"Bleed for me!" he said.

Iggy said, "You know I will!"

"Also, the drugs cost me five hundred bucks."

"So?"

"You owe me money, you fuck!"

Iggy snapped on his dog collar. He took a jar of peanut butter and smeared a great gob onto his bloody chest.

"I don't owe nothing!" he said.

Pollack dove into the crowd. He landed on me. I was in the front row with my notebook.

"Where's your old lady?" he said.

"She's at home," I said. "All alone."

The drugs started. Pollack felt the drops of sweat on his neck mutate into living reptilian globules with mouths and teeth like knives. Or so he thought. The floor rose toward him. His knees sank. Iggy, ripping it up on stage, grew to eight feet tall, but his voice sounded faint and thin. The guitars softly cut through Pollack's veins.

Iggy was straddling a photographer, who took shots of his crotch. People in the crowd were beginning to hit one another, spurred on by the screech of a saxophone and the horror-thwack of untutored bass. Pollack twitched wildly. I shook him, but he was lost in a drug spasm.

I looked away. When I turned back around, Pollack was gone, as though he'd drifted into the heating ducts. There was no way anyone could get through this crowd, I thought. How the hell . . .

Iggy dove into the crowd. He splattered us with his sweat and blood and filth. Where was Pollack? An amp blew up. Iggy's pants came off.

Suddenly, I knew. Shit! I parted the crowd with my fists and tore for home.

On a windless night, Barbara heard the wind. Our white chenille drapes fluttered. The gusts grew louder and rattled the window. Louder still and the room filled with a cacophony of gale. In her doorway stood Neal Pollack, naked. His eyes lived with fire.

"Oh, god," Barbara said.

She opened herself to him.

Consumed by weeks of desperation, loneliness, and desire, they humped. Barbara had never known passion like this, and Pollack had been without passion like this for at least a month. He had a lot of energy.

I appeared in the doorway.

"Pollack, you sonofabitch!" I said.

I wrenched Pollack from my wife. He was on the floor. I pounded him. He drew his hands to his face. Barbara threw off the sheets.

"Leave him alone, Paul!" she said. "He's more of a man than you'll ever be!"

I was smacking Pollack with a frying pan.

"Untrue!" I said.

"It *is* true! And he's a better writer, too!"

Then I, Paul St. Pierre, ordinarily a kind man of mild temperament, did something. I grabbed Neal Pollack's feet and dragged him to the window. Pollack was barely conscious.

"Uh . . ." he said. "Unnnnnnh . . . ."

Barbara reached to stop me, but I slapped her away. I lifted

Pollack up, edged his body out the window, and let go. It was four stories down.

Pollack was falling, falling, falling. Eternity opened beneath him, a gaping mouth of darkness where A&R men sharpened their long knives. As the world went black, Pollack heard the end of music.

"Clambone," he said. "Don't let me die."

INTERLUDE
MIDNIGHT DRIVE ON A HIGHWAY STREET

1971–1972

With a moan and a grunt, I sit upright in bed. My lower back wrenches. The bottle of Maker's sits half empty on the nightstand. Through my boxers and undershirt, I can see the permanent paunch. I haven't shaved in several days. It feels like flies are buzzing inside my head.

Ruth appears in the bedroom doorway. She's holding her overnight bag.

"Paul," she says.

"What?"

"I'm leaving you."

I lay back down.

"No," I say.

"We haven't spoken in two months."

"That could change."

"You went to Detroit without telling me."

"I had research."

"You have children."

Speaking of children.

"Oh, god!" I say. "Where are the children? What about the children?"

"They're at my parents' in Connecticut," she says. "They've been there since January."

Well, I think. No wonder I haven't seen them.

"Good-bye, Paul," she says.

Have my months of immersion in Neal Pollack's world caused

me to become like him? Am I losing human feeling, intellectual integrity? The assignments have slowed to a trickle, and then a drip. Suddenly I find myself living off my book-contract scraps, and spending most of those on booze.

Aw, fuck it, I say, and roll over.

When I wake again, it's dusk. Across the river, into the New Jersey marshes, I hear Bruce calling to me. Somehow, I know where I'll find him. I hope Ruth left me one of the cars.

Three hours later, I park in front of an abandoned factory in a forlorn field on the outskirts of Asbury Park, New Jersey. There, atop a rusted blast furnace, sits the Boss, holding his acoustic guitar. He's crying.

"Hello, Bruce," I say.

"Look what they've done," he says. "Look what they've done to America."

"Why are you sitting here?"

"Man's gotta sit somewhere," he says.

He sings in an authentic voice that reflects all our pain, with lyrics that make the universal particular and the particular universal. Because whenever we hurt, as Americans, Bruce is there. Whenever we feel, he feels with us. In our darkest, coldest hour, we call out to him, and he answers:

> *Hey there mister can you tell me*
> *Whatever happened to the dreams we had?*
> *We were feelin' good, now we're feeling bad.*
> *I'm just driftin' now from bar to bar.*
> *With my workin' hands.*
> *And my old guitar.*
>
> *Johnny came back from Kuwait*
> *In the summer of '92.*
> *He was alive, he had survived*

His buddies taught him how to drive
A tank.
Uncle Sam said Johnny just you wait.
We'll find you an important job to do.
Well Johnny waited patiently
He kissed his wife beneath the tree
He was a metaphor
For you and you and me.

Johnny moved to Oklahoma
In the spring of '95
He leased a house, he was a renter
His wife got a job at the Federal Center
For life.
Uncle Sam said Johnny see,
We took care of your children's mom.
Well Johnny hopped onto the public bus
He watched along with all of us
As his wife got killed
By a patriotic homemade bomb.

Hey there mister can you tell me
Whatever happened to the jobs we had?
We were feelin' good, now we're feeling bad.
I'm just driftin' now from bar to bar.
With my workin' hands.
And my old guitar.

Johnny moved to New York City
With his kids and his broken heart.
He was an also-ran, but he had a plan
To become an urban fireman
At last.

Uncle Sam said Johnny you're a zero
No benefits.
We'll make you quit.
Your life is not worth turkey shit.
Then America blew up.
And Johnny was a hero.

Hey there mister can you tell me
Whatever happened to the world we had?
We were feelin' good, now we're feeling bad.
We're just driftin' now from bar to bar.
With our workin' hands.
And our old guitars.

Bruce finishes. Bows his head. The Jersey night is still, out of respect.

"Wow," I say. "That really captures the tenor of the times. We need you, Bruce. We really do."

"Yeah," he says. "I've just been sitting here a long time and thinking that the world isn't what they promised us, back then, in the storybooks. I mean, you look at how hard my old man worked, and his old man, but we escaped that somehow, didn't we? Because of the songs we heard on the radio. And then it all just falls away, the American dream."

"Tell me about Neal Pollack."

Springsteen looks confused and bitter, but he always does.

"Aren't you that guy from the *Nation*?" he says. "The one who appreciates and understands me?"

"No," I say. "I'm Paul St. Pierre. Remember? After you played Boston the first time, I wrote about you in the *Phoenix*. If I remember correctly, the piece said: 'I have seen Bruce Springsteen, and he may just have a future in rock 'n' roll.'"

"Didn't read that one," says the Boss.

"Oh."

The Boss strums his guitar and starts to hum.

"Please tell me about Pollack," I say. "Please. I had a hard one today. My wife left me."

He pauses mid-strum.

"I've been there, man," he says. "Marriage isn't what they promised us, back when promises were made. When they sent Frankie off to 'Nam, his woman said—"

"Pollack," I say.

"Oh yeah," says Springsteen, his voice raspy. "I met him, uh, about thirty years ago, maybe thirty-one, about this time of the year, around August. I was working in this bar down on the Shore. I worked there for three, maybe four months. Place called the Broken Coaster."

He starts ticking off a rhythm.

"So it was me, and it was Steve and Garry. And Southside Johnny. Do you get down to the Shore much?"

"No," I say. "I have a place in the Catskills. And I go to Mexico."

"Well, I'll tell you that the Catskills never had a band like Southside Johnny's band. Yeah, the Dukes. Anyway, we were all working in this bar, and we were feelin' real discouraged. Because no one would give us a gig or nothin'. This guy had just bought the Broken Coaster. He was blind and had one leg, and didn't know nothin' about runnin' a bar. That was the dingiest, dirtiest dump any of us had ever set foot in. It was empty and it smelled like dead animals. We say we'll play for the door. Charge a dollar. We had an eighteen-piece band at the time, and we brought 'em in. That night, we must have made . . ."

Out of the night shadow steps a hook-nosed man wearing a white suit and a broad-rimmed white hat.

"Five dollars," says the man.

"Thank you, Stevie," says Springsteen. "Five bucks, maybe. And a bunch of guys quit. The next week, we had a fourteen-piece band, then a ten-piecer, and then we were down to six, then we had to dump this guy Eric 'Little Picker' McGonigle, he's a bus driver in New York now, until finally it was four of us, and we all wanted to quit, too. Seemed like in this world we had no hope, no fans, and no friends. Nothin'.

"One night after the gig, we was all feelin' down in the dumps and we'd each had about eight beers. It was one of those nights when we were sayin': 'Man, I'd rather work in a damn *factory* than do this.' Even sadder was that we all did work in factories. 'How come we ain't got no record out?' I said. Steve said, 'Because we ain't got no recording equipment,' and it was all very mournful. None of us had a car that night, and we were gonna walk home along the boardwalk.

"It was a nasty night. Rain comin' down in big old sheets and the wind whipping in off the Atlantic, gettin' salt in our hair and our eyes. It was late, too. It musta been three in the morning. Steve was playin' his guitar, tryin' to get some chords right. He worked damn hard. Like all Americans. We work hard, but what do we get in return? Nothin'. It's all just broken promises and forgotten dreams."

He began to sing:

> *Under the overpass*
> *Down by the sea*
> *Hiding from reality*
> *Prayin' to be free . . .*

I find myself growing frustrated with the Boss.

"Damn it, Bruce," I say. "Would you please finish the story?"

"Yeah," he says. "We see something rumblin' toward us, on the boardwalk, really fast. 'What the hell is that?' I said. 'I don't know *what* it is,' Garry said, 'but we better get out of its way.' We jumped onto the beach. There was water up to our ankles. We hid under the boardwalk and looked up through the cracks. Turns out it was this maroon van, brand-new. It brakes to a halt right in front of us. These two burly guys, both white, almost albino, but both dressed all in black, get out of the front seat, and they open up the back. We're looking on, real quiet, and they pull out this skinny naked guy. He has a big gash in his forehead. God knows if he was even alive. They toss him headfirst onto the beach. Guess they figured by the time high tide hit, he'd wash out to sea. Now none of us were gonna mess with guys like that. As they got back in the van, one of them said, 'Cheap-ass rock critic didn't pay us enough to *finish* the job,' and I'm thinkin', 'rock critic? How're we gonna get one of those to our show?'

"The naked guy starts twitchin' and moanin' in the sand. He couldn't have weighed more than a hundred and twenty, a hundred and fifty pounds. Steve said, 'We just can't leave him out here to die.' Among the four of us, we managed to get him to his feet. 'What's your name?' I said. He was twitchin' and droolin', and I think he started to cry, though I couldn't tell because it was rainin' so hard. He said, 'I . . . I . . . I . . . I can't remember! My true identity is a mystery to me!' He passed out right there in my arms.

"We just stood there for a few seconds, in the rain, all confused. Then I said, 'Boys. I think we've got ourselves a roadie.' "

The man might have been dying. He lay on a cot at Bruce Springsteen's house in Freehold, New Jersey, for almost two weeks, not moving, just sweating in his bandages. Springsteen's family had long since left for California, so it was only Bruce and the occasional band member living in the place. They fed the man soup and soda through a straw. Occasionally, he would bolt up and scream, "I WANNA DIE! LET ME DIE!" Then he'd collapse again in his fever.

"Ain't no way I'm gonna let you die, pal," Springsteen said.

After a while, the man started sitting up in bed, asking Bruce to put records on.

"I wanna hear Jerry Lee," the man said. "And Warren Smith. Don't know why."

Springsteen didn't know who this man was, but he certainly knew about the early days of rock 'n' roll.

Eventually it was safe to move him. Springsteen had rented an apartment over a drugstore in Asbury Park. The mystery man went with him, but as soon as the move was done he sat in an easy chair and stayed there. Sometimes at night Clarence Clemons would come over and lull him to sleep with gentle saxophone lull-abies. Other nights, the honky-tonk songs of Southside Johnny drifted up from the boardwalk and filled his dreams with abstract, almost generic images of an all-night party.

At a club called the Upstage, every Friday, Saturday, and Sunday night, Springsteen and the boys would play shows. They'd start at three in the afternoon and sometimes go until three in the morning. All that summer, they'd line up four thick at the door to see the band that everyone was calling "that band that Springsteen's in."

The man with amnesia woke up one night to the sound of thunder. How far off? he sat and wondered. It sounded like it was coming from down the street, maybe two blocks. He swung his legs over the side of the bed. He could stand! His knees felt solid. But he had no clothes. He'd been naked all summer. Guess he'd have to borrow some of Bruce's clothes. He looked in the closet. There were four black leather jackets, six identical pairs of blue jeans, and about twenty sleeveless white T-shirts. Also a blue denim cap. Well, it was something. He wore one of each, and the cap, along with one of Bruce's eight pairs of black leather work boots.

He got to the club. Women were spilling out the door. The band was ripping through a twelve-minute version of "Green Onions." Inside, the air was dense with smoke and sweat and good old-fash-ioned rhythm and blues. Bruce was onstage, leading the crowd in a merry, rollicking chorus of "Jambalaya."

"Whoo!" shouted the amnesiac. "Good old New Orleans boogie-woogie! Yeah!"

The band moved into a slow, steady rhythm. Bruce smiled that smile, that shit-eating world-swallowing grin. He said:

"Now, I'm from New Jersey."

The crowd cheered.

"Is anyone else here from New Jersey?"

"Yeah!" the crowd said. "We're all from New Jersey!"

"Now a lot of people out there put New Jersey down. They say it stinks."

BAM! went the band, on the one beat.

"They say people here are stupid!"

BAM!

"They say it's dying and it's hopeless!"

BAM!

"Well, I'm here to tell you, New Jersey is not dying!"

BAM!

"It's not hopeless!"

BAM!

"It does stink! But we're working on that!"

BAM!

"New Jersey has the most beautiful women in the world!"

The crowd was whipping from side to side now, frenzied.

"And let me tell you one more thing about New Jersey!"

BAM!

"New! Jersey! Knows! How! To! Rock!"

And so the song began:

> *Midnight drive on a highway street*
> *Jenny's got her blue jeans*
> *Crumpled at her feet*
> *One hand in her crotch*
> *One hand on the wheel*

I'm cruisin' 'cross New Jersey
While I'm coppin' me a feel!

Jenny Jenny, Jenny Jenny Jenny
Jenny Jenny, Jenny Jenny Jenny
Beautiful American
So hungry and so free
I haven't got a job
I've just got you and me!

Midnight layoffs at the automotive plant
They're downsizing my cousin
My uncle, and my aunt
Dad's got one hand on the bottle
One hand on the gun
While I'm cruisin' 'cross New Jersey
Runnin' wild and havin' fun!

Jenny Jenny, Jenny Jenny Jenny
Jenny Jenny, Jenny Jenny Jenny
Beautiful American
So hungry and so free
I haven't got a job
I've just got you and me!

Midnight burglars at the Watergate
While my hometown is boiling
With anger and with hate
I've got one hand on the Bible
Little Jenny's in the pew
She says with a name like Springsteen,
You've just got to be a Jew!

Jenny Jenny, Jenny Jenny Jenny
Jenny Jenny, Jenny Jenny Jenny
Beautiful American
So hungry and so free
I haven't got a job
I've just got you and me!

Three hours later, the show ended. The band sat around drinking cheap beer, understanding one another as no men have ever before or since. The amnesiac joined them. Springsteen slapped him on the back.

"That was a great show, guys," said the amnesiac.

"Thanks."

"It seemed to embody the living mythos of rock 'n' roll, as though you were creating a fresh universe from stale parts. Somehow, in the fetid Jersey night, you encapsulated the hopes and dreams of a generation, living out the fantasy of every kid who ever saw a guitar in a store window or listened to a record alone in their bedroom or saw the Rolling Stones on television, who said, 'I wish that were me.' A hard sound, yet a soft sound, a shout of pain and celebration, of communal joy yet also utter isolation."

The band was silent.

"Your critical acumen is remarkable," Springsteen said.

"You understand us so well," said Clemons. "But how?"

The amnesiac shook his head.

"I don't know," he said. "I just don't know."

On May 2, 1972, Bruce Springsteen played an early-evening acoustic set at the Gaslight, a club in Greenwich Village. He walked into the club with his manager, Mike Appel. Spread about three tables, a dozen people sat. The amnesiac stumbled in, carrying all of Bruce's bags, and also his guitar.

"Man," the amnesiac said, "this place is fucking DEAD!"

At one of the tables sat the legendary John Hammond, of Columbia Records, the man who had given Bob Dylan his first professional break.

"Oh, dear God," he said.

The amnesiac porter dropped all his bags on the stage in a thud, which cracked the guitar frame. He sat down next to Hammond and scratched himself.

"Neal Pollack," Hammond said. "I would rather have died ten years ago than ever seen you again."

"What'd you call me?" said the porter.

"What'd you call him?" Springsteen said.

Also in the room was Peter Knobler, the editor of *Crawdaddy*.

"I thought you were dead, Pollack," he said. "You owe us a profile of Syd Barrett."

In his mind, the amnesiac porter heard a vague call from down a dark road. He gripped his skull with both hands. "Ohhh," he said. "It hurts!"

Pollack stood up from the table, knocked over some drinks, and lurched toward the door. With a howl, he threw it open, bursting into the late-day Greenwich Village sun. Inside the club, they could hear his sad banshee wail.

"Pollack," Hammond said. "The singin' fishin' cowboy."

"The greatest rock critic alive," said Peter Knobler.

"Can I sing now?" said Springsteen.

That day, in his blue jeans and white sleeveless T-shirt, unwashed and bearded, Neal Pollack looked like much of lower Manhattan. But the whole borough veered out of his way as he lurched uptown, magnetically drawn like mercury toward Times Square. Four decades of guitar ripped at his brain as the memories of a life that may or may not have been his flashed like thunder in his mind.

"Urgh," he said.

Down the street, oozing from the basement of a seedy hotel, he heard a guitar screech, or was that in his mind? No, this was definitely external, with drums. Something that sounded suspiciously like rock 'n' roll was crawling out of that basement, slithering down the sidewalk, and into Pollack's pants.

He had an erection.

"Hello, old friend," he said.

His boner led him into the hotel and down the stairs. In front of an audience of a few fourteen-year-old girls, a couple of A&R guys, and several dozen rock critics, five men dressed like women yet somehow also like men were thrashing about in their platform shoes and white pancake makeup and bouffant-manqué hairdos and aluminum pants and tight striped shirts open to the navel. There were also garbage bags involved. The music sounded elementary, even impoverished, but to a rock critic's ear, it was sweet nectar.

Jesus, Pollack said to himself. That's "Showdown," by Archie Bell and the Drells. Wait. How could he possibly have made that connection? Why were these fairy queens playing this song? Why were they drinking Schlitz? Goddamn, they sounded good! They sounded better than anything he'd heard in a long time. He threw himself into the show, raised his arms, sweat and stench and all, and rocked out.

"I KNOW WHO I AM," he said. "AND I AM ROCK 'N' ROLL!"

The lead singer spat in his face. Pollack spat back. Prodded by the New York Dolls, he was seized by raw sexual desire, and he groped through the crowd.

"Get your hand off my ass, dickwad!" said a girl.

She kneed him in the nuts, and he fell.

He was whole again.

PART FOUR
NEVER MIND THE POLLACKS

1973–1979

One floor below me, my mother putters across brown-and-ivory shag, gossips into her lime-green rotary phone, watches *Wheel of Fortune,* mixes almonds with the green beans. In the evenings, we walk around the artificial pond and feed the ducks. On weekends, we go to Costco. I eat a hot dog. She buys detergent, toilet paper, tuna packed in water, garbage bags. Then home, always home, where the private airplanes flying into Palwaukee regional buzz overhead from 5 A.M. until sundown. On earth, there are few places less rock 'n' roll than Wheeling, Illinois. Yet here I am, drying out with mother, seeing my book contract through.

Ruth doesn't call. She doesn't e-mail. No one does, anymore. My project is simultaneously losing steam and focus. Pollack's been dead eight years now, but it seems like eighty. Writing about the 1970s feels like writing about the 1870s. It's a vast, absurd gulf of time.

Still, the manuscript and memory summon me back.

It was Memorial Day weekend, 1973, and we'd all been invited to Memphis for the First Annual Association of Rock Writers Convention. One hundred and forty tickets paid by Ardent and Stax records to promote Black Oak Arkansas and Big Star. Neither of the bands had any commercial viability. I'd said so in the *Voice.* Still, I took the trip to support my old friend Greg Shaw, who was trying, against all hope, to unionize America's rock critics. When he told me on the phone, I laughed.

"That's like trying to lasso the wind," I said.

"What a crummy metaphor," he said.

The air in Memphis was thick and viscous. A mosquito flew up my nose. My linen shirt instantly soaked through with sweat.

Shaw met me at the gate and was nice enough to carry my typewriter.

"They're all here," he said. "Meltzer showed up, and Lenny Kaye."

"What about Lester?" I said.

"Lester doesn't miss a party," Shaw said. "The whole staff of *Creem* drove down, in a stolen van."

Then he was silent.

"What?" I said.

"I don't know how to tell you this."

"What?"

"Pollack got in this morning."

My first reaction was shock, followed by surprise. It couldn't be. Pollack was dead. I'd had him killed, by goons, two years earlier. Yet he wasn't dead, or so Greg was telling me.

"Are you sure it's Pollack," I said, "and not an impostor?"

"Unmistakable," Greg said.

Somehow I wasn't angry. Barbara had been relentlessly unfaithful to me, according to the detective agency I'd hired. Her cineaste persona was a front; she'd slept with every half-baked Lothario in rock, including James Taylor, who gave her free cocaine. Over the course of two weeks, through relentless therapy, I'd come to blame Barbara for the incident, not Pollack. After all, I realized, he was driven by a relentless priapism beyond that of normal men. My second divorce hadn't been his fault.

We got to the Holiday Inn. Pollack was atop a coffee table, slugging Jack Daniel's, while the other rock critics gazed at him in awed rapture.

"A toast to Memphis, the city of my youth!" he said.

He belted the bottle.

Lester Bangs hopped onto the table next to him.

"Fuck you, Pollack!" Bangs said.

He took a great chug of cough syrup.

"I'm the King of Rock Critics!" Bangs said.

"No," Pollack said. "It is I!"

"Me!" said Bangs.

"Me!"

"Me!"

"Me!"

Bangs saw me at the check-in desk and bounded over.

"Paul St. Pierre!" he said. "Oh, Paul! How I've longed to see you again, you sweaty bastard!"

He wriggled like a puppy and wrapped me in an obnoxious hug. His right hand slipped a joint into my breast pocket. His left hand patted my butt.

"Put in a good word for me at *Fusion,*" he said.

Behind us, Pollack hovered, like a one-headed Cerberus.

"Hey, Paul," Pollack said.

"Hey."

"I'm sorry I nailed your wife."

"That's OK," I said. "I'm sorry I pushed you out a fourth-story window."

"You gave me amnesia."

"Sorry."

We hugged. Pollack smelled worse than ever. He sobbed in my ear. But that moment passed, as all moments must, and I had the porter carry my bag upstairs.

Later, buses waited outside to take us to a show where Black Oak Arkansas was going to play nude by the Mississippi. The buses were appointed with buckets of free booze and fried chicken. They were monuments of Payola on wheels.

In the front of the bus, Furry Lewis played acoustic.

"This is a song by an old friend of mine, Willie Jefferson," he said.

Lester threw an empty plastic bottle of Romilar at him.

"Shut up, old man!" he said. "I hate the blues! Jim Dandy to the rescue!"

Furry Lewis looked genuinely sad, almost frightened.

"Naw," Lester said. "I love the blues!"

Pollack stood in the aisle, bottle in each hand, and told stories.

"So Johnny Thunders and I were in the back room at Max's, and I said to Bebe Buell, you can blow me, but only if we figure out a way to take heroin anally. Todd Rundgren was really pissed, and he threw his fur coat on the floor. . . ."

I sat in the back, ignored and unrespected. Here I was, an increasingly wealthy and respected academic and a lover of some of the world's best, most original music. I'd lived a life full of adventure, or at least in proximity to it. Of all the people who'd ever breathed, I counted myself among the top one percent in terms of income and comfortable circumstance. And there was Neal Pollack, a disgusting, poverty-drenched slob, a professional loser. This pretentious bloated nightmare of a man was despised by all but his small coterie of pasty disciples.

I was jealous of him.

The attempts to organize the critics went nowhere. Seventy-five of us showed up for a Saturday meeting, seeking air-conditioned shelter from a sticky wind, which was the first sign of an apocalyptic tornado bearing down on Memphis. Seventy-three of us, including me, were drunk. Meltzer stood on his chair and demanded that the liquor companies pay rock writers from now on. "We're their best customers!" he said. You could never tell if he was joking or not.

In the end, we concluded that writers didn't get paid enough.

"No shit," Pollack said. "I've made ten dollars since 1970, and

I'm the best writer in the room."

But Pollack joined the union anyway. It immediately dis-
banded over an argument about David Bowie. An hour later, we
reformed, and he joined it again. Later, at a Big Star show, he leapt
onstage, kicked over an amp, grabbed the microphone from Alex
Chilton, and said, "This is useless! They're taking advantage of
us! We're all a bunch of industry whores! But the music is pretty
good!"

Next to me, a nineteen-year-old sophomore from Oberlin University gasped.

"My god," the kid said. "I never thought of it that way before.
Rock *is* an industry."

"Didn't you read my piece in *Rolling Stone*?" I said. "I figured
that out two years ago."

"Neal Pollack is brilliant," said the kid.

Lester Bangs came up behind me, shirtless.

"Fuck this," he said. "Let's take some acid."

Later, Lester, Meltzer, Stanley Booth and I got into a brand-
new Cadillac the color of pea soup. Neal Pollack was in the driver's seat.

"You can't drive, Pollack!" said Lester.

We roared out of the parking lot.

"Where'd you get this thing?" Booth asked.

"My friend Sam Phillips lent it to me," Pollack said.

"You don't know Sam Phillips," I said.

"Oh, yes, I do."

About then, my acid kicked in. Pollack's head grew to three
times its normal size. His jaw unhinged, revealing cragged valleys
of bug-strewn teeth and a flabby leechlike tongue. His words drew
out long and deep.

"SAM PHILLIPS IS MY FRIEND," he said.

Through the night, I imagined shiny gold records whipping
toward the car, smashing into the windshield but not breaking it.

Above us, on a flying motorcycle, a cackling figure, guitar strapped to his back, waved a six-foot scythe.

"Shit," I said. "I'm trippin'."

It was dawn. The car had stopped. No one else was inside. I wondered how long I'd been curled on the floor, behind the front seat, shivering, naked. I looked up.

Graceland.

Meltzer and Bangs, one hand on the gates, one hand each at their respective flies, were pissing through the bars onto the driveway. Stanley Booth was running around in circles. He had a Confederate flag wrapped around him like a cape. Pollack leaned against a tree, bottle of whiskey in one hand, bottle of gin in the other. At least *he* seemed to be in control.

"Mornin', sleepy," he said to me.

The ground rose up, my knees sank toward it. My mouth was desiccated.

"Need . . .clothes," I said.

"You need a drink," said Pollack.

I felt like someone had driven a steel spike into my back. But the whiskey was strong and the spike softened a bit. Pollack produced a joint, and that also helped a lot.

From down the road, we heard the clomping of hooves. Meltzer and Lester, who were still pissing, zipped their pants. Stanley dropped his flag. I picked it up because I was cold, and wrapped it around my shoulders. Pollack squatted by the tree, waiting.

Over the hill came a horse the color of cream. Its coat had a shine that could only have been created by a groom from Austria, or maybe Kentucky. The air was thick as butter, and full of flies. It was goddamn hot already.

Atop the horse sat a man, or what had once been a man, or, as I described him in my second book of Elvis criticism, *The Man Who Was Once a Man,* "once he was a man, but to us, he was now a god, or meat, to us, that is. He had multiple meanings, this Elvis, but no meaning to us meant as much as the meaninglessness of no meaning. He was decay and mystery, and because of that, he contained clues about our death. The Elvis we saw then is the Elvis we hear now."

The King approached, on his white horse. Lester fell to the ground. Meltzer crossed his arms, skeptical. Stanley fainted. Pollack stayed against the tree. I took mental notes.

"Oh, my King!" Lester said.

"Rise, Lester Bangs," said Elvis.

"You know my name!" said Lester.

"Of course," Elvis said. "I read *Creem*."

He clapped his hands. From the bushes came two stable boys. They helped him dismount. I rubbed my eyes.

"You aren't hallucinating," said Elvis. "The acid has left your system."

Elvis knew everything, and it frightened me.

The sun began to cut through the haze. Neal Pollack stepped into the light.

"Hello, Elvis," he said.

"Hello, Neal," said Elvis. "It's been a while."

"Wha-wha-wha?" Bangs said.

"Yeah," said Pollack. "Jesus, you look terrible."

"So do you," Elvis said.

Elvis put an arm around Pollack's shoulders.

"Come in," he said. "I'll make you breakfast. You can bring one friend."

Pollack turned around to see Lester's pleading face. Meltzer had started walking down the road. He was already putting rock behind him. Under a maple, Booth babbled like an idiot about his deadlines.

Pollack pointed at me.

"St. Pierre," he said. "Let's go."

The cape only covered my shoulders. Elvis looked down at my

crotch. I felt stirring against my will.

"The South shall rise again," he said.

The gates opened. Thanks to Pollack, I set foot on the sacred grounds. Behind us, Bangs held the bars, whimpering.

"Fucking Pollack," he said.

Lester Bangs tried to urinate again. But he was all tapped. He would soil Graceland no more.

We sat in Elvis's breakfast nook, eating eggs, slabs of Kentucky ham, and stacks of pancakes as big as my head.

"Damn, I was *starving*," said Pollack. "Elvis, man. You can cook!"

"It's all I have left," Elvis said. "For what am I to America anymore? Just a celebrity slab onto which people can paint their own grief, fury, and desire."

I took a heaping mouthful of okra.

"Don't sell yourself short, Elvis," I said. "You can still come back."

"No," he said.

He stuck a Quaalude into a bran muffin.

"My useful hours have ended."

Elvis pressed a button on the wall. Next to the refrigerator, a panel opened into a secret room.

"My atelier," he said.

I never really thought I'd have access to Elvis Presley's work space. In my febrile imaginings, I figured it would contain some recording equipment, a few guitars, a keyboard, maybe evidence of songs attempted but abandoned in despair. Instead, it was nothing but records, thousands of them, alphabetized, and also categorized by genre.

"The only good thing about being Elvis Presley is that people send you their records," he said.

The discography in that room was almost beyond imagining.

Elvis had every record ever put out by Ernest Tubb, Rufus Thomas, Hank Snow, and Bobby Blue Bland. There were a thousand Okeh disc recordings alone. I spotted a Capitol album that I'd never seen before: *Merle Haggard Sings the Songs of Other People Singing Merle Haggard Songs*. And the soul music: the Orioles, the Flamingos, Ivory Joe Hunter, Little Willie John, and a rare copy of *The Underappreciated Sam Cooke*. Singles of Jackie Moore's "Personally" and Eddie Floyd singing "Never Get Enough of Your Love."

"My word," I said. "Black people certainly make a lot of music! Why doesn't this stuff get played on the radio?"

"It does down here," Elvis said, sadly.

Pollack wasn't paying attention. Hungrily, he flipped through a different stack of records.

"You have Alice Cooper's first album!" he said.

"Derivative," said Elvis.

"And the Velvet Underground's *Murder Mystery* bootleg, recorded live in Cleveland in January 1969!"

"True."

"And the complete Jonathan Richman sessions recorded at Fowley! How'd you get those?"

"I'm a huge Modern Lovers fan," Elvis said.

In one corner of the room sat a desk, with typewriter, and sheet of paper, with words. I read them aloud: "Do you think *White Light/White Heat* is a revelation? Are you going to turn to salt if you look over your shoulder at Lou Reed? Have you ever stood knee-deep in the Delta at midnight, the devil's green mud licking at your thighs?"

Elvis looked ashamed.

"Why," Pollack said, "that's rock criticism!"

We gazed upon the King. His eyes gained a life that they hadn't seen in years, and never saw again. He said:

"Yes, I want to be a rock critic. I've often read the music press with awe and wonder. No matter what I've achieved in my life, I don't feel that I've gained true artistic perfection. Alone above all the arts, rock criticism stands. At its best, criticism topples music, because, at its best, it's music combined with literature. How I long to make people read, to make them understand. Would that I could discard my fame for a humble, yet consistent, byline!"

"It's not too late," said Pollack.

"For me, it is," said Elvis. "My fate's been written. But yours hasn't. I beseech you, Neal Pollack, take care, for the music industry has become something voracious and codified. The true critic must stand above and seek the unknown bands that do not care about fame. He must go beyond. And he can make music himself, but it has to be godawful."

"I understand," Pollack said.

"What about me?" I asked.

"You don't matter, Paul," Elvis said. "Let's get you some pants."

We sat there for a while, listening to bootlegs, taking notes like true professionals. Inside the main house, a bell rang. Elvis looked at his watch.

"My doctor's here," he said. "It's time for my injections."

He walked us to the gate. Lester was still there, face pressed against the bars. We all took a good-bye 'lude. Elvis gave Pollack a hug. Lester rolled his eyes. The King drifted back toward his mansion shrine, a ghost ahead of his time.

"Stay the course," Elvis said. "Don't debase your noble calling."

It was Sunday, and we had planes to catch. Halfway to the airport, Pollack stopped the car. A Dream Carnival was underway in W.C. Handy Park. Geeks wrestled in the street, half watched by their trainers, almost totally ignored by the indifferent, stoned crowd. Black transvestites pistol-whipped one another behind the Porta-Johns. Everywhere, you saw guns and whiskey waved with cavalier glee and total lack of regard for human dignity. The tornado lurked just miles away; the air swayed and whipped frenetically. Music screamed from every corner of the debased grounds, terrible and wonderful, rock and soul and blues and the last decay of folk. None of the other critics were there. We were the only ones who stood on the true hallowed lost plain of American music, and it was all because of Neal Pollack.

"Memphis, Tennessee," he said, "is the greatest city in the world."

Those were Neal Pollack's golden years. They were the times when times were good. Punk had descended onto New York like a vampire bat on a possum, and Pollack felt a thrilling rush in his veins. The skies seemed to rearrange themselves nightly. Pollack published magazines no one read, and wrote poems no one published. And for once he made dimes off his criticism. He wrote for *Creem* and *Punk* and *Melody Maker* and *Hit Parader*, *Rolling Stone*, *Fusion*, and once, only once, for *New York Rocker*. They were stories, many of them made up, about his new friends with whom he often posed, sullenly, for group pictures. For three years, no one smiled, but they took a lot of drugs and fell down stairs. And they were all so happy. "We are everyone's rejects and everyone's nightmare," he wrote. "We have no talent, but lots of ambition. We may have read a book or two. We're gonna be stars, and you can't stop us."

He and Patti Smith fell in love after meeting at a poetry reading at the Mercer Arts Center. He was dressed like a woman, and she like a man. "You're so transgressive," she said. Like Baudelaire had in his time, Neal and Patti and Richard Hell and Tom Verlaine broke open the dress codes of genre, sometimes by wearing floppy hats, or by ripping their T-shirts in two separate places. "It got to the point," Pollack wrote in his diaries, "where everyone wanted to hang out with us. And by everyone, I mean no one."

He lived in a windowless room in a residential hotel on the Bowery, with wire mesh for a ceiling and no potable water. "All I ever wanted, needed, or cared for," he wrote, "were a typewriter and three solid walls. It's all a true man requires for happiness. That and drugs, of course." There were definitely drugs. At night or by day, Pollack and Jim Carroll and sometimes Iggy if he was in town would stumble through the streets looking to score. Pollack called Lou Reed from time to time, looking to reconcile or mooch, but Lou was never home. The streetlamp across the street from Lou's apartment reflected a thoughtful silhouette. Pollack stood for hours, shouting his name, but he knew that there was no home in Lou Reed's mind or heart for him.

"Why, Lou, why?" he said.

By day, he would walk through a bankrupt, wasted city, among the contraband vendors selling their trinkets on reclaimed cardboard, past the sticky-fingered gold-chain-wearing con men, the bat-and-knife-wielding hooligans, the depressed and confused and insane. By night, he hung out at Max's and Mother's and a hundred other bars that didn't get the same amount of press. His head nodded; his arms opened to the world. Boys made out with boys and girls with girls, and the in-betweens with whomever they wanted. The air scorched with pills and fellatio and poetry and music and the knowledge that it was all going to burn, burn, burn. Pollack, at the center of it all, would stand up on a table, any table, and shout, "Whaaaaaaaaaaaaaaa!"

It was the battle cry of a generation without a name.

A great party was under way at Gerard Malanga's apartment, largely involving beautiful young men making out in groups. Pollack burst through the door, clutching his beloved kittens, Max and Kansas City, who he'd recently rescued from a fire at the Mercer. He needed a fix.

"What's rockin', you sick fucks?" he said.

"Oh, no," said Malanga.

The music stopped. So did the kissing. Lou Reed sprinted for the back door.

Pollack looked around: Lots of glitter, lots of platform shoes.

Men were wearing lipstick and hair spray.

"GLAM IS DEAD!" he said.

Patti was there. She kissed him on the lips.

"Where've you been, baby?" she said.

"I was on deadline," said Pollack.

"For two months?"

"It was a long piece."

In a corner of the room, a slivery individual tied off alone. He was done up in full glam: ripped T-shirt, platform shoes, leather pants, sailor hat and all.

Pollack instantly wanted to be this guy's friend. He leapt upon him. They cuddled all night, sometimes with Patti, sometimes without, while all about them New York in the '70s swirled, a skanky paradise of strung-out negative possibility. At two A.M., Iggy appeared, and asked Malanga if he could take a bath. Pollack and the guy, who said his name was Dee Dee, got into the tub as well.

"Man, I'm sick of glam," Pollack said. "All the good bands are in the Midwest, anyway. Fuck New York. Everyone's trying to be Mick Jagger all the time. Just fun, fun, fun. Look around you. Are these people having fun?"

"I'm having fun," Iggy said.

"You don't count," said Pollack.

Patti had curled into a ball by the toilet. She was writing poetry.

"I'm not having fun," she said.

Dee Dee's makeup leaked into the water. He was tired of the hustler's life, he said, sick of going back to Queens Boulevard and throwing things at the old ladies. Where was the rock 'n' roll he used to listen to on the radio?

"That's a good question," Pollack said.

Pollack launched from the tub and grabbed Patti's notebook. He took a bottle off the sink, swallowed whatever was in it, and began writing an essay called "Where Is the Rock 'n' Roll We Used to Listen to on the Radio?"

After a few minutes, he had ten or so usable pages, and he got back in the bath.

"I agree with you completely," he said. "We need a raw, stripped-down music that takes rock out of the hands of the artists and brings it back to its amateur, working-class roots."

Iggy belched.

"All you need are jeans, a T-shirt, and a guitar," Pollack said. "Why didn't I see it before?"

He later described that event as "the most important bath in the history of rock 'n' roll."

"Let's go to Manny's Guitar Shop," said Dee Dee Ramone.

If you knew Joey Ramone, you were lucky. If you knew Dee Dee Ramone, you were a little less lucky, but still somewhat luckier than the average person. The other Ramones, as of this writing, are still alive. There's still time to know them, but who has that kind of time, really? Neal Pollack, however, knew them all at the time we wish we'd known them. He knew them in the beginning, when the world was young.

Dee Dee had invited Pollack to a recording studio. Pollack didn't want to go, but Dee Dee slipped some Tuinals into his gin-and-tonic, so Pollack would follow him anywhere. Dee Dee couldn't play his guitar. The drummer, some skinny longhaired freak, was worse. He really didn't know how to play at all. The bassist wasn't much better.

"Stop this noise!" Pollack said.

And they stopped.

"You can do better," he said. "Let's hear you play together."

They started doing a Bay City Rollers cover. It sounded like Max and Kansas City getting fed to a meat grinder. Pollack stopped them again.

"You're not gonna get anywhere as a band unless you let me

play bass," he said.

"Who are you?" said the longhaired guy.

"I'm Neal Pollack."

The longhaired guy kneeled and bowed his head.

"I'm sorry to have insulted you, great one," said Joey Ramone.

"Ah, you're all right," said Pollack.

"You can be in the band, but you've gotta give us drugs," Joey said.

"No problem."

"And you have to have a Ramone name."

It was just another stupid band gimmick, like a thousand others Pollack had seen. But they went through a list anyway, dumping Ritchie Ramone right away, even though it sounded cool and alliterative. There were lots of other possible Ramones: Archie, Spanky, Slinky, Go-Go, Mikey, Ziggy, Crunchy, Georgy, Frodo, Tinky, Winky, Petey, Kitschy, Henry. None of them seemed to suit Pollack.

They broke open a bottle of Boone's Farm and tried some more.

Kinky, Willy, Dicky, Lachlan, Rupert, Junkie, Alkie, Nicky, Talky, Lumpy, Hedwig, Chalky, Horny, Wally, Kobe.

Nah.

"Grumpy?"

"That's pretty good," Pollack said, "but no. None of the Seven Dwarfs."

"I kinda like Dopey Ramone."

"Then take it yourself."

They smoked and popped pills and drank until the sun came up. Joey nodded behind the drum set. Dee Dee and the other guy collapsed into heaps on the floor. It was 7 A.M. when Pollack's brain sparked on.

"I've got it!" he said. "I know what my name should be!"

The other Ramones barely stirred. Pollack started kicking

them. If they were going to make it in rock, they'd better start having some discipline.

"And my name shall be . . ." Pollack said.

"Mmmmm. Whuh?" said Joey.

"Smokey Ramone!"

Pollack went downstairs and got coffee. The Ramones had written a bunch of songs, with titles like "I Don't Wanna Clean My Room This Weekend," "I Don't Wanna Go for a Ride in the Country, Stupid," and "I Don't Wanna Eat a Bag of Cheese." Pollack tried to play them. He wasn't sure if the other guys were trying or not. The songs got faster and faster, sludgier and sludgier. Joey fell off his stool, and they kept going. He just flailed stupidly at the drum set. They needed a real drummer, bad. But it was still the best band of all time.

Joey groaned. "I don't wanna play the drums anymore," he said. "Please let me sing, please."

He threw a snare out the window. They started playing a song that they later named "I Don't Wanna Play the Drums Anymore." An amp blew up. The room filled with smoke but they all choked through it and kept on playing. It was a goddamn mess of dirt and noise.

"God, this is horrible!" Pollack said. "Isn't it wonderful?"

The original Ramones—Joey, Marky, Dee Dee, Tommy, and Smokey, the elusive fifth Ramone—took the stage at CBGB for the first time on August 16, 1974.

"I figured that club had no chance," Pollack later wrote for the newly formed *Punk* magazine, after it was newly formed. "No chance at all."

They played the first note of the first song. A string broke on Pollack's guitar. They played the second note. Another string broke.

"Fuck!" Pollack said.

"Man," Joey said, "you're messing up our gig."

"Screw you!" said Pollack. "I quit."

He stormed off the stage, and the music started again. Five seconds in, Dee Dee broke a string.

"I'll kick your ass," Joey said.

"Fuck you," said Dee Dee.

They started swinging at each other. Pollack came running back to the stage, with fresh guitar strings. He handed them out and rejoined the band. They started again. An amp blew up. A drumstick flew out of Tommy's hand.

They played a lost Ramones song, which Pollack later claimed that he'd written. No one argued with him, because it wasn't very good.

Dee Dee said, "Onetwothreefour!"

Riding on the Cyclone
Seeing lots of Mermaids
Eating all the corndogs
Whack-A-Mole
Riding on the Carousel
Blowjobs on the boardwalk
Nearly reaching third base
By the pier

Coney Island is the place to be
Coney Island whitefish
Swimming up from the sea
Coney Island is the place to go
I'd rather visit Coney
Than spend a weekend at the Jersey Shore.

I will be with you
Whoa-oh-oh

On Coney Island!

Getting in a bar fight
Beating up the Irish
Drinking with the Russians
All night long.
Whistling at the hookers
Buying stolen furniture
Never ever wanting
To go home.

Coney Island is the place to be
Coney Island whitefish
Swimming up from the sea
Coney Island is the place to go
I'd rather visit Coney
Than spend a weekend at the Jersey Shore.

I will be with you
Whoa-oh-oh
On Coney Island!
One Two Three Four!

Going to the freakshow
Gazing at the Lizard Man
Heckling contortionists
For five bucks
Kiss the bearded lady
Kiss the tattooed lady
Kiss the lovely lady
Who breathes fire!

Coney Island is the place to be

Coney Island whitefish
Swimming up from the sea
Coney Island is the place to go
I'd rather visit Coney
Than spend a weekend at the Jersey Shore.

I will be with you
Whoa-oh-oh
On Coney Island!

After the show, as the Ramones packed up their gear, a bearded guy loped toward them. He was walking two dogs.

"I'm Hilly Kristal," said the guy. "I own this bar."

"Oh yeah?" Joey said.

"I thought you were good. But no one else is ever gonna like you. If you want, you can play here again."

"Great!" Pollack said.

"On one condition," said Kristal. "You've got to lose Smokey."

Pollack raised his guitar over his head and said, "Fuck you, you shit-brained country-music-loving Jew-ass motherfucker. . . ."

A bouncer flung Pollack onto the Bowery. His career in the Ramones was over. He pounded on the door.

"Let me in, goddamn it!" he shouted. "I made this band what it is today!"

A hand was on his shoulder. Pollack turned around to face me. There was a lovely young woman on my arm. I immediately saw that this wasn't a good time for him. The Ramones incident had brought on another one of his long, slow declines. Two years of very hard living had suddenly taken effect.

"Hello, Neal," I said.

"What do you want, Paul?" Pollack said.

"Just to say hello. That band was great!"

"Thanks!"

"Except for you."

"Oh."

Pollack stood there in the summer heat, shivering.

"This is my third wife, Ruth," I said.

"So?" Pollack said.

"Ruth, this is the legendary rock critic Neal Pollack."

"I've read your work," said Ruth.

Pollack stopped twitching momentarily.

He kissed Ruth's hand.

"My dear," he said. "How do you do?"

For weeks, Pollack and Patti Smith had been living in the artist Arturo Vega's loft on Bowery with the Ramones. Nights meant an endless wandering from avant-garde theater to poetry venue to rock club to bar and back home for something up the nose. Then they were back on the town until dawn and pancakes. Noon passed, and two P.M. When they woke, Patti would read Rimbaud aloud. Pollack pet his cats. He was getting bored.

Patti twirled about the room in her long skirts, stopping only to cross her arms. She gazed at Pollack dramatically.

"How I long to lose myself," she said, "in a sea of possibility."

"I long for a blow job," Pollack said.

"How old are you?" she said. "Grow up."

Pollack looked at his watch, which he'd stolen recently. He studied the minute and second hands very carefully. Maybe the answer to her question was embedded in the watch face somewhere. Then he remembered.

"I'm thirty-four," he said. "I'm old. Very old."

"I'm so young," Patti improvised, twirling and twirling. "I'm so young. I'm so goddamn young. I'm so young. I'm so goddamn young. We created it: Let's take it over."

"Shut up," Pollack said.

Patti flopped next to him. She pounded on her chest, and then his.

"You shut up!" she said. "I hate you! I hate you!"

In a far corner of the loft, a hideous she-creature stirred beneath a great mound of black clothing. On either side of her, a Ramone snored. The creature raised herself, her face smeared with horrible multicolored goo. She was wearing the same dress she'd worn all week, had been asleep for two days, and she was hungry. Her blurry eyes saw two shapes entwined across the room. A little focus revealed that the shapes were wrestling, and not happy. She lurched toward them.

Pollack and Patti looked up at her.

"Oh, Nancy," Patti said. "You're awake."

"I'm starving," Nancy Spungen said.

"Go back to Philadelphia, you whore!" said Patti.

Patti resumed hitting Pollack.

"I hate you!" she said. "I hate you!"

Pollack's erect penis protruded from his pants. Nancy leapt upon it like a jungle beast. She began sucking. Patti tugged at Nancy's hair.

"Get off him, bitch!" she screamed.

Pollack moaned with pleasure. He slipped a finger into his ass, and then inserted his whole hand, as he was wont to do. Patti beat at him and Nancy simultaneously. In a distant corner of the loft, Arturo Vega was painting a Day-Glo swastika on the wall. Joey Ramone grabbed the spray can from him.

"Cut out that Nazi shit, you fascist!" he said.

Vega hit him in the head with the can. Two other Ramones were swinging guitars at each other for no reason. Iggy Pop burst out of the bathroom. He broke a window and started cutting himself with the glass. Two people who no one had ever seen before fucked under a blanket in the middle of the room. Nancy Spungen sucked harder and harder. Pollack felt himself soaring toward the brink of something.

Johnny Thunders burst through the door.

"Hey, everyone!" he said. "Guess what? I've got heroin!"

The fighting stopped. So did the sucking. Patti's arms dropped to her side.

They all began licking their lips.

Two hours later, everyone lay on the floor of the loft, looking at the ceiling, except for Pollack. He sat on his mattress, staring coldly at the wall.

"Ohh," he said. "I think I have an infection."

No one paid him any mind. The world was for the young now. He was getting old.

On July 16, 1975, the Neal Pollack Invasion played its only show ever. Pollack had formed the band from castoffs from other bands that had never played live. It was the most authentic collection of working-class musicians ever assembled. His bassist worked as a security guard at the Fresh Kills landfill. His lead guitarist was a gravedigger, and his drummer a copy editor at *Harper's*. They had no money, no identity, no talent, and no hope.

They got a gig at the Coventry, a club in Queens, opening for the Dictators, who Pollack described as "the greatest rock 'n' roll band of all time," a superlative he only handed out every two or three years.

At first, the Dictators had been reluctant to book the show.

"No," said Andy Shernoff.

"Please please please please please?" Pollack said. "I'll write about you. . . ."

Unfortunately for Pollack, on that same night, Blondie, the Ramones, and the Talking Heads played a show in Manhattan for the opening of CBGB's first summer music festival. In Queens, Pollack looked into his audience. There were seventeen people, all of them wearing cotton headbands. They'd obviously been lured in by the "Free Headbands" promotion.

"Let's make some rock 'n' roll!" Pollack said backstage. "Let's give 'em a night they won't forget!"

Handsome Dick Manitoba drank beer from a can.

"Let's get this over with so we can go home and watch TV," he said.

The Neal Pollack Invasion took the stage. The crowd booed, except for one girl, maybe fifteen, who moved her head to a music that hadn't even started yet. Pollack knew then that he'd reached her, and that he'd done the right thing. Out there, he knew, were dozens like her, maybe hundreds, sad smart kids who needed him to express their unheard hopeless voices.

America was a desperate place, plagued by rising unemployment, decaying, bankrupt cities, and rapacious, impersonal corporate greed. The land careened toward imminent ecological catastrophe. Government was in the hands of buffoonish, plutocratic dinosaurs obsessed with power and self-preservation. Popular culture had become loud, clownish, distracting, hideous in its lack of meaning. People were afraid, and they expressed their anxieties through blind, stupid, meaningless patriotism. Unknown enemies seemed to lurk around every corner, waiting to wrench away the comforts of empire with unholy apocalyptic fire. There was fatality in the air, decay, oblivion, disintegration, and a secret longing to die.

It was nothing like today.

Pollack climbed atop a speaker. He said:

"Here's our generational anthem!"

The band kicked in an incoherent grind, and Pollack moaned, shrieked, gurgled this:

> *New York City is a pile of shit!*
> *New York City is a pile of shit!*
> *New York City is a pile of shit!*
> *Ahhhhhhhhhhh!*

New York City!
Andy Warhol is a pile of shit!
Andy Warhol is a pile of shit!
Andy Warhol is a pile of shit!
Ahhhhhhhhhhh!
Andy Warhol!

CBGB's is a pile of shit!
CBGB's is a pile of shit!
CBGB's is a pile of shit!
Ahhhhhhhhhh!
CBGB's!

Fidel Castro is a pile of shit!
Richard Nixon is a pile of shit!
Jalapeno bagels are a pile of shit!
Barbara Walters is a pile of shit!
The whole damn world is a pile of shit!
Fuck you, David Bowie
You're a goddamn
Suck-up whore
Pile of shit!

Pile of shit is a pile of shit!
Pile of shit is a pile of shit!
Pile of shit is a pile of shit!
Ahhhhhhhhhh!
PILE! OF! SHIT!

Pile pile pile pile
Pile of shit!
Pile pile pile pile
Pile of shit!

Pile
Pile
Pile
Pile
Pile pile pile pile
Pile of shit!

Pollack stood center stage, arms extended, drenched in sweat and blood. The crowd silently moved toward him, emitting a low, sinister hiss. Their eyes were crazed and evil. The band dropped their instruments and ran like hell. The girl Pollack thought he'd touched opened her mouth wide, extended her right arm. She pointed toward Pollack.

"KILL!" she said.

They charged toward him, ready to tear him apart. He looked around. They were closing in on all sides. He dove, smacking a boot into some kid's midsection. Arms flailing, he descended into the swarm. Then the cops came, batons flaring, and the crowd's rage turned on them. Twenty people kicking the snot out of the cops, Pollack thought. Now that's rock 'n' roll.

Pollack squirted from the crowd and headed for the exit.

"My work here is done," he said.

As they ran down the street in terror, the box office manager handed Neal his night's take, ten dollars, and a telegram that had come to the theater during the show.

Pollack read it:

NEAL. NEW YORK IS DEAD. YOU'RE NEEDED IN
LONDON. COME IMMEDIATELY, AT YOUR OWN
EXPENSE. MALCOLM.

Pollack rubbed his chin thoughtfully. He pulled his cats Max and Kansas City out of his duffel bag, where they'd been suffocating. They panted feebly and scratched at him.

"Well, kitties," he said. "London again! Won't this be a delightful adventure?"

Neal Pollack sat atop a box, which was atop another box, which was atop another. The boxes were all painted black with the letters S-E-X in white going down their fronts. They were supposed to have spelled SEX, naturally, but someone had arranged them wrong, so they actually spelled out XSE. Still, for London, late 1975, that was pretty radical.

Pollack wore a black rubber vest, no shirt underneath. His eyes were ringed with black eyeliner, and he had a red clown nose on. At either side of him sat his cats, also wearing rubber. Their fetish suits were lined with fish oil to keep them from complaining.

Inside the shop at 430 King's Road, Malcolm McLaren tapped a table loudly. In front of Pollack, in a circle, sat a dozen or so young men, middle-class or working-class, angry, desperate, malleable, and ready to party. They were all named John. Pollack looked down at them. I'll be running this country within a month, he thought.

"Now kids," McClaren said. "We have a guest speaker today. He's a great rock critic from the United States of America."

"Ohhhhh!" said the boys.

"He knows David Bowie," McLaren said.

"Ohhhhhhh!"

"And he has many important things to say to you about fashion and politics. Please welcome Neal Pollack."

Pollack rubbed his chin thoughtfully.

"The Queen is a cunt," he said.

The Johns gasped.

"And the world is lit by fascism. Your government is trying to destroy you. If you still have parents, they don't understand you, and they'd rather see you dead. We are puppets, pawns, automatons, shivering fearfully in the shadow of the machine. The ground is poisoned, and the air is foul. The British empire has been revealed for the farce it always was, and we've been thrown the feeble scraps."

Now the boys were sobbing.

"But there is an answer," Pollack said.

"Hooray!" said the boys.

"It's called rock 'n' roll. "

"Ohhhhhh."

"If the world becomes fucked up, only a raw protean yawp from youthful bowels can save it."

One of the Johns raised his hand. He was wearing a white Pink Floyd T-shirt. Above the logo, he'd written "I HATE."

"What are you talking about?" he said.

"You have to start a band," said Pollack.

"Anger is an energy," said John.

"Yes, yes," Pollack said.

"I am an outcast and unwanted."

"I know, I know."

"Because my friends and I are all extremely ugly, our only recourse . . ."

The Johns began to buzz. Their innocent faces had taken on revolting sneers. Before Pollack's eyes, they were transforming. They rose and began to pace the store restlessly. Malcolm McLaren rubbed his hands. His eyes took on the glint of an entrepreneur. Excellent, he thought to himself. They're furious and they don't know why. My master plan is working.

"Who wants benzedrine?" Pollack said.

A few months later, Pollack, by now an established columnist for *New Music Express*, was at the 100 Club, nodding off in the back with Chrissie Hynde. McClaren walked by him.

"Hey, Malcolm," Pollack said.

McClaren ignored Pollack and moved away. A male ghost with

bristly hair walked behind him. He kicked Pollack in the shins. The club was crowded, so Pollack figured it was an accident. The guy came back. He kicked Pollack again.

"Who's that guy?" Pollack said. "And why does he keep kicking me?"

"That's Sid," said Hynde.

Pollack popped two bennies.

"Screw him," he said.

Sid was following Lydon around like a shadow. Lydon came up to Pollack and pushed him in the chest. Pollack pushed back. Lydon pushed back in return.

"What's all this shit you've been saying about us in the papers, then?" Lydon said. "You're trying to get us banned, aren't you?"

"It's good to get banned," said Pollack.

"Balls! I didn't go to art school just to get banned!"

Pollack put a finger to Lydon's lips.

"Shhh," he said. "This is part of a plan."

Johnny Rotten bit down on Pollack's finger, hard. Pollack felt a little crunch of bone, and a snapped tendon. He dropped to his knees. Rotten and Sid squirted away, leaving behind a legacy of sneering, angry, macho violence.

That night the Sex Pistols performed a new song:

> *Never mind the Pollacks*
> *Never mind them all*
> *Kick them in the bollocks*
> *Punch them in the balls*
>
> *Pollack is a tosser*
> *And so's his sainted mum*
> *London Bridge is falling down*
> *So kick him in the bum*

Neal Pollack!
Neal Pollack!
Neal Pollack's dead!

We haven't got a future
We haven't got a past
We haven't got a byline
Kick Pollack in the ass!

Neal Pollack!
Neal Pollack!
Neal Pollack's dead!

Pollack heard from the back. He ripped toward the stage. Some-one had written a song about him! Someone cared! He needed this! Sid stood directly in front of him. Pollack tapped him on the back.

"Excuse me," Pollack said. "Could you move over?"

Johnny Rotten lobbed a gob from the stage. Sid ducked. It hit Pollack in the monobrow and dribbled down his nose.

Sid uncrouched. He faced Pollack, his breath like hell-air. He had a bike chain in one hand, a knife in the other.

"I don't like your trousers," he said.

Sid cracked Pollack on the left temple. Pollack felt a hot flash on his right cheek; he swung out blindly, but Sid was gone. Blood poured everywhere. Guitars screamed into the night. Johnny Rot-ten screamed back:

Never mind the Pollack
He don't really exist
A worthless alcoholic
He's gonna slit his wrists

Neal Pollack is a junkie

He's shacked up with the Queen
He mounts her like a monkey
He pissed in her canteen

Neal Pollack!
Neal Pollack!
Neal Pollack's dead!

Pollack fell, awash in his own blood. He got up and dove in a bum's rush for the stage, connecting with Johnny Rotten's midsection. Someone tossed a burning cigarette onstage. Pollack stubbed it out on Rotten's hand. Sid Vicious charged him, brandishing a crowbar. Pollack caught him with a leg sweep. Vicious sprawled, hitting himself in the face with the bar. He stood up, looked at the cheering crowd, and hit himself again. Fights were breaking out all over the room. The music couldn't drown out the shouts of pain and fear. The police charged in, brandishing nightsticks. They started busting heads. Rotten looked at Pollack with nothing less than awe. This was the true essence of rock.

James Osterberg sat in his kitchen and gazed upon the ghost city of Berlin. Magnificent, decadent Berlin! Fading home of Weimar dreams! And, at last, a room of Iggy's own. A tinpot stove, a bowl of cereal, a wooden table, stuffed parrot hanging above on a wooden swing, postwar wallpaper, prewar tile, a Kraftwerk album on the hi-fi, and a couple of chairs. These things made him happy, along with good-looking drag queens, which Berlin didn't lack. Iggy Pop was breathing true freedom for the first time. Gone was the jail time in L.A., the 5 A.M. wanderings down Sunset Boulevard. Vanished were the ritual concert humiliations of a thousand tossed fruits and vegetables, the angry confrontations, the meaningless groupie sex. His mind was clear; a ten-minute walk in Berlin was as cleansing to him as any sauna. He was at home here.

Nothing could tamper with his serenity anymore.

The doorbell rang. Iggy put down his copy of Christopher Isherwood's *Berlin Stories*.

"Yes?" he said.

"Iggy," said an unmistakable voice. "It's me."

"Shit," Iggy said.

"Iggy! Iggy darling . . .I'm writing about you for *Slash*! Please let me in."

"Go away, Pollack," Iggy said.

"Oh, come on, Iggy. Please?"

"Leave me alone."

"Iggy . . .I've got cocaine. . . ."

No. He couldn't let Pollack into his life. Not now. It would annihilate everything that he and Bowie had built there in Berlin, wipe out all shreds of joy, take him down that evil river of pestilence that he'd tried so hard to abandon. Not this time. No more tragic ballads. But he heard it anyway, in his mind's ear.

From behind the door: "Iggy? Iggy. Let me in, Iggy."

Iggy clutched his temples. "No!" he said. "Please, no!"

"Iggy . . ."

From deep within, Iggy felt a roar in his stomach. It wafted into his chest and blew up his windpipe, launched into his throat and emerged from his mouth full-throttle. He grabbed a cheap glass vase from a side table, threw open the door, and swung, hitting David Bowie smack in the jaw.

Bowie dropped to the ground.

"What'd you do that for?" he said.

Pollack stood next to prone Bowie.

"Hi, Iggy," he said.

Then they were unleashed onto Berlin, Pollack and Iggy and Bowie. They pranced through deserted streets to the robotic drone of the Trans-European Music Express. They found themselves in a whorehouse cabaret called Long Tall Sally Bowles, lying faceup on an ermine rug while a six-foot drag queen, better look-ing than Jerry Hall, took turns grinding their nipples with her spiked heels.

"You are beautiful," she said to Iggy.

"You are elegant," she said to Bowie.

"You are disgusting," she said to Pollack.

"Ah, yes," Pollack said, "but I have the cocaine!"

"Then I am yours for the night!" she said.

During the days, Pollack sat in Iggy's apartment, typing the letter "l" thousands of times on hundreds of sheets of paper, an experiment in what he called the New Literature. He drank copi-ous quantities of Pernod, blew through kilos of cocaine. Iggy was trying to be responsible. He wrote songs that would later become commercials. Pollack would sneak up behind Iggy, put his hands over his Iggy eyes.

"Guess who?" he'd say.

"Neal Pollack," Iggy would say.

"Do you want some coke?"

"Yes."

Then it was off to the recording studio, and sex with transves-tites. More cocaine. Iggy got two albums done. He and Bowie planned a tour. But he was frying now, living in perpetual confu-sion. Pollack was like a worm burrowed in his mind, his greatest fan but also his final destroyer. Iggy had been created, in some way, by Pollack. But like all creations, he longed to free himself from his master, to become a whole man, alone.

Pollack put on a Question Mark & the Mysterians album. He danced on Iggy's breakfast table, naked, smoking a joint. Iggy moaned into his coffee.

"This is the greatest band of all time!" Pollack said. "Can't you hear it? Can't you feel it in your soul?"

No, Iggy wanted to scream, he didn't.

"Will you please get the hell out of my life?" Iggy screamed.

Pollack looked at him strangely.

"OK," he said.

He kissed Iggy on the forehead.

"But you'll miss me."

And just like that, he was out the door, disappeared into the rainy Berlin morning.

Bowie emerged from the bedroom, yawning, resplendent in a purple silk kimono. He also kissed Iggy's forehead.

"Where's Pollack?" he said.

"Gone," said Iggy. "Gone forever."

"Thank goodness," Bowie said. "Now we can start planning our life together."

Iggy said nothing. Instead, he had a drink. He *did* miss that stinky little rock critic, despite himself.

Tampa, Florida, sometime in 1977. Pollack was on tour with the Patti Smith Group. He'd gotten tangled in some wires backstage at the sports arena and was whining softly. A familiar tweeded figure, improbably handsome, appeared. He pulled Pollack out of the mess.

"Hey, Paul," Pollack said. "What's rockin'?"

"I'm here to do a profile of Patti," I said. "A think piece for *Rolling Stone*."

"About what?"

"Patti. Her significance."

"Right," Pollack said. "Is Ruth here?"

"She's smoking in a dark corner of the parking lot all alone," I said. "She's completely unsupervised, which is fine, because I trust her."

Pollack picked up his Black Russian and staggered toward the load-in dock. He hopped down, found a Dumpster, and puked. Man, that felt good. He puked again.

"Hello, Neal," said a gilded voice.

Pollack turned to see Ruth in a burgundy knee-length skirt and leather boots. She wore a single carnation in her hair. A graduate student had never looked so beautiful to him. He wiped puke on his sleeve, stumbled over to her, and began to cry.

"Ruth, nobody understands me," he said. "I'm a really sensitive guy, and everybody thinks I should be happy fucking all these chicks and being a rock critic. But I'm hurt and I'm lonely and I need someone stable in my life like you."

She stroked his hair.

"There, there," she said. "I understand."

They held each other, for minutes that felt like hours, while Pollack sobbed out whatever miseries and lost hopes had lain buried in his soul all those years.

"If they don't appreciate what I've written about them," he said, "I'll fucking kill them all."

I wandered into the parking lot and saw them together.

"Oh," I said. "I didn't realize."

"I was just consoling him," said Ruth.

I picked up a two-by-four.

"Come inside, Ruth," he said. "Bob Seger wants to meet you."

The hug ended. Pollack's face contorted with rage. He raised his arms and shouted into the humid night: "Rock doesn't deserve me!"

"That's enough, Neal," said Ruth.

Pollack wept. "I'm sorry," he said. "I'm sorry. I'm so sorry for everything."

Pollack was in the front row, glaring, as the Patti Smith Group began their set that night. She and her band performed their first song. The audience stood silently, no applause, no enthusiasm, not even hatred. Pollack grinned and pointed, and he knew Patti could see him. He wanted her to see him, because he hated her just like he hated all women, except for those who loved him, and Patti had never loved him. He'd been just another peg on which she'd hung her fur coat of stardom. This was the truth, this was what he knew, and this made him hurt all the more.

He said to himself, "I was just sleeping with you, Patti, to get into shows for free."

They started playing their second song, "Ain't It Strange." Pollack had always hated that song. Midway through, Patti started twirling. "Come on, God, make a move!" she shouted. She whirled in broad swoops and the band played a wobbly beat.

One twirl took her to the lip of the stage, and the next right off the stage. Patti fell. Two guys in the pit tried to catch her, but they missed. Her head hit the floor with a loud crack. Blood pooled at the back of her head. She started twitching. Pollack pointed and laughed.

"Who's the poet now?" he said. "Who's the prophet now? Someone won't be reading Rimbaud for a while."

A roadie looked annoyed.

Pollack turned to face the crowd.

"Come on!" he shouted. "Let's finish her off!"

The roadie looked at him with pity and disdain.

"Go away, old man," he said.

The crowd didn't seem to be lusting for blood. They were only concerned, and concern was not what Neal Pollack liked to see at a rock show. The wheeled stretcher came, and then the ambulance, and then it was the middle of 1977 and Pollack was tired. He loped backstage, where Ruth and I were both standing around looking as concerned as everyone else.

"Forget about her," Pollack said. "Punk is dead."

"I don't know, Neal," I said. "You might be wrong about this one."

"I'm never wrong."

Pollack heard the ringing. Did he have a phone? Well, he must if it was ringing. He reached above him to where the ringing was coming from. Yes. A phone.

"Hello," he said.

"Neal," said the voice.

"Who is this?"

"It's me, Claude."

"Who?"

"Claude. Claude Bessy."

Oh, yes, Pollack thought. A lesser critic. From Los Angeles.

"What do you want, Frenchy?"

"Just thought I'd call."

"Where am I?" said Pollack.

"I don't know," said Bessy.

"Mmm," said Pollack. "Listen, Claude, I'm really sick and I'm going back to bed now."

"No, you listen," Claude said. "You need to move to L.A. immediately."

Los Angeles!!!! Pollack thought. "You have got to be kidding! I'd rather die than move to L.A.!"

"There are bands here," said Bessy. "Really good ones."

"So?"

"Bands with chicks in them. Chicks that have their own chick groupies."

"See you in two weeks," Pollack said.

The next afternoon, Pollack held a sidewalk sale to get rid of his possessions. After a couple of hours, he had twenty-five bucks, and he was free. He shoved the cats, an ounce of weed, a bottle of Jack Daniel's, one clean pair of underwear, and his sainted copy of *Trout Mask Replica* into a backpack, and went to the East Village looking for a motorcycle to hot-wire. It didn't take long, and soon he was on the West Side Highway, leaving the bankrupt city behind him, hopefully forever.

New York is so dull and predictable, he thought. Out there, on the American road, there has to be a fresh approach. Somewhere, he just knew, culture was being created with no hope of making a profit. People were putting out records that corporations would never discover. He wanted to be there to chronicle those many births.

His motorcycle neared the Bronx now.

"No good music will ever come out of New York City again," he said.

He turned his head toward the city one last time. In that moment, a barely discernible interstice that seemed to last forever, he heard a break, a beat, a pop. He saw everything, somehow. There, in an asphalt park, an island of beauty in a lake of decay, an old man wearing long African robes stood behind two turntables. A stack of records sat beside him on an overturned milk crate. Around him, a bunch of kids were doing a loose dance, more like a grind. The music revved and screeched. It sounded like the future.

"Freaky," Pollack said.

Behind the turntables, the man, pretty hip considering how old he was, rhymed into a microphone. The words whipped from his mouth freely. For 1979, it was an astonishing verbal display that seemed completely unrehearsed. It went like this:

> *Hey, party people (are you ready to drop it?)*
> *Hey party people (are you ready to pop it?)*
> *Bop it (don't stop it!)*
> *Tip-tip. Top-hop. Don't stop till your body pops*
> *I wanna see your hips hop!*
> *Rock the block*
> *Do it in your socks*
> *Rip. Slip. Clip-clop and knock your cocks.*
> *Hop On Pop and a Fox in the Box*
> *Slip. Slop. Get down on the long mop.*
> *We're gonna have a party*

And we're gonna do the body rock.
Just bust it, trust it, clean it up and dust it
and say Ho!

The man stepped out from behind the turntables, removed his robe and dashiki, and Pollack gasped.

"Clambone," he said.

At that moment, in 1979 or so, rapping debuted on the earth. As Clambone said:

> *Now I'm MC Clam and I'm twice as juicy*
> *As Dick Van Dyke or I Love Lucy*
> *Your brain is fried, your mind is blown*
> *I'll beat your ass with my microphone.*
> *I birthed the blues, I invented the funk*
> *I sold Charlie Parker his first hit of junk*
> *If you stole my music, you best repent*
> *Or give up plagiarism for Lent*
>
> *Come on everybody and start to move*
> *'Cause I'm the lord of eternal groove*
> *Come on, everybody and start to dance*
> *And hit me with your underpants*
> *So let's party!*
> *And let's party some more!*
> *We may be in recession*
> *But at least we ain't at war!*
> *Here we go! Here we go now*
> *Here we go go go go go go go go now!*

Was Pollack dreaming? Was Clambone creating yet another form of African-American musical expression, this time one that was so unique to the black experience that white people would never be able to co-opt it? He needed to rap himself, just to test. He tried:

> *Now I'm Neal Pollack, and I'm here to say*
> *I'm the best rock critic in the USA*
> *I like to write, and I take drugs*
> *I have three dildos and four buttplugs.*

God! He sounded like Tim Conway! This form of music was simply beyond him. Black people had done it, at last.

The world froze. Clambone hovered over the basketball court, bathed in a golden light. He gestured toward the highway.

"Pollack," he said.

"Clambone," said Pollack

"Rock is changing," he said. "From now on, you must Do It Yourself."

"Yes," Pollack said. "Of course."

"But beware She Who Shall Not Be Named for Fear of Lawsuit."

"What do you mean?"

"Beware," Clambone said. "And don't stop 'til your body pops. . . ."

The world unfroze. Clambone and his break beats were gone; Pollack was in the wrong lane. A truck bore down on his motorcycle. He swerved and smacked the median, then swerved the other way and smacked the other median. Shit, he thought. I should have worn a helmet. Inside his backpack, the cats howled. The bike smacked the median again and Pollack flipped over the handlebars.

"I'm free," he said.

He broke an oncoming windshield with his face, and the world went dark.

PART FIVE
THE COPS WILL HAVE YOUR HEAD

1980—1991

T he '80s were fun, at least for me. With great pride, I can now claim to have been the first mainstream critic on the mailing list of SST Records, writing, of their initial Black Flag issue, "This record, a relentless wall of noise that is never less than noisy, sounds unlike anything else I've heard this year." Even more impressively, I wrote in my seminal record guide *Paul St. Pierre Reviews the '80s* that "Ian Mackaye may be 'straight edge,' but his music roars down the road like a trucker on speed. What a nice young man."

But then the weirdo music paradise that I'd helped publicize was first co-opted and then totally corrupted by the recording industry. Capitalism reigned triumphant. As I wrote in a 1993 *Spin* article that was nominated for a National Magazine Award, "They say 'we won,' and they think we don't know who they are or why." Observations like that kept me on top long after my generational peers had faded away toward Margaritaville.

All the while, Neal Pollack vexed me. As sharp as I remained in the early '90s, he was even sharper. Researching this manuscript, I found a prophetic quote from his late diaries that made him seem less like a critic and more like a musical seer from the future: "You can take your Misfits T-shirts and stick 'em in a drawer, and run over your Soundgarden lunchbox with a pickup truck, because the future of music will come from Beck, the Fugees, Moby, and Outkast," he wrote. "I also predict a rise, in the Midwest, of a white hip-hop artist who stupid critics like Paul St. Pierre will compare to Elvis."

I don't appreciate the personal potshot, and I stand by my assessment of *The Eminem Show* as the greatest album released in the last twenty years. Still, Pollack's predictions have proven to be eerily accurate. While going through his personal effects, I found an old issue of *Maximumrocknroll* devoted to praise of Mudhoney. Pollack had written the entire contents. Scribbled on the back cover, in thick black marker, were the words "Blink 182 SUCKS." Pollack was so right. But how did he know that a band, not yet even formed, sucked? How?

To discover the truth, I now find myself interviewing people at least twenty years younger than I, or more. It makes me uncomfortable, because I want to sleep with all the women, especially Sleater-Kinney, who can make beautiful noise that seems abstracted from their mouths, fingers, bodies, and instruments. They make me want to suck in my gut and remove my chin fat with a surgical hose. Well, do you blame me? They're hot.

But somehow Pollack seemed to have the distance necessary to see that world as it formed around him. In 1990 he wrote, "A chick band is going to come out of Olympia, Washington, that makes Bikini Kill sound like Melissa Manchester." Also, he said, "Beware She Who Shall Not Be Named for Fear of Lawsuit. Because she's been sent from an evil place to destroy us all."

Never in my life have I found myself face-to-face with She Who Shall Not Be Named for Fear of Lawsuit, or, as my friends call her, the Widow. Now the time of our encounter is nigh. She knew Kurt better than all of us put together. Kurt knew Pollack better than anyone in both their waning days. So I've come, at my own expense, to Los Angeles, where the Widow lives. I've already been here far too long.

It's been a dispiriting few months. The Widow has thwarted all my attempts to speak with her. She uses a vast army of lawyers, publicists, bodyguards, personal assistants, salon employees and bouncers to deflect attention from her daily routine. One night, at the Viper Room, I saw what looked like her ankle step out of the back of a Bentley, but one of her behemoths had me in a head-lock before I could take out my tape recorder. Another afternoon, I left a message with her messaging service's messaging service, and a few hours later, this was on my voice mail:

"Listen, you fucking prick. This is the Widow. I don't know who you think you are trying to talk to me, but if you try to get anywhere near me or my family, I promise you that I will hunt you down, cut off your balls with a chainsaw, and grind you into fuck-ing horsemeat. You sexless asshole, I will destroy you and then I will eat you and lick the blood off my fingers and laugh and I won't go to jail because no one cares about you and I'm a fucking superstar. And you ever reprint this message in a book, I promise you that I will hunt you down again and kill you again, and this time, I won't leave any evidence. Don't fucking mess with me. I mean it. Good-bye."

I shivered when I heard the message.

"Ruth, listen," I said.

But the apartment was empty. Ruth had left me months before. I wept and cursed my former wife.

Someday, I thought, she will ache like I ache.

Now, a year past deadline, running out of money, barely shaven, wearing the same rumpled khakis and blue oxford shirt two days running, I must speak with the Widow. There are holes in my story that need to be filled. Only the Widow can fill them.

An occasion has arisen. I read in the *Los Angeles Times* that the ACLU, the Sierra Club, the NAACP, Food Not Bombs, and the Spartacists Youth Brigade are honoring the Widow for "relentless lip service to unpopular causes." This is my opportunity. The Widow would never surround herself with goons while the left was watching.

She appears early, in a flash of glamour. Everyone wants to

touch her. She's an honored guest among people who are normally reluctant to honor guests. Her smile is wide. Her eyes glisten. This is all she ever dreamed about in the heroin dens of Portland. She's a star.

"Widow!" I shout. "Widow!"

"Hi!" she says.

This is my chance to ask her all the questions I've ever wanted.

"Are you glad to be here?" I say.

"I am," she says. "It's all about being liberal, which is very important."

"How's your new album coming along?"

"Great!"

"Oh, that's really cool. Listen, I'm writing a book about Neal Pollack, and I was wondering . . ."

The Widow's eyes fill with cold, hard hate. She looks at my tape recorder.

"Is that on?" she says. "Because I'm not talking to you anymore if it is."

"Buh, buh, buh," I say.

She grabs my recorder and throws it against the wall. Her goons appear. They toss me onto the street. My pants rip at the knee. They're the only pair I have left.

Because I have nothing else to do, I walk, which is easier in L.A. than you might imagine. Wandering past all the coffee shops, record stores, and empty furniture warehouses, I look into the hills at a million lights. Neal Pollack probably walked these same streets when he arrived here in 1980. He knew L.A. better than anyone, just as he subsequently knew Seattle and so many other points on the open American road. There was nothing glamorous about Neal Pollack's L.A., Neal Pollack's America.

Pollack and his Do-It-Yourself message defined the '80s, the true, noncommercial '80s. He didn't care how anyone felt about him, which was good, because everyone wanted him dead. As Jello

Biafra said during an early Dead Kennedys show in someone's basement in Colorado Springs, "Don't hate the media! Become the media! Unless the media is Neal Pollack. Then you can hate the media."

The list of bands he influenced and subsequently alienated in L.A. alone is almost too long to believe: the Alley Cats, the Avengers, the Bags, Black Flag, Black Randy and the Metro Squad, the Controllers, and the Dickies, with whom he was once stuck in a pagoda with Tricia Toyota. Then there were the Dils, the Eyes, F-Word, and the Flesh Eaters. Every night for one memorable week at their pad in the Cambridge Apartments, the Go-Gos blew Pollack beyond an inch of his life. He also befriended and betrayed Hal Negro and the Satintones, the Mau Maus, the Nerves, the Randoms, the Screamers, the Skulls, the Last, Wall of Voodoo, the Weirdos, X, and the Zero.

"But Darby Crash and the Germs were the greatest of them all," he wrote in *Slash*. "I remember one night I was dry-humping Lita Ford in the alley behind the Masque, and Darby came up and said, 'I need a ride to the Whisky A Go-Go.' Then he threw up all over me."

At midnight, I'm still walking, lost in memory. A limousine pulls up. The Widow pops out the sunroof.

"Neal Pollack was a liar and a thief!" she says. "And he still owes me five dollars! Put that in your book!"

Well, at least I got one quote out of her.

In the summer of 1982, Neal Pollack started sponsoring a monthly "Make Your Own Fanzine" workshop in the basement of the San Bernadino garage in which he was living illegally. The first two months, no one showed up. The third month, because of a promotional article in *Flipside,* fifty people stopped by, but Pollack told them to come back the next day because he was in the middle of a nap. When they did, he wasn't home.

The fourth month, he got two kids in their early twenties, one of them an enormous Native American of some stripe, the other a pimply, nondescript white guy. Pollack blearily opened the garage door and found them arguing. They were both holding guitars.

"America is a fascist police state!" said the fat one.

"No, it's a bourgeois democracy," said the other one.

"We live under an oppressive regime. Open your mind!"

"All of us are capitalists at the core!"

"Your ideals have been corrupted by the network news!"

They looked up and saw their hero. He was pondering them carefully.

"Oh, wow," said the fat one. "Neal Pollack!"

"We're huge fans," said the other guy.

"Who are you?"

"I'm Mike Watt. This is D. Boon. We read your stuff in *Creem* and *Punk*."

"I'm sorry," Pollack said.

"We started a band," said D. Boon, the big Indian. "I wrote a song. Wanna hear it?"

Before Pollack could reply, the guys began to play. Pollack looked at his watch. By the time he looked up, the song was over. The guitar work was very sincere, the lyrics heartfelt:

> *How can you have a girl*
> *When there's war in Nicaragua?*
> *Is Ronald Reagan your President,*
> *Or is it Che Guevara?*
> *That's the question I ask myself every day.*
> *And it hurts my feelings.*
> *Punk rock changed my life*
> *It made me what I am today.*
> *Three hundred years of French racism*
> *But I still want to see the Eiffel Tower*

Go on tour in England
And make more SST Records
Television fills my head with contradictory images
I hate new wave music
But I love you.

The song ended.

"French people aren't racist!" said Mike Watt.

"Yes, they are," said D. Boon.

"What have I created?" said Pollack to himself.

"What'd you think of our song, Neal?" asked D. Boon.

"Very nice, boys," Pollack said.

"Is it going to make us rich, like the Rolling Stones?" said Watt.

"No," Pollack said. "Rock shouldn't make you rich. That's a myth. You need to Do It Yourself. You must live econo."

A few weeks later, Pollack approached a basketball court next to a half-pipe, where a hardcore show was scheduled to take place. His aesthetic had changed, to suit the changing times. Now his head was shaved. He wore athletic shorts, no shirt, hi-top sneakers, and long socks pulled up to his knees. On his chest was a tattoo of a skull, with pus and worms oozing from its eyes, and the words "WEALTH IS RACISM." This is what Elvis would have been doing if he were a kid today, Pollack thought. We are his legacy.

In front of Black Flag, a young man prowled. He was the band's ninth lead singer in three months. Four had quit because of "creative differences" with Greg Ginn, two had OD'ed, and one had stolen six dollars from the SST Records cash box. The latest had accidentally gotten locked in the freezer of the Pizza Hut where he worked and suffered severe frostbite. Ginn subsequently fired him because he wasn't working for an independent pizzeria.

Pollack could see, though, that this new kid was different. For one, he and the kid were wearing the exact same clothes. For two, the kid exuded an air of authentic menace. The crowd stamped its

feet like bulls about to be released from the chute. The sound
check alone could have stripped the asphalt off a convenience-
store parking lot.

Pollack took a hit of nitrous and plunged into the throng.

The first note sounded a tsunami. The singer launched himself into the crowd. He punched someone in the nose. The crowd
launched him back. He grabbed the microphone and screamed.

THE CITY IS DEAD
LET'S PAINT IT RED
I NEED SOME MORE
LIFE IS A WHORE
YOU'VE NEVER BEEN
THE GIRL NEXT DOOR
THE COPS
WILL HAVE
YOUR HEAD

BEER AND WEED
BEER AND WEED
ALL I NEED IS
BEER AND WEED

I'VE GOT A GUN
I'M HAVING FUN
I'M SO AFRAID
THIS IS A RAID
THIS COPS WILL BEAT YOU
WHILE THEY GET PAID
YOU'LL ROT
UNDER
THE SUN

I NEVER READ
I NEVER BLEED
I NEVER NEED
GIMME SOME WEED
GIMME
SOME GODDAMN
WEED!

BEER AND WEED
BEER AND WEED
ALL I NEED IS
BEER AND WEED

JACK IN THE BOX
ASSES AND COCKS
CALIFORNIA DREAMING
CALIFORNINA SCREAMING
THE COPS WILL GIVE YOU
A CALIFORNIA REAMING
THEY'LL STRIP
YOU TO
YOUR SOCKS

Henry Rollins, who was once Henry Garfield, pointed at Pollack in the audience. He emitted a long, low, guttural moan.

"Traitor!" he shouted. "Rock critic!"

The crowd closed around Pollack. He was caught in a steel-booted gauntlet of pain. He felt a tooth loosen, then another, and then his liver. Never before had he seen so much hate and frustration in youthful eyes. This was more anguish than he'd bargained for. These kids were evil.

Something sharp stuck into his upper thigh.

"I'm going to die," he said. "And I've never had a son."

The band kept grinding. Rollins kept screaming. A wail of sirens, and the cops charged. Some of the kids ran in one direction, some in another. Some of them ran at the police phalanx. The cops brushed them aside. It was the band they wanted. They bashed Black Flag over their heads, but Black Flag kept playing. The cops cuffed them, but Black Flag kept playing. Nothing could stop Black Flag.

Pollack was bruised, bleeding, and confused. He stood on the edge of the playground. A van pulled up. The side door opened. Pollack smelt seven unwashed young men.

D. Boon poked his head out.

"Neal!" he said. "We're the Minutemen! We're going on tour! We're doing it ourselves!"

"Uhhh," Pollack said.

Mike Watt was driving.

"You look terrible!" he said. "You've inspired us! Get in the van!"

In an interview years later, Watt said, "Bringing Pollack on tour with us was the dumbest decision our band ever made."

Nothing has been written about the Minutemen's first U.S. tour. Years later, Mike Watt was to say, "We left L.A. young and sincere with such high hopes, and returned beaten cynical old men." They fell into a trap that so many bands had before. They gave Neal Pollack control.

For the first twenty-four hours, everything went great. Pollack didn't drink anything, not even water. They did a show in San Diego in the backyard of a guy D. Boon had met at a 7-Eleven, in front of almost two hundred kids, and made thirty dollars each.

"Let me handle the money for you," Pollack said. "Also, I'll book all your shows."

In Phoenix, on the second day, Pollack arranged for the band to play in a downtown parking lot. They unpacked their gear and started playing to their audience, comprised of five men who were in line for the Salvation Army soup kitchen next door. Boon insisted on doing the full set. "These are the guys we're trying to reach," he said. "They're working-class." Within minutes, they'd all been arrested, except for Pollack, who'd easily blended in with the soup kitchen clients. He spent all the San Diego profits on bail.

That night, in his journal, Pollack wrote, "There's never been a less rock 'n' roll place on earth than Phoenix, Arizona, and no music will ever come from here, except for the Meat Puppets. It is a godforsaken baked asshole of ignorance and blind consumerism, a festering nightmare. If god picked the lice from his armpits and flicked them to earth to die, he could find no better resting place than Phoenix. Now I have to go rob a liquor store so we can get to Albuquerque."

No one showed up at the Albuquerque show. It was at a Hardee's. The next night's San Antonio taqueria gig went marginally better, because the band at least got free tacos. In Austin, they played at Liberty Lunch in front of 350 people, and sold albums to every one. Watt sold three guitar picks to one guy for a hundred dollars.

"Man," he said, "Austin rules! We should move here!"

"No," Pollack said. "It's too gentrified."

"No, it's not," Watt said.

"It will be," said Pollack.

Still, they'd made enough money in Austin to keep them going, and the tour really began. Pollack had them on a grueling schedule. They played sixty-five shows in thirty-two days, eating on the fly and sleeping in the van, or, occasionally, onstage. They had six pounds of pot in the van, which, in retrospect, wasn't a very good idea. From Austin, they drove to Houston, and then to Baton Rouge, New Orleans, Memphis, Nashville, Knoxville, Asheville, Winston-Salem, Raleigh, Durham, Chapel Hill, Charlotte, Columbia, Charleston, Jacksonville, Tampa, Miami, Ft. Lauderdale,

Atlanta, and Athens.

"Stop the car," Pollack said. "Do you hear that?"

"Hear what?" said D. Boon.

"It's the sound of a music scene coming together."

"There's no music scene in Athens, Georgia," said Watt.

"Oh," Pollack said, "you're wrong. In fact, I attended a house party here on Valentine's Day, 1977. A band played a six-song set twice in a row. You may have heard of them. The B-52's."

"They suck!" D. Boon said.

"Yes," said Pollack, "they're authentic."

He grabbed the wheel.

"Turn left!"

"Goddamn it!" Watt said.

"Now a sharp right! Here. Drive down that street. There's a dirt road at the end of that cul-de-sac. Go down that."

"Why?"

"House party," Pollack said.

Sure enough, at the end of the dirt road was a house party.

"Who's playing tonight?" Pollack asked the door guy.

"Tiny Toy, Love Tractor, Pylon, and the Side Effects," the door guy said.

"Fuck!" said Pollack. "I love those bands!"

The stage was outside. The keg was in the kitchen. On the couch sat a skinny, abstract guy with two women on either side of him. He was talking to them about many things.

"We're sitting on a couch," he said. "Or maybe we're not. It could also be a dream, or a waking thought. There are things that we just take for granted and things that we are very quick and very easy to dismiss and not think about or say, 'Oh, that's bad and I don't want to go there' or, 'Oh, I don't know what I must've eaten to make me dream that.'"

"Bullshit!" Pollack sneezed.

"Excuse me?" said Michael Stipe.

"Nothing," said Pollack. "Please continue."

He did.

"Most people miss the point that I'm trying to make in my songs, but that's OK. I'll accept that it's a beautiful song and I'll let it be one. I'll change MY take on it to allow it to be that. For instance, when I sing about a moral kiosk—"

"What's a moral kiosk?" Pollack asked.

"It's a phrase I thought of while listening to Patti Smith's *Horses*."

"Get bent!" Pollack said.

"What's that?" asked one of the girls, who was looking at Stipe with a twinkle of love.

"A beautiful album," Stipe said. "I have it right here on cassette."

He went over to the stereo and put *Horses* on. Patti Smith screeched from the speakers. Pollack dropped to the ground and twitched.

"No! No! No!" he said.

From his back jeans pocket he produced a copy of *Van Halen II*.

"Now *this* is music!" he said.

He ripped the Patti Smith cassette from the player. A spool of magnetic tape spilled onto the floor. Within seconds, Van Halen was ripping through the party.

Michael Stipe stood up. Pollack looked at him. Jesus, he was tall. What was with that stupid cap?

"That music promotes rape," he said.

"Well, I hope so!" Pollack said.

"I know who you are, Pollack," Stipe said. "And you're not welcome at this party."

Neal Pollack punched Michael Stipe in the face. It was an action, Stipe later said, that prompted him to take Pollack's name out of "It's the End of the World As We Know It (And I Feel Fine)." Stipe staggered backward, but he didn't fall. The band outside stopped playing. A whole mess of country folk with a somewhat hippie aesthetic moved toward the patio door. Pollack glanced over his shoulder. The Minutemen were backing up toward the front of the house.

"Run!" he said.

They played Richmond, Annapolis, Baltimore, Washington, D.C., Philadelphia, Trenton, Jersey City, and Newark, skipping New York City because Pollack didn't feel like seeing anybody he knew there. That was when the band realized something was awry. But they kept going because they had no other way of getting home. Pollack had taken all their driver's licenses and put them in a locked box, he said, "for your protection."

So they hit Boston, Burlington, Buffalo, Pittsburgh, Cleveland, Columbus, Toledo, Lexington, Bloomington, Indianapolis, Detroit, Chicago, Milwaukee, Madison, Minneapolis, Iowa City, St. Louis, Kansas City, and Lawrence, where the show was attended solely by William S. Burroughs, followed by Omaha, Denver, Boulder, Colorado Springs, Fort Collins, Laramie, Salt Lake City, Boise, Eugene, and Portland.

In Seattle, they played at a construction site at midnight.

"There aren't any clubs in this town that book unsigned bands," Pollack said. "Believe me, I looked."

After the show, the band held a meeting. It was decided to slip two Valiums into Pollack's whiskey. About an hour later, the van moved slowly down a small-town Washington state highway. The side door opened and Pollack tumbled out.

The van screeched away. Pollack rolled down a hill, but still he slept. A few hours later, it was dawn. He woke to the sound of timber mills shutting down because of the recession.

He stirred, barely, and knew what had happened. Like always, once a band got big, they dropped him. It was OK. He'd see the Minutemen in the afterlife for sure, and then he'd get them, those ungrateful bitches.

He looked up. A sign read "Aberdeen, Washington. Abandon Hope All Ye Who Enter Here."

"ABERDEEN?" he said.

Man, he thought. I could really use a donut.

The front page of the *Aberdeen Desperate Shopper* drifted by him in the wind. He could make out the headline: "Last Donut Shop In Town Closes."

"Shit," he said.

Thin raindrops fell, followed by thick ones. Pollack sat by the side of the road, waiting for the rain to stop. It didn't. An hour later, he decided he'd wait another hour. It still didn't stop. He didn't care, until about four hours after that, when it was still raining. Max and Kansas City were soaked to the bone, their wet fur pasted against his chest.

"I'd better go find a bridge to live under," he said.

Great wind gusts blew sharp sheets of rain under the bridge. Pollack's mouth felt silty and rotten. His pants and coat and hair were caked with slime and mud. The cats, terrified beyond imagining, had burrowed into a hole in the concrete. Crap, Pollack thought. I've lived for seven men. Enough. He looked at his wrists, which were in need of slitting.

Then, from the other side of the Young Street Bridge, he heard a voice, soft and young and sweet and full of hope. He looked to the embankment on the other side. There sat a young man, stringy blond hair cascading over his face, in a Kermit the Frog T-shirt. He played a guitar and sang.

> *I'm unconscious*
> *In the darkness*
> *I'm unconscious*
> *So alone*

> *Crawling crawling on the floor*
> *A cigarette consumer whore*
> *Eating from the feedbag*
> *Living by the sea*
> *Feel the needle, Mr. Flea*
>
> *I'm unconscious*
> *In the darkness*
> *I'm unconscious*
> *So alone*
> *My aloneness*
> *In the darkness*
> *I'm unconscious*
> *So alone*
>
> *My family is a famous lie*
> *You want to live*
> *I want to die*
> *Patriotism*
> *Made of jism*
> *It's a prism*
> *I'm in prison*
> *I'm in prison*
> *I'm in prison*

Pollack swore he saw a halo shine around the young man's head. He had come at last. The golden one had come. I've lived my whole life for this moment under a bridge

in Aberdeen, Washington, Pollack thought. Suicide? Bah! I must wade across that river to my destiny.

"Come, kitties," he said. And they miraculously swam together, while the boy sang, penetrating the dawn fog.

From the river, young Kurt Cobain heard a voice shout, "Your voice is sentimental nonsense!"

Kurt saw a man's head and shoulders barely bobbing against the current. Two cats clawed desperately at the man's scalp. The man swam toward the tiny rotting island where Kurt sat.

Kurt thought, I need some weed.

Pollack emerged from the river a muddy, rotten, wasted, confused-looking junkie wreck. He bore the scars. But somewhere, in the bag of bones that was Neal Pollack, lay the essence of rock.

"I've been searching for you," Pollack said. "For you are the chosen one."

"Ch-ch-chosen?" said Kurt. "Me? But I'm just some stupid kid who says he lives under a bridge!"

Pollack took the guitar from him.

"I like your singing," Pollack said, " but your guitar is all wrong. I want to play you something."

Pollack took the guitar. He began to thrash as young Kurt had never heard thrashing before, and he screamed:

> *On Wisconsin*
> *In the darkness*
> *On Wisconsin*
> *So alone*
> *In the darkness*
> *On Wisconsin*
> *In the darkness*
> *I'm alone*
>
> *On Wisconsin*
> *On Wisconsin*
> *On Wisconsin . . .*

The guitar ripped through chords of unbearable grief and anger, the very sound of savage rebellion being born. Pollack sang.

He created a wall of noise like nothing Kurt had ever heard before. When he finished, he said:

"Bad Brains! Bad Brains! Fucking rock 'n' roll!"

"You totally got my lyrics wrong, dumbass," Kurt said.

He made quote marks with his hands.

"Whatever."

Kurt's flip, ironic tone hung in the air, becoming a poison gas of cynicism that withered everything it touched. It diminished our national character, nullified debate, and across the country, people prayed for it to end. But like most diseases, irony lingered, a festering sickness on the body politic. Would sincere discourse ever be possible again after the withering pessimism of Generation X?

"Human existence is pitiful and meaningless," Pollack said. "All we can do is chronicle it with agonized mockery."

"Will you be my dad?" asked Kurt.

"Sure, kid," said Pollack. "Let's go get some smokes."

There was, between Neal Pollack and Kurt Cobain, an instant, pure, and total love. All his life, Kurt had sought a man to replace the man who thought he was his father, and all his life, Pollack had sought a son to replace the man who had been his father but failed. In Pollack, Kurt had a mentor and friend. In Kurt, Pollack had a willing, naïve tool, a boy of raw mental clay. Pollack could, at last, create his perfect rock machine.

That afternoon, Kurt took Pollack home. Kurt's mother was sitting at the kitchen table, smoking, drinking whiskey by the glass. She gave Pollack a sly look.

"Dude," Pollack said to Kurt, "your mother is hot."

"Stay away from my mother," Kurt said.

In Kurt's bedroom, Pollack looked through the LPs and cassettes.

"These aren't very good," he said.

"I keep all the records for my favorite band in my closet," Kurt said.

"What's your favorite band?"

"Judas Priest."

Pollack brought a fist down on Kurt's head.

"Ow!" Kurt said.

Pollack hit him again.

"Stop it!"

And then he hit him again. Kurt fell to the ground, unconscious, an experience that he would later chronicle in an early song, "Unconscious." It went, *I'm unconscious, in the darkness/I'm unconscious, so alone* . . .

When Kurt awoke, it was night, and he was on his bed. Pollack sat in a chair next to him, daubing his forehead with a cold cloth. He said, "You'll probably have some minor brain damage. Which is good."

Pollack produced a large red box, on which he had written, in thick black marker, the words "RECIPE FOR ALIENATION."

"I have a gift for you," he said.

Kurt opened the box. Inside were old copies of *Creem* and *Punk* and *Crawdaddy, Slash* and *Bomp,* and many English magazines of which no other copies existed in North America. Every one of them contained at least one story with Pollack's byline. Also in the box were albums from X, the Germs, and the Dickies, to which Pollack had contributed the exact same liner notes, word for word.

"Wow!" Kurt said. "You even gave me a dirty needle!"

"It belonged to Nancy Spungen," Pollack said. "Don't touch it without gloves."

That night, and all through the weekend, Kurt read the history of rock as told by Neal Pollack. Kurt had never heard of half these bands. Pollack told him that the corporate media wanted it that way so they could sell him inferior musical products that would keep him from thinking for himself. As Kurt read, he got angrier and angrier. Nothing was going to control him from now on. He wrote that night in his dream diary:

> Neal Pollack is meaner stronger less susceptible to disease and more dominant than a male gorilla. He comes to me at night. Without warning, he bends the bars on my brain and infects my mind with his words. He is costing me my sanity. I see his cats and I want to slit their throats and drink their blood. He comes to me in my bedroom, appearing in a pillar of fire, and he sprouts horns. His body is covered with thick black greasy hair. He stands in a pool of his own semen and vomits bile. I lick it up, and vomit out my own. He laughs. He mounts me. I'd like to kick his hotstinking, macho fuckin' ass.

An American poet had been born.

Around midnight, from his mother's bedroom, Kurt heard a man moaning. Not again. He was tired of the men his mother brought home, all of whom wanted to be his dad. But he only had one dad, now, a rock dad, Neal Pollack, who'd made his life weird.

"Neal, oh, Neal!" he heard his mother say.

"Crap!" said Kurt.

He ran to his mother's room. The door was open. Pollack wore nothing but an L.A. Dodgers baseball cap, backward. He was sitting straight up, riding Kurt's mom, howling like a beast.

"Damn it!" Kurt said.

"Sorry, man," Pollack said. "Your mother's hot."

That night, in his journal, Kurt Cobain wrote the word "kill" for the first time.

Days passed, as days do, and then they turned into months. Pollack and Cobain lived with Cobain's mom. So he wouldn't hurt Kurt's feelings, Pollack only slept with his mom when Kurt was at work or at school or running errands or out of the house for any other reason. When Kurt's mom finally found another man, who called them both pansies, Pollack and Cobain were forced to move from house to house, Kurt sleeping on the couch, Pollack on the floor. Every well-meaning person in Aberdeen put them up, and subsequently booted them out. Kurt got a job at a pet-food store so he could steal grub for Max and Kansas City. Pollack drank copiously and worked on the first sentence of his novel, *The True Story of How Rock 'n' Roll Smacked Me in the Mouth Until I Bled Real Tears.* In the evenings, they would go see the Melvins play at the Thriftway. Before bed, as they nodded out on lithium, Pollack told Cobain stories.

"I once lived with the Rolling Stones," he said.

"No!" said Kurt.

"Yes," said Pollack. "They attached electrodes to my testicles."

"Wow!" Kurt said. "Oh, wow!"

"Those were the days. With the old sounds. We had real bands then, like the Yardbirds."

"I've heard of them."

"And the Monks."

"I haven't heard of them."

"They were these American soldiers in Germany in the mid-sixties. They didn't have anything better to do, so they started a band. Their heads were shaved like monks' tonsures, and they just thwacked away at their instruments like idiots. One of them cut a hole in a banjo and stuck a microphone inside. I saw them play once at an army base in Hamburg. They were horrible."

"Right."

"But they were also the greatest band of all time. They were the first punk rockers. And they taught me an important lesson."

"What's that?"

"Remember, Kurt," Pollack said. "There's nothing more important in life than being cool, except for making music on your own terms, unfettered by corporate constraints. If you live by these principles, you'll be happy. You have my guarantee."

Neal Pollack had lucked into one of the greatest cultural flowerings in the history of the world. Fifth-century Egypt, the golden age of Athens, Greece, the Italian Renaissance, the Babylon of Hammurabi, none of them had much on western Washington state in the late 1980s. The area's relative geographical isolation, high concentration of colleges, and cheap weed all contributed to what Pollack called "the largest gathering of talented morons in human history." Every day, a new band crossed Pollack's ears. He wrote about them in *Brand New Age,* and in his journal. The March 1, 1988, entry read, "Screaming Trees is the greatest band in the world." The March 2 entry read, "Jesus. I can't believe this new Green River record. They're the greatest band in the world." On March 3, he simply wrote, "Mudhoney, Mudhoney, Mudhoney! Motherfucking Mudhoney!" The next week, in an article for the *Rocket,* he wrote, "Mudhoney has sold out like the troglodyte college-boy indie-rock posers that they are. They never rocked at all." Then he wrote, "Shonen Knife, Shonen Knife! Shonen Knife! TAD TAD Fastbacks Walkabouts! Swingin' on the flippity flop!"

Pollack and Kurt moved to Olympia, and Pollack named himself Kurt's manager. When Kurt complained, Pollack said, "First of all, I'm your dad, so you do what I tell you to. Second of all, I have a lot of experience in this business. I know what works."

Despite Kurt's protesting, Pollack named the new group Kurt and the Cobains. He said that the world was ready for a return to eponymous garage bands. Using a stolen mixing board and "borrowed" amps, he recorded a seven-inch single of "Unconscious," which he considered Kurt's best song. He arranged for a meeting with Calvin Johnson, founder of the band Beat Happening and also the boss of Olympia's own K Records. Johnson was the ultimate proponent of honest indie-rock business practices. Pollack despised him.

Kurt and Pollack cut their hair short, shaved at the bus station, and wore clean T-shirts and blue jeans.

"No flannels," Pollack said.

They met Johnson at a coffeehouse. Over decaffeinated tea, they made their pitch.

"Um, I'm really ethical," Kurt said.

"He is," Pollack said, "the most ethical musician in all of Olympia."

"And I'm a vegetarian," said Kurt.

"Vegan," said Pollack.

"Right," Kurt said. "Locally grown produce."

Johnson studied them carefully for signs of weakness or sell-out potential.

"Do you know how to play your instrument?" he asked.

"No," Kurt said.

"Do you hurt girls when you dance?"

"No."

"Do you believe in purity?" he said.

"Oh, yes," said Pollack. "We are rigidly pure. We fly in the prevailing winds of rock decadence."

Kurt vomited.

"Shit," he said. "Sorry."

"I don't think you're for us," said Johnson.

Outside the café, Pollack considered the situation.

"Fuck it," he said. "We'll just sign with Sub Pop."

Kurt nodded off while standing up.

Pollack shook him by the shoulders.

"Goddamn it, Kurt, you've got to stay off the junk!" Pollack said.

"Huh?" said Kurt.

Pollack scratched his forearm hungrily.

"Hey," he said. "Do you have any?"

The tour van raced down the autobahn from Hamburg toward Berlin. There were ten of them in that Fiat minibus: Pollack, Kurt, and the rest of Kurt's band, which, to Pollack's disgust, he'd renamed Nirvana. There were also a couple of roadies, and another band called Tad, fronted by a three-hundred-pound behemoth named Tad Doyle. Nine countries, ten men, thirty-nine cities in forty-two days meant the van could smell like only one thing: ass.

"Damn it," Pollack said aloud. "What am I doing here?"

"You wanted to come," Kurt said.

"Well," said Pollack. "I AM your manager."

"Wish you weren't," Kurt mumbled.

Pollack grabbed him by the shirt.

"WHAT DID YOU SAY TO ME, YOUNG MAN?" he said.

"Nothing, sir," said Kurt.

"YOU'D BETTER CALL ME SIR," said Pollack.

It was the worst fight they'd ever had. Neither of them spoke for the rest of the drive. Kurt looked out the window at the Black Forest and wept. When would he no longer be poor? When would he find true love? When would the soul-sucking vampires stop haunting his dreams?

They got to Berlin at 2 P.M. Soundcheck wasn't until 7. The show didn't start until midnight. Kurt looked terrible. Well, he always looked terrible, but this time Pollack saw that he'd really hurt the little guy's feelings. Usually, he didn't care if he hurt someone, but Kurt was his son, after all.

Pollack started tickling him. Kurt started giggling. He could never resist when Pollack played Tickle Monster.

"Tickle tickle monster!" Pollack said.

"Quit!" Kurt said.

"Tickle tickle too!"

"Stop!"

Pollack put an arm around his son. He said, "We've got a few hours. I want to show you something."

A quick subway ride and short walk later, they were knocking on an apartment door.

"Who lives here?" Kurt said.

"I don't know," Pollack said.

A woman answered. She was holding a baby.

"Yes?" she said.

"Excuse me. My name is Neal Pollack. I'm an American rock critic."

The woman said, "So?"

"You speak excellent English," he said.

"That's because I grew up in Manchester, England," she said.

"Oh," said Pollack. "Well, I just wanted to show my son this apartment, because I used to live here with Iggy Pop, about twelve years ago."

"Bullshit," said the woman.

"Bullshit," said Kurt.

"No, seriously," Pollack said. "I can prove it. There's a loose tile in the bathroom to the left of the sink. You should find a mouse skeleton. We buried it there in case something like this came up."

The woman went back into the apartment. Pollack and Kurt heard a scream. They looked at each other.

"Let's blow," Pollack said.

A few blocks later, as they caught their breath in front of a department-store display window, Kurt looked at Pollack with renewed wonder.

"You knew Iggy Pop?" he said.

"Know," said Pollack. "I know him well."

"Iggy rules!"

"Yes," Pollack said severely. "Yes, he does."

A few weeks later, the band was in New York City, where they were scheduled to play a show at the Pyramid Club. Kurt was reluctant. As he ground away in front of a pit of bobbing hipsters, he saw a familiar figure, bony and desolate, moving in the crowd. Could it be? No. Someone like that would *not* come hear him play.

Pollack was in the crowd, and he saw the figure, too.

"Iggy!" he said, after the set. "Oh, Iggy!"

Iggy Pop approached Kurt instead.

"Hey, man!" he said. "Great fucking show! I fucking loved it!"

"Thanks, man," Kurt said.

Pollack was tugging on Iggy's sleeve.

"Iggy, Iggy, Iggy," he said. "Hey, Iggy."

But Iggy and Kurt were deep in conversation.

"You've gotta look up at the audience more," Iggy said.

"Yeah," said Kurt, "I know."

Pollack said, "I've been telling him that for months!"

"Come on," Iggy said to Kurt. "I'll buy you a beer."

They walked toward the bar. Pollack moved after them, but the crowd seemed to close in around him, as if it was protecting Kurt and Iggy. But from what? Pollack just wanted to be their friend. If they acted like a couple of sellout rock stars that only hung out with other rock stars, fine. Who needed them?

"Hey, Iggy!" Pollack shouted. "Your new album sucks!"

One afternoon in the spring of 1990, Pollack returned home to Olympia. He'd been in Los Angeles, where he'd stolen the original masters of Wire's *Pink Flag* LP, an album that he frequently referred to as "the greatest record of all time," especially after he finally got around to listening to it. He hadn't been to L.A. in seven years, and was disappointed in how things had changed. In his journal, he wrote, "Everyone's into glam metal. All the rock stars now are these shitty farm boys with long hair who fuck porn stars. Not like back in the day, when L.A. was free from artifice and posing. But the rap scene is pretty cool. Thug Life 4 Ever!"

Back in the Pear Street apartment, Pollack found Kurt and

another guy decapitating toy soldiers.

"Hey," Pollack said.

"Hey," said Kurt. "You want some Quaaludes?"

"No, thanks," said Pollack. "I had a big breakfast. Who's the dude?"

"This is Dave," Kurt said. "He's our new drummer."

"Hey," said Dave.

Kurt and Dave were listening to a record. The music was very loud. A crazy man screamed something about American Airlines.

"Who is this?" Pollack asked.

"Wesley Willis," Dave said.

"Who's that?" Pollack said.

The music seemed to stop. In Pollack's mind, time froze, because he knew this was the key moment. Punk rock had finally passed him by. Kurt cannon-launched a gaze of withering sarcasm that exploded, full on, in Pollack's face.

"*You don't know?*" he said.

"No," said Pollack.

"He's from Chicago."

"Figures," Pollack says. "Chicago's not a real rock town. Fuck Steve Albini and his elitist indie attitude! If I had a chance, I'd—"

Kurt stood up and grabbed Pollack by the shirt.

"Don't disrespect Steve Albini in my presence again," he said. "Steve Albini is a god."

Kurt's eyes filled with an eternal hate, but Pollack felt his own demons slipping away. He was, once again, a scared little boy, running from his own father, down that Chicago alley so many decades before. The fight was gone from him.

"Dude," Dave said, "chill out. Our girlfriends are coming over."

Kurt let go.

"Hooray!" Kurt said. "Hooray! Our girlfriends! Our girl-friends!"

He started running around the apartment, picking up animal

turds.

"Got to clean this place up," he said.

Pollack heard a loud, discordant guitar note. The front door blew off its hinges. Two chicks were standing in its place. One of them wore a Misfits T-shirt. The other wore no shirt, and had painted the word "SLUT" across her belly. They looked ready to make music on their own terms.

"Yay," Kurt said. "It's our girlfriends!"

"On your knees, gentlemen," said the shirtless one, who was obviously a lead singer.

So Neal Pollack and Kurt Cobain and Dave Grohl and their girlfriends Tobi Vail and Kathleen Hanna went out on the town. They were on the guest list for the Nation of Ulysses show, which featured eight bands playing seventeen minutes each. The kids all seemed to like it, but Pollack had his earplugs in by 9 P.M. By 10:30, he was smoking a cigarette in the parking lot. It was all too loud and rowdy for him. Now X, or the Ramones, or Television, *those* were bands. This was nonsense passing for a music scene, in his opinion, and it would never have an impact on the larger world.

After the show, they went to another show, and then they went to a bar. The girls did all the talking. Tobi, the drummer, said: "-We're gonna start our own band and our own record label, and I already publish three fanzines. Chicks can rock and they should control their own destiny. Punk isn't about control. Punk is freedom."

"I understand," Pollack said. "I knew Wanda Jackson."

"Shut up, old man," Hanna said.

Kurt looked at Tobi moonily. On his napkin, he wrote the words "Tobi, Tobi, Tobi," over and over again.

"Punk is freedom," he repeated. "Freedom, freedom."

The girls went to the bathroom. Pollack went to the cigarette machine. He was bent over, trying to coax an extra pack out of the slot. As the girls were coming out, he heard Tobi say, "Let's ditch these wimps and go fuck some bikers."

The bitches! They sounded just like men!

At dawn, Pollack woke on the floor. In the bed above him, Kurt was moaning loudly and muttering in his sleep.

"Tobi," he said. "Tobi, Tobi, Tobi, Tobi, Tobi, Tobi, Tobi, Tobi. Let's go get tattoos, Tobi."

Pollack got up and shook Cobain by the shoulders.

"Snap out of it, boy!" he said. "You can't lose yourself like this over a woman!"

Kurt woke up.

"But I love her!" he shrieked. "She's perfect! I love her so much she makes me sick!"

Kurt started weeping. Pollack looked on, concerned. The crying grew more intense. Pollack put his arms around him.

"There, there, son," he said.

"Why didn't she sleep over tonight, Neal?" Kurt said. "Why?"

Pollack hated seeing Kurt in so much pain. Young love sucked, it really did. He had to find him another girlfriend, one who would take his mind off Tobi, because Tobi was obviously going to break Kurt's heart in such a way that he'd never write lyrics again. But who would be right for Kurt? He could be so picky. Then, suddenly, he just knew.

He rocked Kurt back to sleep, went to the bus station, and bought a ticket for Oregon.

Pollack walked into Satyricon, a small dimly lit club somewhere in Portland. A sign out front promised a three-band lineup: Hazel, Drunk at Abi's, and the Village Idiots. Satyricon was red-bulbed lights, a few booths, a stage, and a back bar that had once served up shots to neighborhood guys on their way to work. Smoke wrapped the room in a hazy crust. The air was thick and choking. He saw her immediately, at a booth, each arm around a different guy. Her eyes prowled the room, looking for more interesting company. She was also with three women who resembled Nancy Spungen, but not as much as she did.

"I am soooooo bored," she said. "Let's go to the Blah Blah Café."

One of the girls put her hand on the Widow's knee. The Widow guided it upward.

"You're nothing but a rock 'n' roll slut," she said.

Pollack went to the jukebox, put in his coins, and flipped around, purposely choosing songs he'd never heard before. From fifty feet away, he could feel her breath on his neck. He turned. They stood toe-to-toe.

"I know who you are!" she said.

"Yeah?"

"You're Neal Pollack!"

"That's right."

"I think your writing sucks!"

"Yeah, well, I think your music sucks!"

"Shut up, Neal," said the Widow. "Why don't you go suck off Joey Ramone in CBGB's basement? I hear you work cheap."

Pollack grabbed her by the shoulders. He swept his right leg across her left ankle. Smack. She was down, and he was on top of her. Pollack had her pinned, but that wasn't going to last. She was four inches taller than he was, and had bigger biceps. Her nails dug into his palms, and he yelped. She left-hooked him in the face the second he released his grip. He went hurtling into a table. Drinks spilled. Her knees were on his chest. He couldn't move and could barely breathe.

"Who sucks, old man?" she said.

"Uhhhh," said Pollack.

"Who sucks? Who sucks? WHO FUCKING SUCKS NOW, POLLACK?"

Pollack was blacking out.

"I suck," he moaned. "I suck very hard."

The pressure let up.

"That's better," said the Widow. "Now what are you doing here?"

"It's Kurt," he said. "He needs your help."

"Who's Kurt?" she said.

"You know who he is," he said.

"Please. Enlighten me."

"Could you let go of my arms first?"

"No."

"OK. He's the guy you call Pixie Meat. He's the guy in Washington to whom you sent a heart-shaped box filled with a tiny porcelain doll, three dried roses, a miniature teacup, and shellac-covered seashells. You rubbed your perfume all over it."

"Nope," she said. "Doesn't ring a bell."

Pollack said, "He's the guy in Nirvana."

"Oh," she said. "Yeah. They're OK, but too metal for me. I like Mudhoney."

"Kurt's always evolving," Pollack said. "He's a true poet."

"He's cute," she said, "but kind of messed up."

Pollack sat up. She hovered over him. He tried another tack.

"He's starting to get famous," he said. "The A and R werewolves are coming to his shows."

The Widow twirled her hair.

"Really?" she said. "Now, isn't that interesting?"

Pollack could see that the fish was on the hook. He didn't want to do this. The pain swelled in him and brought him nearly to crying. But his son was an emotional wreck back in Washington. For some reason, he knew that this woman was the only glue that could mend Kurt's heart. Pollack gulped and prepared for the ultimate sacrifice.

"You two should hook up sometime," he said.

"Maybe," she said. "I have to check my schedule."

"Check fast. He's in love with someone else."

The Widow froze. She snarled. Pollack, in his diaries, later wrote, "I swore I saw her nails grow two inches right there."

"No bitch is gonna steal my man," she said. "Let's call him."

Outside, in a thick drizzle, Pollack dropped eight quarters into a pay phone. He dialed Kurt's number. On the sixth ring, Kurt answered.

"Tobi, is that you?" he said.

"For god's sake, Kurt," Pollack said. "Be a man. Someone here wants to say hi."

"Tobi?" Kurt said.

"No, not Tobi," said Pollack.

The Widow took the phone.

"Hey there, sugar lumps," she said. "Why don't you come on down here and pierce my cunt for me?"

A silence on the other end.

"Hello?" she said.

"I . . .I . . .I love you," Kurt said. "You're amazing. I think you're the coolest girl in the whole world."

"What's he saying?" said Pollack.

"Get outta here," she said. "I'm talking to my boyfriend."

About a year later, at the Palladium in Los Angeles, Kurt and Pollack were hanging out backstage during an L7 concert. They passed around a bottle of Romilar. Pollack took a long chug.

"I always loved this shit," he said.

"Tastes like cherries," said Kurt.

From behind them, they heard, "Watcha drinkin', boys?"

It was the Widow.

"Cough syrup," said Kurt.

"That's not cough syrup," she said.

She reached into her purse and pulled out a bottle of Romilar Extra Plus PM Cold Relief, Now With Liquid Barbiturates.

"This is cough syrup."

She drank the whole bottle in one smooth gulp.

"I'm fucked up," she said.

Kurt stood up.

"D . . .Do you have any more?" he said.

She tackled him. They fell to the ground. His hands moved toward her breasts. This was a private scene, and Pollack didn't want any part of it. Somehow, he knew that he was done. Kurt had found his heart's home, his sweet love. Pollack moved toward the exit.

Kurt and his bride tumbled. Pollack opened the door. The sunlight hurt his eyes, as always. He looked behind him. Kurt's mouth moved.

"Thanks, Dad," he whispered. "Thanks for everything."

Pollack waved.

"Good-bye, son," he said.

He's in good hands, Pollack thought. The Widow is a safe, loving harbor. My boy will be all right.

A bunch of antiracist skinheads were hanging out in the parking lot, looking for racists to beat up. Pollack hated the smug looks on their faces. They didn't get it, these damn kids. A lot of people had taken boots to the face so these schmucks could disrupt Klan rallies. He said: "Fuck you, skinheads!"

They moved in. Their blows and kicks peppered Pollack's torso and skull. It felt good to bleed and bruise again. Pollack didn't fight back. Let it come, he thought. I'll endure this as I've endured the rest of my life. I'll prove it all night. You bet. Nothing can finish me off. My retirement years have arrived.

I'll go to Brooklyn, Pollack thought, as he spit out a tooth. That should be a safe place for me to write my novel, dictate my memoirs to a college student, and compile two volumes of my best record reviews. Yes, Brooklyn. Perfect. The kitties will love it there. I can be free.

Rock 'n' roll will never come to Brooklyn.

EPILOGUE

This brings the narrative to 1992, but Pollack's life still wasn't over. Why and how did he die, like he was born, in obscurity? Who was this man, and what did he really leave for the world? Was he an easily forgettable answer to an obscure trivia question, a brief blip on the weak radar of a self-styled underground? Or was he even less, a cipher in the back row of a high school graduation photo? The Butthole Surfers, with whom Pollack lived for a few months at their ranch outside of Austin, referred to him in a 1985 song as "Nailed Penis," but even to them he meant almost nothing. Pollack spent his life trying to legitimize rock's existence. Yet rock, by its very destructive essence, negates him.

I feel like it's negated me as well. My family is gone, and I've given up my home. Ruth is teaching at Oberlin College, in Ohio, and she's taken the kids. I call her.

"Ruth, it's me," I say.

"Me who?" she says, and hangs up.

She's blocked me from her Instant Messages, and from her AIM. I can track her movements in Michel Houllebecq chat rooms, but her opinions on contemporary French literature don't interest me. I want to know what my children are learning, who their friends are, if they've read Daddy's books and enjoyed them. And I still love Ruth. I long to hear her whisper my name in the same sentence as Jean Baudrillard's. Sometimes, I think of the face she used to make when she pretended to have an orgasm while we made love, and I hope that she'll return. But she won't.

That world is closed to me now.

And the world of journalism has locked its revolving door as well. Since *Rolling Stone*'s redesign, my freelance work there has vanished. There's no place for a prose stylist like myself in *Blender*. I'd be an oil tanker of prose in a sea of two thousand monthly record reviews, five words each. And like anyone at *Vibe* would ever talk to me. Even that last repository of great media intellect, *Salon*, has canceled my column, "Five Elementary Things About Rock by Paul St. Pierre." Why? I'd only missed three deadlines. These young editors treat me like a worm.

Damn it. I'm an out-of-work rock critic with a drinking problem. The last I heard, those aren't desirable qualities for any employer, not even for employers who post on Craigslist.

My research on the ghost of Pollack is all I have left. Hellhound on my trail, I've come to Chicago. This is where Pollack's life in rock began. Sometimes, as Milan Kundera wrote, to discover endings, you must rediscover beginnings. And rock 'n' roll in America had only one true starting point: Maxwell Street, the ultimate urban bazaar and the immigrant crossroads of the Midwest. In its heyday, Maxwell was the hub of the world.

I can't afford a cab, and everyone knows that public transportation in Chicago sucks. So I find myself walking to Maxwell, stopping at Manny's delicatessen for my day's only meal, a corned-beef sandwich thick enough to kill a moose. Two blocks and the purchase of one package of discount hosiery later, I arrive at the corner of Roosevelt and Halsted, gateway to the truth. A wrought-iron arch loops over the street. On either end, among decorative curlicues, are guitars, each emitting two musical notes. The words "UNIVERSITY VILLAGE" bump out in fake copper. At the base of the arch is a sign. It reads, "The University of Illinois at Chicago, committed to the city's multicultural heritage, is proud to present a new concept of student living in one of Chicago's most historic neighborhoods."

As I walk, I discover that there is, literally, no more Maxwell Street. The city has renamed it Thirteenth Place. Where ancient Jewish tailors once pressed pants awash in steam and peeling lime-green paint, a seven-story dormitory now stands. The zoot-suit emporium has become a coffeehouse. There aren't any vendors, period. The streets are clean and freshly paved. But there's no one on them; it's as quiet as a strip mall in a second-ring suburb.

I see another plaque, on the brick façade of a copy shop that also serves Italian subs. It reads, "No one unusual ever lived here. Our neighborhoods are safe for your children. Richard M. Daley, Mayor."

I wonder what Pollack would make of these changes. Then I think I know. He'd just say, "Who gives a shit? Let's go have a beer."

The neighborhood is completely silent, perhaps for the first time ever. There's no one around. But from across the street, I hear the faintest guitar twang. The music grows slightly louder. It appears to be coming from a parking lot next to a baseball field. Wait. I see a vague outline of someone, or something.

I duck under the entry gate, moving toward what now distinctly sounds like the blues. The vague outline grows clearer, thicker, becoming the shape of a man, old as time. He's sitting on an overturned wood crate. He sings:

> *Woke up this morning.*
> *And my boots were full of blood.*
> *Yeah, I woke up this morning,*
> *All my boots were full of blood.*
> *Shouldn't have stayed up all night.*
> *Getting nasty in the mud.*

I'm directly in front of the man now. He's come into full focus. He wears a tan cowboy hat with silver studs around the brim, a red cowboy shirt, brand-new cowboy boots, and a star-spangled bandana. Suddenly, I recognize him.

"Holy shit!" I say. "R. L. Burnside! What are you doing here?"

The playing stops.

"Son, I ain't R. L. Burnside," says the man. "I wouldn't record no album with no Jon Spencer Blues Explosion."

He starts playing again.

Then I recognize him for the second time.

"Clambone," I whisper. "Clambone."

Again, he stops.

"Now that's right, Paul St. Pierre," he says. "I've come for you."

"You know me?" I said.

"Oh, I know you," he says. "I know you. You're trying to tell the story of rock 'n'roll. The Neal Pollack story."

"Yes," I say.

"Your tale is not complete," he says.

"I know."

"That's because you've been untrue. You've been untrue to the truth."

"My research skills are impeccable," I say.

"No doubt," he says. "But your story has no ending. I'm here to tell you that it must end. The truth is not true if it's incomplete."

"What ending?" I say.

"You know," he says.

I clutch my head in my hands. I begin to weep.

"NO!" I say. "I DON'T KNOW THE ENDING! I CAN'T FINISH MY BOOK!"

"Yes, you do, Paul," says Clambone. "And yes, you can."

"Ruth," I moan. "I did it for you, Ruth."

"You owe it to Pollack," Clambone says. "You owe it to memory. The world needs to know. Tell the folks the truth."

Clambone is right, of course, because Clambone is always

right.

And so the ending shall be told.

I went to the address in Brooklyn I'd written down. Williamsburg? What the hell? I'd never heard of this neighborhood, though I'd been to Brooklyn a few times before. Some friends lived in Park Slope, where we met monthly to discuss the future of book reviewing, and I had a cousin in Brooklyn Heights. But no. There was no way Pollack could be living here, in the basement of a poultry-processing plant on a dead-end street with a view of the East River and the BQE.

The air was dense with shit and feathers. I peered into a thin grease-stained window with bars. An enormous cat peered out back at me and hissed mightily. That was one of Pollack's bitches, all right. The door was open. I went inside.

"MRRROWWWWWW!"

The cat was on my head, clawing, within a second. Another one was crawling up my leg, dug in for the duration, ripping flesh, seeking bone. God, it hurt. But I was used to dealing with these creatures. I shook a little conical container.

"Kitties," I said. "I have treats!"

The cats released immediately.

It was dusk outside and the room was lit like a tomb. But I'd come prepared for that as well. There were matches in my pockets, and three candles. I lit one and saw a cheap wood veneer kitchen table covered with crumpled sheets from a yellow pad, and album covers, and discarded nitrous-oxide canisters. My research sense was tingling. I uncrumpled one of the papers. It read, "When is the new My Bloody Valentine album coming out? Must get free copy to review."

Pathetic.

I chose another one. Pollack had written:

"My favorite bands right now, in no particular order, are,

Swervedriver, Jawbreaker, Seam, the Breeders, the Jon Spencer Blues Explosion, Royal Trux, Sonic Youth, Verve, Beat Happening, Sebadoh, Superchunk, Tsunami, Unrest, Belly, Pavement, and Beck, whose *Mellow Gold* is the best record I've heard in many a day. Thank god I'm alive. I really think this is the year my writing is gonna break out."

I realized that there was music playing in the room. Some kind of hip-hop, but not the slick stuff you heard on the radio now. It was old-school music, with meaning. Between the candlelight and the music, the room seemed to pulsate slightly. It stank in there, of chickens from the factory, and of cats, but also the faint whiff of unwashed human flesh. I gagged into my sleeve, lit another candle, and moved forward.

Neal Pollack was naked on the filthiest futon that I'd ever seen. His legs crossed at the ankles, and his arms formed the upper half of a T. He lay among a mess of needles and plastic bags, discarded cough-syrup containers and rubber tubing, pills of diverse color and shape, a half-drunk bottle of isopropyl alcohol, pipes of partially smoked weed. I moved the candle closer. Pollack looked pale and gaunt. Dried streams of drool caked on either side of his mouth. I felt Pollack's arm, and recoiled immediately with a preternatural shiver. Pollack was freezing to the touch.

"So much senseless death in the world," I said.

I picked up a pipe and sparked. Pollack usually had good stuff. I sucked a sweet inhalation of narcotic earth, held it for about ten seconds, and then exhaled. The air instantly smelled better.

Pollack shot up like a bolt from hell.

"DON'T DO IT, KURT!" he screamed. "YOU'RE TOO YOUNG!"

I dropped the pipe, which clanged on the concrete floor. The force of Pollack's reanimation had been enough to blow out the candle. I scrambled in his pockets for the other one. Pollack was sniffing the air.

"What is this?" Pollack said. "Does my nose deceive me?"

A moan rose out of Pollack, low at first, but then it became almost a bray.

"WHO THE FUCK IS SMOKING MY WEED?"

I lit the third candle. Pollack was patting around the mattress for something. He found a pill and popped it in his mouth.

"Oh," Pollack said. "Hey, Paul. What're you doing here?"

"You called me," I said. "From a pay phone. And begged me to come over."

"I don't remember that."

"You said you were going to kill yourself."

"Naw," said Pollack. "I wouldn't do that."

"Well, you seemed dead when I came in."

"I was just tired," said Pollack. "I've been remembering."

"Remembering what?"

"My whole life. It's been pretty interesting."

Without being asked, Pollack began to tell me everything. For the first minute, which was basically the unhappy boyhood with immigrant parents section, my eyes glazed. But then Sam Phillips entered the narrative. No, I thought. Pollack didn't know Sam Phillips. It wasn't possible. But by the time Pollack got to the point where Elvis was playing his Bar Mitzvah, I was taking notes on whatever he could find, detailed notes, with underlining and asides to myself to make follow-up calls. This was a rock 'n' roll story unlike any I'd ever heard.

Pollack talked and talked, seemingly in a trance, about the mysterious bluesman who'd haunted his dreams since he was a boy. He told me about his mother's disastrous marriage to Jerry Lee Lewis, about his unverifiable folksinger wanderings across the earth, his symbiotic friendship with the young Bob Dylan, his crush on Brian Jones, his brief stint as head songwriter at Pickwick Records, his days as a hairless androgyne, meeting Iggy before he became Iggy, and about the story he'd heard about the spaceship in Detroit during the race riots. Forward the narrative moved, forward into the fog, toward Asbury Park and amnesia and then the stuff I knew about, the Patti Smith stuff and the Ramones stuff and the glam period, and then veered away from my knowledge, to the secret indie days in L.A. and Athens and Olympia. Pollack talked for hours that seemed like days that seemed like seconds.

It was nearly dawn. I needed to get home. The family had a plane to Mexico that afternoon. It was time for my annual sabbatical, which I'd dearly earned. I looked at his notes. More than a hundred pages. I'd have to do some digging, look at the newspaper clippings, and conduct hundreds of interviews, naturally. But the outline was all there. I had his book, perhaps my masterpiece, there in front of me, scribbled on yellow pads, prescription slips, and the backs of cereal boxes. I would make Pollack's life's work my own, get a huge book contract, making sure that Pollack got between five and ten percent of the advance. It was the least I could do.

"So then I woke up here, and you were in this room, smoking my weed," Pollack said. "That's the last thing I remember."

"This is great, Neal," I said. "A really great story."

"Yeah," said Pollack. "Well, you didn't have to live through it. Next life, I'm going to dental school."

I got up to leave.

"Wait," Pollack said. "I left out one detail."

"What?"

"I fucked your wife."

I sighed.

"I know," I said. "I forgave you for Barbara long ago."

"No," said Pollack. "Not Barbara. The other one."

"You fucked Commie Girl?"

"Oh yeah, her too. I forgot about her."

That left only one wife, my beloved Ruth. No. She was my dearest possession. She *belonged* to me. There's no way she'd ever have sex with Neal Pollack.

"You . . ." I said. "With Ruth?"

Pollack took a long toke from his favorite pipe.

"Shit," he said. "I've been banging her for years. She once said something to me like, 'Paul is my husband. But you're my man.'"

I dropped my notes, shaking.

Pollack laid his head down. He blew out a puff. He turned and looked at me.

"Hey, Paul," he said. "Guess what? I fucked all your wives."

Without a thought, without a pause, I ripped the pillow from underneath Pollack's head.

"You . . ." I said. "You . . ."

"You married well," Pollack said. "Ruth's a hot lay."

I shoved the pillow in Pollack's face.

"Mmmph!" Pollack said. "Cut it out!"

I flipped the pillow vertically, and pressed down, hard. Where had I read about asphyxiation? Probably in some heavy-metal liner notes somewhere, and now I was going to try it myself. My left thumb pressed into Pollack's larynx. I could feel it vibrate; Pollack was trying to scream. Pollack jerked and twitched, but the drugs had slowed his reflexes. It only took ten, maybe fifteen seconds, before he relented. His body went slack, twitched, and went slack again. His chest was heaving, but irregularly. I pressed harder. I'd never felt so much strength and power, so much anger. It was like a wicked guitar solo, only murder. A throat ligament snapped beneath the pressure. There was no more sound, not a ripple of movement.

Pollack was done.

I removed the pillow. Pollack's eyes had rolled up into his head. There was a thick blue bruise near his Adam's apple. I had to cover that, so I took some rubber tubing and tied it around Pollack's neck. Then I jabbed a used needle into the bruised area. There. Now it looked like an overdose. Everyone had expected Pollack to OD anyway. I was just fulfilling a prophecy.

Pollack's eyes opened. Then his mouth. I gasped.

"Take . . .care . . .of . . .my . . .kitties," he said.

And then he died.

Max jumped on my back. Kansas City attached to my side. They clawed and they started to bite.

"OK," I said. "I'll take care of your kitties, Pollack."

I staggered toward the futon, removed the case from Pollack's pillow, put it on the floor, opened my kitty treat container, and tossed it in the case. The cats detached themselves from me and burrowed. Quickly, I tied the case shut. I ran outside, taking care not to slam the door. The cats screamed. I dashed half a block, scrambled up on some concrete. With a desperate heave, I threw the cat-filled pillowcase into the river. It splashed and sank.

"Fucking cats," I said. "You deserved it."

I had to wash off the blood and grime. Maybe I'd stop at the Y on the way home. Then I had to call my agent. I would still do the book, but I was going to tell the truth about what an asshole Pollack was. Now I knew what questions to ask. Oh, it would be so juicy! I thought of the title. *American Rock Monster: The Lies and Betrayals of Neal Pollack.*

But first, home to my wife, who belonged to me and only me. Screw Pollack, I thought. And now, vacation.

I stood in the middle of a parking lot next to what had once been Maxwell Street, sobbing. Clambone looked at me without emotion. He strummed absently on his guitar.

"I'm a murderer," I said.

"Yes, son, you are," said the Clam. "But so am I. We've all murdered at one time or another."

"I'd blocked it all out," I said. "It was the only way."

"But you can be whole now," he said. "Because now you've told the true tale. Your story is accurate. But more importantly, you've learned the Message."

"What Message?" I said.

"The Message that has been embedded in American soil since the beginning of America."

"Oh," I said.

"Would you like to know the Message?" he said. "After all, you've learned it."

"Sure."

Clambone opened his arms wide to the sky. He closed his eyes, tilted his head upward, and said, "Blind, unfocused rage is the emotional core of all great art. And once you've experienced it, you can make rock 'n' roll."

He began to fade.

"Wait!" I said. "Don't go! What am I supposed to do now?"

"Make rock 'n' roll . . ." he said.

He kept fading. Even though he wasn't singing, I could hear his voice anyway. The sky was growing cloudy, the wind whipping and bitter.

"Please!" I shouted. "Don't tell anyone I murdered Pollack."

Clambone laughed, a cackle twinged with kindness. He'd broken down into a spectral outline, and was receding backward across the parking lot.

"Shit," he said. "I've got better things to do. Like my three P.M. date with Josephine Baker in heaven . . ."

With that, Clambone vanished, and I was alone.

Thunder clapped. Seven bolts of lightning struck around me like an electric cage. A chill rain pelted from the unforgiving heavens, and I found myself seized by a wave of blind, unfocused rage, just as Clambone had predicted. My wife had left me. I had an alcohol problem. I was a murdering bastard, a biographical leech. I was broke and I smelled like shit. Without knowing, I knew where I needed to go. I said:

"ARRRRRRRRGH!"

I tore down Halsted to Roosevelt, and then down Roosevelt to Michigan. I ran in the wind and the rain, down the Magnificent Mile, past the popcorn shops and the boutiques and the malls that bore the façades of other malls, and the Hancock Building and the Water Tower. I ran all the way to Oak Street, where I encountered a police barricade, so I turned left and ran to Clark. I ran eight more blocks and then I stopped, stunned. I looked to my left and saw a playground, a shopping center, and a new branch library.

"Holy shit," I said. "They tore down Cabrini Green."

Something said to me, run, Paul, run, and so I did. Past Planet Thai, My Thai, and Thai One On, six neighborhood bars that used to be theaters, and six theaters that used to be neighborhood bars, on into the district that sold incense, ironic lunchboxes, and spiky dog collars. I'd never run forty-five blocks in my life, but I still had all my breath. My eyes burned with bloody anger. Then I saw it. The Guitar Center. In the window was propped a 1956 Les Paul Fender Stratocaster.

I threw myself into the window. It shattered. The guitar was mine. I ripped it from its perch and launched myself down the street, an unstoppable force of one. The sky had darkened with rain mixed with sleet. The wind was unbearable and the air felt like it was full of knives. I held the guitar over my head and shouted,

"ROCK 'N' ROLL! ROCK 'N' ROLL! MOTHERFUCK-ING ROCK 'N'ROLL!"

Everyone got out of my way.

I stopped to take a piss on the Harry Caray statue, and I just kept running. This neighborhood had so many restaurants. Past the cemetery and the International Leather Museum, I ran and ran. At the door to a bar in a yellow-brick building, I stopped.

Inside, I heard the distinct beginning guitar notes of "Your Cheatin' Heart."

I needed whiskey, now.

The bartender was a squat middle-aged blonde woman who looked just off the truck from Appalachia. She wore a T-shirt bearing the image of a beautiful young thing playing honky-tonk music. The text read, "Wanda Jackson: The First Lady of Rockabilly."

"Whaddya have, darlin'?" she said.

"Whiskey," I said. "Make it a triple."

She noticed my guitar.

"Nice Les Paul Fender Stratocaster. Is that a 1958?"

"1956," I said.

"Ah," she said. "You should play. It's open-mike night."

I looked around. In a room next to the bar was a stage. Between both rooms, there were about twenty people in the place. Half of them were old men asleep, heads on the bar. There was a middle-aged Chinese woman, face heavily made up, glancing around nervously over a glass of white wine. The rest were bikers or shit-kickers of some sort. They watched the house band wrestle with Hank Williams cover after Hank Williams cover.

Blind, unfocused rage, I thought. OK. I can do this.

The song ended, and the bandleader said: "Our sign-up sheet is empty. Doesn't matter if the mike is open if there's no one behind it."

I approached the stage with my guitar.

"I'll play," I said.

"Well, all right," said the bandleader.

I got onstage. Took off my shirt. Plugged in the guitar.

"What's your name?" he said.

I held my guitar above my head and said: "MY NAME IS PAUL ST. PIERRE! AND I AM ROCK 'N' ROLL! STAND BACK!"

A chord progression flashed through my mind. Even though I'd never played an instrument before, somehow I was ready. I hit the first note.

A sound louder and more dissonant than anything ever heard before on earth came out of that guitar. Someone in the room shrieked. I hit the second note. It was even louder, and more dissonant. Holy shit. My heart was full of fire. I was a goddamn punk rocker, at last.

"Fuck you!" I heard from the audience.

I stopped.

"What's that?" I said.

"You suck!"

My music had clearly agitated the crowd. Two of the old men lay dead on the floor. The Chinese woman was sobbing. The bikers and shit-kickers moved toward me, grinding their hands. I couldn't tell which one of them had called me out.

Three guys twice as big as me bum's rushed the stage. They were on me before I could swing the guitar at their heads. One of them ripped the strap from my shoulder and smashed the guitar in two. I felt something metal smack into my skull, and then a sharp pain in my abdomen. A pinprick of blood appeared on my shirt. It widened quickly, and then it began to gush. The guy who'd stabbed me put his knife back in his sheath.

He picked me up by the collar and carried me through the bar. The pain was greater than anything I'd felt before. A thick stream of blood oozed behind us. The bartender trailed with a mop soaked in vinegar.

The guy tossed me onto the sidewalk.

"Die in peace, man," he said.

I tumbled twice, and settled into the flooded gutter. My blood mixed with the rushing rainwater, washing me in a fetid stew. I moaned.

Die in peace? What was he talking about? Oh. I guess I was

dying. And fast, too. I die. You die. We all die, die, die.

A rumbling came from below the street, followed by a cracking. A guitar note sounded, a hundred times louder than what I'd played in the bar. I saw the pavement buckle, and then it gave way. An enormous cat's paw, eight feet wide, burst through the concrete. An unearthly moan blew up from below.

"MRRRROWWWWW!"

"Oh, shit," I said.

The earth tore open with a mighty roar. Two monstrous devil-cats launched themselves into the air. They pulled a bright-red chariot, which carried a man. He wore black jeans, black socks, black steel-toed boots, and a black T-shirt with red lettering: "MURDERER." His chariot flung into the sky. He said:

"I HAVE RETURNED TO CLAIM MY KINGDOM!"

"No," I said. "Please, no."

Neal Pollack hovered several feet above me. A ball of flame launched from his palm. In the street, a car exploded.

"Paul St. Pierre," he said. "I see you!"

"I'm dying, Neal," I said.

"You killed me, you bastard!"

"I'm sorry!"

"No, you're not. Admit it!"

He launched another ball of flame. It exploded just behind my head.

"OK," I said. "I'm not sorry!"

A third ball of flame exploded in my face. Oh, god. My head was on fire.

"The rock apocalypse has arrived!" Pollack said. "I am its herald! From below I have been sent to announce that after nearly a decade of throwaway candy pop, rock is returning to achieve its ultimate dominion over the earth!"

"Well," I said, "I like the Strokes."

Pollack threw fireballs from both palms.

"Fuck the Strokes!" he said.

A thunderclap.

"What about the White Stripes!" I said.

"They're a different story," he said. "It's hard to tell if the music's sincere, but Jack White is a genuine . . ."

He shook his head.

"Wait! That's not the point! The point isn't whether or not you like the Strokes or the White Stripes or the Hives or the Vines, although if you like the Vines, you're a total idiot."

"What about Interpol?" I said. "Or the Yeah Yeah Yeahs?"

"Same old annoying New York bullshit," said Pollack. "Goddamn it, Paul, you don't understand, and you never have! What I'm trying to say is this: You don't know anything about rock 'n' roll! You don't know where it comes from or where it's going! Its true path cannot be predicted and cannot be packaged or marketed! And it *is* returning! Somewhere in some basement or some garage or some parking lot, someone who you've never heard of and never will is making music that you'll hate! It may not be the most sophisticated music of all time, but it'll be sincere and loud and fun, and it will kick your ass!"

"Tell me some bands," I said. "So I can write about them."

The greatest rock critic who has ever lived or ever will raised his arms. My lifeless body levitated toward him. In a voice as loud as the creation of the universe, Neal Pollack said:

"No! You'll never know! You'll never know! No one cares what you think! Rock doesn't belong to you, or anyone like you, anymore! Rock critics of the world, I have destroyed you! Renounce your profession as I carry you to hell! Your time on earth is done!"

SELECTED DISCOGRAPHY

Obviously, a selection of this sort is going to be subjective and bounded by my personal taste, which is better than yours. It's therefore intended to provide you with the best possible musical education. None of these records are available commercially. In fact, only two copies of each exist, on LP, and I've hidden one of each in various secret locations around the world. If you find them, well, bully for you. Anyone who doesn't have time for a crazy treasure hunt and is interested in obtaining a copy of *Merle Haggard Sings Songs of Other People Singing Merle Haggard Songs, The Underappreciated Sam Cooke,* Black Flag's *Butt Muscle* EP, or any of the other albums mentioned here, call the *Chicago Reader,* ask for Peter Margasak, and leave a voice-mail message.

ONE: COME ON OVER TONIGHT

The Untold Elvis Essential Master Recording Demos: B-Side Remixes (RCA 84838). Some of Elvis's most moving performances have vanished, like everything else that's good in the world. These are no exception. Includes a capella renderings of "Ezekiel Saw The Wheel" and "Boogie Woogie Bugle Boy."

Clambone Jefferson Sings Lost Songs Of Haiti (Folkways 23576). Alan Lomax coerced these songs out of the Clam one afternoon. A personal favorite of Baby Doc Duvalier.

Warren Smith: I Got Screwed! (Sun 29304). Bitterness breeds great hillbilly boogie.

The Billion Dollar Septet (Sun 89032). More than an hour of Elvis, Jerry Lee Lewis, Carl Perkins, Roy Orbison, Tom Petty, George Harrison, and Bob Dylan, singing together for the first and only time.

Elvis Fat and Old (RCA57483). Nineteen gospel songs for a CBS special preempted by the moon landing.

TWO: THIS STATE HOUSE OF DETENTION

The Shitkicking Bob Dylan (Bootleg recorded in secret location, 1961). Not actually an album, but rather outtakes from a different album.

Joan Baez Live at the Apollo (Folkways 29402). Essential listening for those who hate music.

Bob Dylan: The Attic Tapes 1967–1969. Selected recordings include:

"Mrs. Jones and Me," first take, Robbie Robertson, guitar, Bob Roberts, piano, Rob Bobertson, bass, Bobby Robinson, drums, lyrics and music by Bob Dylan from marriage ballad inspired by murder.

"Smoke the Long Bone." Dylan obviously not caring what anyone thought about him in lyrics advocating man-boy love, said to have derived from William McKinley campaign song, New Orleans, circa 1896.

"Lo and Behold!" v. 6, 8.2.45.29. Very, very different from all the other "Lo and Beholds."

"Rally Round the Whiskey, Mister." Stolen from Clambone Jefferson.

THREE: GYPSY TIGER IN MY SOUP

The Velvet Underground and Nico Get Loaded (Verve 6868). April 1967 (USA), October 1967 (UK), November 1967 (Australia), December 1993 (Canada).

The Stooges Live in Paris (Elektra 1971). Mercifully, before Bowie got his hands on the songs.

"Kick Out the Jams." MC5, Thirty-seven-minute live version, *Lost Midwest Garage* bootleg, circulated in secret among badly dressed long-haired nerds.

Lou Reed Is God (Verve 8906). An album so great that no one was allowed to play on it but Lou.

"Sweet Love, Love Your Woman." Soul Barbers, Revilot Records, 1965.

Interlude: Midnight Drive on a Highway Street

Anyone who still gives a shit about Springsteen already owns everything he's ever recorded.

FOUR: NEVER MIND THE POLLACKS

Live at the Hippodrome. The worst recording ever made of a New York Dolls concert, and that's saying a lot.

Patti Smith: Pretensions. Lost singles, including live versions of "Mother's Little Helper" and "Riders on the Storm." Hard to find. Before you die, you hear her sing.

"I Don't Wanna Shit Blood for a Week." Recorded live by the Ramones at the Rocket Tavern in Washington, D.C., before the dawn of time.

Eat, Eat, Bang, Bang Rock 'n' Roll Patrol. Invaluable six-volume UK First Wave post–Sex Pistols compilation including Buzzcocks, the Clash, the Damned, Slaughter and the Dogs, Eater, the Adverts, the Saints, Snatch, Cortinas, Penetration, the Lurkers, and a hundred other bands you never saw.

"Don't Stop Till Your Body Pops." MC Clam, 1979.

FIVE: THE COPS WILL HAVE YOUR HEAD

Tin Whistle. Fugazi EP, 1988 (Dischord Records). Available only in very ethical record stores.

Only About 15 People Showed Up. Mission of Burma, (Ace Of Hearts Records).

Pink Flag. Wire EP. The greatest album of all time.

Husker Don't! Husker Du (SST Records). Bob Mould moans, and the world weeps for him. Growing up is hard.

Death to Fame, Self Promotion Sucks, Volume 2 Compilation 1989 (Sub Pop). Available in CD, 8-track, LP, cassette, MP3, DVD. Don't buy it. What, you already did? We're all such sellouts, I swear.

If Courtney Hears That You're Distributing This Nirvana Bootleg, She Will Hunt You Down and Kill You. Someday, we will defeat her.

We Are Rich Assholes with Nothing to Say: Songs Of Williamsburg. (Capitol 2003). The sound of today.

Until the next book, then, I remain,
Yours in the Revolution,
Neal Pollack
PS: Fuck off!